A Tough One To Lose

A BLACK BAT MYSTERY

BY THE SAME AUTHOR

The Only Good Body's a Dead One

A TOUGH ONE TO LOSE

by Tony Kenrick

THE BOBBS-MERRILL COMPANY, INC.

Indianapolis / New York

The Bobbs-Merrill Company, Inc.
Indianapolis • New York

For Timmy, who missed out the first time

Contents

Chapter

PART ONE

PART ONE

Prologue

He still had a few minutes to kill.

He rinsed his hands under the tap so he'd be doing something if somebody came in and slowly dried them on a paper towel. He straightened his tie in the mirror and patted his pockets for a comb. There was a dispenser on the wall; it wanted a dollar fifty for nail clippers and seventy-five cents for a comb. Seventy-five cents? Who were they trying to kid? He could go into any drugstore in the . . . Wait a second. That was pretty funny. Here he was on the verge of two million bucks, and he was getting uptight over a lousy six bits. He was going to have to get used to the idea of spending. He fed three quarters into the machine, pulled out a drawer, picked up the comb and walked back to the mirror, tearing the wrapper away. He ran the comb through his hair a couple of times, unzipped the flight bag at his feet and dropped it in next to the rest of the things: tweezers, a nail file, a hand towel, a toothbrush, a small tube of Gleem, a paperback, a black plastic case. Inside the case a barber's straight razor lay doubled up on a bed of red velvet. It was brand new, the thin, ice-cold edge untried. There wasn't any shaving cream. If anybody asked he could say he'd forgotten it. But nobody would ask; it was a hundred to one they'd even look at him twice. He zipped up the bag, went through the door and mounted the stairs to the concourse. From speakers somewhere over his head a man's deep, comforting voice broke like a wave of warm syrup over the terminal: Calair announcing the final call for Flight 422 non-stop to New York. He gave it another ninety seconds, then started toward the departure gates. He wanted to time it just right.

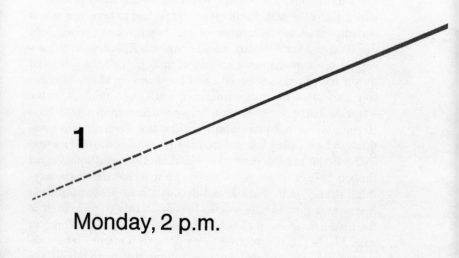

1

Monday, 2 p.m.

The Fleishhacker Tower is on the south side of Montgomery Street, just about in the dead center of the financial section of the city of San Francisco. It was built in the late Twenties when American architects were still dreaming of the glories of Chartres and Amiens and Notre Dame, and if you're a broker or a lawyer or an accountant it's a very good address to have. William Verecker was a lawyer, and he had an office there but only because he did some legal work for the renting agents now and then and was getting a break on the rent. If he hadn't been he could never have afforded it; he couldn't afford much these days. His law practice was only three months old, and nobody was knocking down the door to retain him, which wasn't so surprising considering what had happened. He'd been a junior partner in an old established firm— an old, conservative established firm—until he'd been involved in an embarrassing incident with a society hostess that the press has picked up. A nude midnight swim, they'd called it, which Verecker said was nonsense. He'd had to borrow a swimsuit that was a couple of sizes too big for him. When he'd dived off the springboard it had come off. The firm hadn't accepted the explanation and neither had his wife, Annie, and they'd both fired him. She'd been his secretary at the firm before and after they were married, until the midnight swim. Verecker had gone to work for another firm for a while, then started up on his own. Shortly after the divorce had come through he'd called her and told her he needed a secretary and asked if she knew a good girl. She'd said yes and applied for the job herself. It floored Verecker, but Annie didn't see anything strange in it. She claimed that as a boss he was terrific— it was as a husband he was so lousy—so they'd gone back to their old arrangement of boss and secretary, although Verecker would have much preferred to go back to the more recent arrangement. He claimed he was telling the truth about the swimming pool thing, but Annie said she knew what the truth was: He'd just got the seven-year itch a few years too soon.

She'd been working in her job for about five weeks and had come to work one Monday expecting to spend the day in the same way she'd spent all the others so far—being sweet to the many people they owed money to and tough with the handful who owed them. But as it turned out, that particular Monday changed her life for quite some time to come.

And Verecker's, too.

She was sitting behind her desk, alone in the office, trying to make sense of the accounts. She had a sandwich in one hand and pecked at a small adding machine with the other. She totaled it, looked at the figure, groaned and lowered her chin into her palm. It was a nice-looking chin and a nice-looking palm. In fact, all of her looked pretty good. A painter would have described her as having good bones, marvelous eyes, a fine mouth, a fluid way of moving. A model agency would have said that although her face was quite lovely, her figure was a little too full. A construction worker would have said that she was stacked.

She'd often complained to Verecker, during their marriage, that she thought she could do with an inch off here and there and that maybe she should diet, but Verecker forbade it. He'd told her she was his and every other red-blooded male's idea of a woman and warned her that lips that touched Metrecal could never touch his.

At the wedding people had said what a handsome couple they made, but they were looking at Annie when they said it. Not that Verecker was ordinary—far from it: five-ten, light-brown hair the law fraternity thought was a little too long, a good strong nose, forceful and honest, above a mouth that looked constantly primed and ready to break into a smile. When it did, the brown eyes would crinkle into a half-squint and two semicircular lines would bracket the smile like parentheses. He was extremely presentable; it was just that, in the looks department, Annie was the star of the show.

The outer door banged and she looked up as Verecker strode into the office, threw his golf cap onto his desk and slumped into his chair. He stared morosely at something he didn't like three feet in front of his nose and said, "It's a humbling game all right."

"Don't tell me," Annie answered. "After you took an eight on the second hole you decided not to keep score but just concentrate on your swing."

"I kept score, don't worry. But so did Rogers. I would have beat him if his last tee shot hadn't rolled into a hole. A hole," Verecker appealed to her. "I ask you, what kind of a club has holes a foot deep on the fairway?"

"Gophers have to live, too."

"Gophers nothing. There was a row of them—some kind of burnt-out fireworks in the bottom. Damn kids."

Annie said, "Wait a minute. *His* ball rolled down a hole and *you* lost?"

7

"Oh, he claimed winter rules and took a drop. Drop? Hell, he hurled the thing about a hundred yards up the fairway. It was his best shot all day."

Annie's eyebrows went up half an inch. "Winter rules? This is May."

Verecker looked disgusted. "He mumbled something about it being a long season. What am I supposed to say to that— 'Listen, schmuck, it's seventy-five degrees, use a wedge'? He's a client, after all."

"Yes, and so far a non-paying one."

"Is there any other kind?"

Annie picked up a wad of bills and waved them like a fan. "We'd better find another kind or this business is going bottom up."

"Please." Verecker turned his face away and held up both hands. "Let's not discuss money so soon after a ninety-four."

"How much did you lose today?"

"Twenty-five bucks."

Annie closed her eyes.

Verecker said plaintively, "You couldn't lend me ten till payday, could you?"

"What payday? Today's supposed to be payday. I haven't had a payday for weeks. I haven't even got my alimony this month."

"Business has been bad."

"Business has been terrible. Honestly, Verecker, we need money."

Verecker got up and squared his shoulders. "There's only one thing for it: I'll become a shyster lawyer—a mouthpiece for the mob, with a hair-line moustache and a badly fitting chalk-stripe suit. Tampering with juries, bribing witnesses, bailing out hoods while the cops grind their teeth—it's steady work and the hours are good."

Annie considered it. "A shyster, huh? Well, you already wear the suits."

Verecker grunted, moved to her desk and picked up the

message pad. "Anybody call while I was out? I mean anybody not after money."

"Someone named Rinlaub."

"Rinlaub, Rinlaub," Verecker said, waiting for a bell to ring. "I used to know a Phil Rinlaub in the Air Force. Was it Phil Rinlaub?"

"He didn't say. But he left a number where he could be reached. It sounded important."

"Better get him on the phone. Somebody close might have died and left me a hundred dollars."

Annie picked up the phone, dialed, waited a few moments, then said into it, "William Verecker returning Mr. Rinlaub's call." She nodded for Verecker to pick up the extension on his desk.

"Bill Verecker here. Hey, Phil! Son of a gun. How the hell are you? I thought it might be you. Yeah." There was a pause. "Sure. Anytime . . . right now's perfect. You got the address? . . . Fine. Looking forward to seeing you then. Right. So long." He hung up and said to Annie, "That's him, Phil Rinlaub, my old Air Force buddy. Wants to see me about something."

"A client?" Annie's face lit up expectantly.

Verecker's smile faded. "No, somehow I don't think so. I got the impression I'm going to be a client of his."

"Oh swell. Have him send his bill in promptly, won't you?"

Five minutes later the outer door buzzed. Verecker slipped out of his cardigan, dumped it into the filing cabinet and put on a jacket. "He got here quick enough," he said to Annie. "O.K., let him in."

She came back with a tall smiling man in tow, showed him into the room and left.

"That's got to be Phil Rinlaub," Verecker said, coming forward and taking the man's outstretched hand.

"Hello there, Billy." His face had got a little fleshier and he'd put on a pound or two around the waist but otherwise he was the same man Verecker remembered: slim, loose-jointed, with the long arms and big hands of a basketball player; slightly

9

sunken eyes under eyebrows that rose toward the ceiling when he laughed, as if he were surprised by the emotion; strong jaw, a good nose.

They spent the next few minutes catching up on each other's history. It turned out that when they'd come out of the Air Force and Verecker had gone back to law school, Rinlaub had got a job as a flight engineer with one of the big international airlines. He'd quit that to work as an air-crash investigator with the CAB for a few years, finally settling down as a trouble shooter for Calair, one of the domestic giants. And it was on his firm's behalf that he'd come to see Verecker.

"But you guys must have a whole barrelful of lawyers," Verecker said. "What do you want with one more?"

The tall man moved into a chair, started to say something, stopped, thought about it, then started again. "Klaus Albrecht is a client of yours, isn't he?"

"Just about the only one. Why?"

"Was he here last Friday?"

"Yes, I think it was Friday. He came in to sign some papers."

"Did your secretary see him, too?"

"Yes, of course she did. Look, Phil, what's—"

Rinlaub interrupted. "Would you mind getting her in here for a second?"

Verecker pushed a button on his desk, looking hard at his friend. Rinlaub smiled. "I'm sorry to be so mysterious, but it's a pretty delicate . . . " He let the sentence collapse on itself as Annie entered the room clutching a pad and pencil.

Rinlaub got to his feet and Verecker said, "I believe you two met in the hall. My secretary, Anne Verecker—Phil Rinlaub."

Annie smiled at him. "Hello again."

"Verecker," Rinlaub said thoughtfully. "Any relation?"

"Not any more," Annie replied.

Rinlaub said a small "Oh" and glanced at Verecker, who made a face and shrugged. They all sat down.

"So?" Verecker prompted.

Rinlaub reached down and clicked open the briefcase he'd

10

carried into the room and came up with a small cardboard box held closed by double rubber bands. He rolled the bands off, opened the box and removed the top.

Inside, a pair of blue-black cuff links rested on a wad of white tissue—silver and onyx cuff links in the shape of a fish.

Rinlaub handed one each to Verecker and Annie. He said, "I want you to tell me if you've ever seen these before."

Immediately Annie said, "One of our clients has a pair like this: Mr. Albrecht. I admired them once and he told me they were from Mexico. Taxco, I think."

"You're right," Rinlaub said. "They are from Taxco. So you'd say they're his?" He watched Annie closely.

Verecker interrupted. "Phil, it would be a lot easier if you told us what this is all about. Has Albrecht gone under a bus or something?"

"No, no bus."

"Then what?"

Rinlaub looked down at the floor. "I'm not really supposed to say."

"Phil," Verecker said sincerely, "you know that anything you tell us won't go any further than the bar at Paoli's."

Rinlaub chuckled. "I'm not worried about you or Mrs. Verecker—"

"Call me Annie."

"O.K., Annie. It's just that if this thing ever got out . . . well, it just better not, that's all."

"This is the Fleishhacker Tower," Verecker explained. "The walls are three feet thick."

Rinlaub sighed. "My head must be, too. All right, purely and simply it's this: Friday night somebody pulled a stunt that makes the Brink's job look like kid stuff. If I felt like being funny I'd call it the Great Plane Robbery."

"Bullion?" Verecker asked.

"A lot worse. People. They're asking twenty-five million dollars' ransom."

"Albrecht's—" Verecker's voice climbed the scale—"Al-

11

brecht's worth twenty-five million? We were only charging him standard rates."

"Not just Albrecht—him and about three hundred and sixty others. Somebody's stolen an entire 747 full of people. And the 747."

There was a moment of absolute stillness in the room while Verecker looked back and forth between Annie and Rinlaub. A slow smile began to build at the corners of his mouth.

"Come on, you're putting me on. You two cooked up—"

"What I'm telling you is for real."

The words pinged round the room like ricocheting bullets.

"Jesus Christ," Verecker said softly.

"But where on earth," Annie started, "—I mean, it's impossible. How could anybody hide so many people, let alone an airliner? It's a jumbo jet after all. They're huge."

"We're having a hard time believing it ourselves," Rinlaub answered.

Verecker said, "I would say that has to be the crime of the month. Not only a gigantic hijack but the world's greatest kidnap as well. Was it a regular scheduled flight?"

"Our seven-fifteen to New York."

"When did you find out about all this?"

"About thirty minutes after the flight took off the captain requested to move north a little to get around what he said was light turbulence. O.K., that's nothing new. But then a traffic-control report comes in that panics everybody: the plane's gone off the radarscope somewhere around Lake Tahoe."

"So you figured the turbulence wasn't so light," Verecker said.

"Not really. The controller said it didn't fall out of the sky but came down fairly slowly, as if it had lost power. Anyway, we couldn't contact the plane—not a peep. And we couldn't search an area like that at night; we had to be content with getting everything ready to go at dawn. Officially, we listed the flight as overdue, although we were pretty sure it was lying on the side of some mountain. We made a grab for the passenger list and that's when we began to suspect something was up."

Annie asked, "What was wrong with the list?"

"We couldn't get it out of the computer. Naturally we figured it was on the blink, but when we went after the ticket duplicates we couldn't find them. And all the copies of the flight manifest had disappeared, too."

Verecker whistled softly. "So you had a missing airplane full of people you had no record of?"

"Exactly."

"What did you do?"

"Got on the blower to New York and told them we didn't think the flight would be arriving on time. If at all."

"But," Annie said, "there must have been people who would have been meeting the plane. What did you tell them?"

Rinlaub shifted uncomfortably and frowned at the memory of something distasteful. "What could we tell them? We couldn't raise the plane—we knew it had lost height over the Sierras—so we had to assume it was down. The bit about the computer and the ticket dupes struck us as more than strange, but nobody in his right mind would have suspected somebody had stolen the flight. I'm afraid our New York office had to fib a little and say that San Francisco was fogged in. Fortunately it was the last flight out that night, so nobody knew it wasn't true. Crack of dawn next morning we had everything that could fly searching the area—as well as half the Highway Patrol. Same thing Sunday. Meanwhile, New York was going crazy. They were getting calls from people wondering what had happened to husbands and daughters and son-in-laws who were supposed to have arrived." Rinlaub stopped talking, blinking his eyes as if he were trying to remember something.

Verecker waited for him to continue and, when he didn't, prompted him gently. "How did you handle it?"

The tall man looked as though he hadn't heard the question, but he answered a moment later: "We took their names and addresses and sent a representative to see each one to explain

13

the position—that we couldn't locate the aircraft, that it was very possible it had crashed and that if, God forbid, that proved to be so, why, then there was always a chance there'd be survivors."

Annie said, "Those poor people. Not knowing either way."

"I know it sounds tough, but we had to give it to them straight."

Verecker asked a question. "How did you manage to keep it out of the papers?"

"We had to pull every string we had. We're still pulling them." Annie looked puzzled and Rinlaub explained. "If that plane had been found in a thousand pieces we didn't want the next of kin finding out about it on the front page of the local rag. That's no way to find out your husband or your wife is dead. We had to keep a lid on it; and seeing how things have turned out, we're awfully glad we did."

"Yeah," Verecker commented, "I can see how you wouldn't want a thing like this getting out."

Rinlaub winced. "Don't even talk about it. Hijackers bug us enough as it is, but if it ever gets around that they've branched out into kidnapping, God save us. All of a sudden hijacking planes to take you to where you want to go will be passé and people are going to try stealing them for money. You can imagine how the airlines would feel about that possibility."

"But how long can you keep something as big as this quiet?"

Somberly Rinlaub said, "We're amazed we've been able to keep it under wraps even this long."

Verecker put the cuff link he was holding down on the desk and tapped it an inch to the right with his finger. "When did you get these?"

"In the mail this morning. They came in a package addressed to the airline along with two wrist watches, a ring, a Parker pen and the names of their owners. Five items in all, just enough to prove they've got those people. And, of course, the ransom note."

"They all check out?"

"Every one, according to the relatives."

"What did you tell them?"

"The truth—that their husbands or wives or whatever were being held for ransom, that the FBI was working on it and that there was no reason to believe they wouldn't be returned safe and sound as soon as the ransom was paid, which the airline would do the moment they had instructions from the kidnappers. Of course, we asked them to keep the whole thing strictly in the family."

Annie said, "Mr. Albrecht's cuff links were the last item on the list then?"

Rinlaub nodded. "Right. The FBI went up to his apartment, but he apparently lives alone. There's a married daughter living up in Canada, but that's all. They found his appointment book and saw that he was supposed to come here late Friday before he went to the airport. They figured you might have noticed the cuff links and could maybe identify them. I told them Bill was an old buddy of mine and offered to run the errand."

Annie looked at Verecker. "He did say something about New York, didn't he?"

"He asked me for the names of a couple of fish restaurants there. He said he was looking forward to the lobsters."

Rinlaub said, half to himself, "I don't think he'll be eating lobster tonight."

Annie put her cuff link next to its twin on the desk and stared at them both. They'd taken on a completely different meaning now, as if they were all that was left of someone after a terrible explosion.

Verecker pushed himself out of his chair and crossed to the window. Outside it was a real San Francisco day: not really warm, but not really topcoat weather either. Down on the sidewalk a crowd of shoppers were filing into a shuttle bus that would take them up to the stores around Union Square— Macy's and Magnin's and Gumps and City of Paris—and not one of them, Verecker knew, had the faintest idea that a planeload of people had been snatched out of the sky. He wondered vaguely how they'd react if they'd been told. Probably wouldn't have believed it.

"How about the package the goodies came in?" he said from the window. "Any leads?"

"Same paper and twine you can buy at any five-and-ten. All kinds of fingerprints on it—all smudged. And you can bet that any that aren't will turn out to belong to the mailman."

Annie asked him if there was a chance of tracing the writing in the note. Rinlaub told her the odds were fantastic. It was very badly printed, as if it had been written in a car while riding over a bumpy road—and, according to the FBI, with the left hand of somebody who was normally right-handed. "Give us a suspect and you could compare the writing, but other than that . . . " He didn't have to finish the sentence.

The room was quiet for a time, the three of them chewing it over. Finally, Rinlaub got up and went over to see what Verecker was so fascinated with outside the window.

He appeared to be watching a dentist in the building opposite who was holding up something to the light and peering at it—a tiny, dark object—an X ray probably.

"Where was it mailed from?" Verecker asked.

"Glenbrook, a small town on the eastern side of Lake Tahoe. It was left like a baby on the steps of the local postmaster's house. He says his doorbell rang and he went down and opened the door and found the package with a five-dollar bill tucked under the twine."

"What time was this?"

"Nine-forty on the dot."

"And the plane went off the radarscope at . . . ?"

"Seven fifty-two."

There was a lengthy silence until Verecker broke it.

"How do they want the cash delivered?"

"They haven't told us yet. And they're not asking for cash; they're smarter than that. They want uncut diamonds."

"Diamonds," Annie repeated. "What's wrong with good old-fashioned money?"

"Too easy to trace," Rinlaub told her. "With diamonds they can have them cut up and sold on the international market. As long as they do it gradually it'll be virtually impossible to track them down."

Verecker said to the window, "Pretty cute. When's delivery day supposed to be?"

"A week."

"A week?" Verecker's head swiveled around. "They figure to keep that plane hidden that long? That's what I call confidence."

Rinlaub said, "They're doing O.K. so far. We've been over every inch of the lake and an area fifty miles around it. It looks like VE Day up there with all the choppers and small planes buzzing around, not to mention a whole task force covering the ground—the Highway Patrol, the local Sierra police, the Nevada police and the countless FBI men. The FAA's up there, the insurance people—boy, are *they* up there. That plane's insured for a fortune."

Annie was fiddling with a ring, an idea growing in the back of her mind. She said, "You know, once you get over the mountains into Nevada there are a lot of flat, wide-open spaces you could land a plane in, even one as big as a 747."

Rinlaub agreed. "Sure, but how do you hide it once you've got it down? And what do you do with three hundred and sixty people for a week? Not that we know exactly how many people are on that jet, except the ticket counter people said it was pretty full. But even if it were half that number you'd still have to take over a summer camp or something."

Verecker said casually, "You checked all the airfields, of course."

"Of course."

Verecker went back to his desk, sat down in his chair, opened a drawer and took out a clean sheet of paper, which he started to fold very carefully. He made a triangle of it, folded that in half, turned down the corners and held up a paper dart. He squinted down the center crease and said, "Would you like me to tell you what I think?"

17

The room waited expectantly.

"I'd say," he said, measuring his words as if he were squeezing them from an eyedropper, "that you've got yourselves a problem."

The room relaxed.

Very slowly, Rinlaub put the cuff links back into their box and locked the box away in his briefcase.

Annie said, "You know, stunts as spectacular as this one don't happen every day. What I'm wondering is just how many people there are who are capable of even thinking this big, let alone having the organization to carry it out."

Rinlaub was nodding in agreement. "That's right, Annie. The FBI says there are only about four people they know of who would even think of trying to pull a job like this. Two of them are in jail, the third's been living in Turkey for the last couple of years and the fourth has been dead for a month."

Annie suggested that the two men who were in jail could still have masterminded the whole thing, even controlled it, from their cells. Rinlaub conceded this but pointed out that, when they'd been convicted, both men's mobs had been broken up and that specialists like these two didn't like working with unknowns.

Vereckers suggested that maybe some new faces had appeared on the scene, people the FBI wasn't aware of. His friend told him that there wasn't very much the FBI wasn't aware of. But he admitted it could be an established group who'd grown tired of knocking over armored cars and had decided to branch out spectacularly.

"How about imported talent?" Verecker asked. "The English have always gone in for pretty showy stuff."

"True," Rinlaub admitted. "But kidnapping is an American specialty. That's why everybody's pretty convinced this thing's home-grown."

"What else are they convinced of?"

"Not a hell of a lot at this stage. It's obvious there was a hijacker on board—probably more than one. And they know

18

that somebody got to that computer and that somebody lifted the ticket dupes and the manifests. But, apart from that, nothing."

"But that must narrow the field for them," Annie proposed.

"Not as much as you might think. Any computer programmer with access to the computer could have done the trick, and there are more programmers around today than you can shake a stick at. And finding whoever took the ticket dupes isn't much easier. They had to be at the airport and they had to have access to the Operations Room and be able to get behind the counter. A lot of people qualify."

"Maybe they were behind the counter already," Annie said.

"Maybe. The FBI are still checking on everyone who was working at the airport that night, but so far nobody's burst into tears and told all. Again, that's a lot of people."

"Which is going to take a lot of time," Verecker put in.

Rinlaub spread his hands. "It's time we're up against. We're facing a twenty-five-million-dollar payoff in five days, and that's just not going to be long enough to break down a couple of hundred alibis."

"What I don't understand," Annie said, "is why wipe out the passenger list? After all, that's what they're ransoming. Why should they try and keep it a secret?"

Verecker waited for the answer. He'd been going to ask the same question.

"Obviously to keep us from knowing all the names on that flight. But don't ask me why. Maybe there's somebody whose name would ring bells with the FBI. I really don't know."

Verecker chimed in. "But it wasn't an international flight, no passports or anything. Anybody could fake his name if he wanted to."

"Maybe he didn't know there was going to be any reason to," Annie said.

Rinlaub said, "Whatever the reason, they don't want us to know who's on that plane, and we'd like to find out why."

Verecked snapped his fingers suddenly and pointed one of

19

them like a gun. "Travel agents. They'd have a record of reservations."

Tiredly Rinlaub said, "Do you know how many travel agents there are in the Bay area alone? Not to mention northern California. It would take ages to check them all. Ironically enough, we did turn up one passenger at the first travel agent we checked—the biggest in town. But he turned out to be an Economy passenger we already knew about." He shot a wrist out of his sleeve, glanced at his watch and said, "Hey, I've got to get out of here." He held out a hand to Annie. "Nice meeting you, Annie."

"Same here."

Verecker walked him to the door and opened it for him. Rinlaub handed him a card.

"Look," he said, "just in case you get any ideas you think could help you can always reach me at this number. And remember, I didn't tell you a thing, O.K.? I volunteered to come over and quiz you, not to tell you more than even the relatives know."

"I appreciate it, Phil. And don't worry. When this thing's all over we'll get together and have a drink. It can't last forever."

"Sure." Rinlaub started down the corridor and called back over his shoulder, "That's what they said about The Hundred Years' War."

Verecker waved, then went back into the office. Annie was taking her turn standing at the window and staring out. Verecker joined her watching the dentist opposite examining X rays. At long last he said, "It's the only way to travel."

"I still can't get over it," Annie told him. "Twenty-five million dollars . . . all those people."

The dentist went away.

Verecker said, "Come on, I'll drive you home. I want to think about this."

They locked the office, rode down in the elevator together and strolled along Montgomery to Clay, where they turned down toward the parking lot at the Ferry Building. Even though they lived only fifteen minutes away by cable car Verecker refused to ride it. He claimed the brakeman's bell clanging was too much for him—he didn't need that much rhythm so early in the morning—so they drove to the office each day. Annie put up with this but insisted they park at the Ferry Building, which was cheaper than Jackson Square. Verecker always grumbled at the walk that that let him in for. He said he'd read in his mother's favorite magazine that walking could kill you. Only the other day a woman had stepped on one end of the long scarf she'd been wearing and strangled herself. Annie had argued that if he'd walk on a golf course, why not a street? He'd said that that was different—there was a bar at the end of a golf course.

They strolled toward the Embarcadero, through a drab section of town that had once been bursting with the flavors and smells of fish and flowers and vegetables but was now a dreary succession of warehouses and corner gas stations. They crossed the little green landscaped park—the stone arch, all that was left of the old market, reminding Verecker of the lone wrecked building they'd left standing in Hiroshima—and went a few more blocks to the parking lot. They climbed into Verecker's three-year-old convertible and started for Russian Hill.

Verecker and Annie had apartments in the same house—a tall, weatherboard house with big, glassy windows and long bursts of white wooden filigree—perched near the top of a street that fell away like a roller coaster on one side. The houses were set into the slope of the hill, stacked one above the other, as if they were standing on tiptoe to get a better look at the bay. The view from Verecker's second-floor apartment wasn't as panoramic as the view from the Top o' the Mark, but it was almost as spectacular. Previously, the apartment had been rented by a stocks-and-bonds salesman Verecker played tennis with now and then who'd given Verecker first refusal on it. When the salesman had married, his bride had flatly refused to live in an apartment she claimed would go rolling down the

21

hill at the first sign of an earthquake, so he'd moved out and Verecker and Annie had moved in. When the marriage busted up, they'd tossed to see who would move out and Annie lost, but being reluctant to give up the view and the great location, she'd wheedled and begged the first-floor apartment from Mrs. Grabowski, the landlady who lived on the third floor. Annie's mother didn't like the arrangement at all; she thought a divorce should be a complete break, and here Annie was not only sharing an office with her ex-husband but sharing a house, too. Annie said she felt about the house the same way she felt about the job: She liked it and didn't see why she should give it up. After all, they lived completely separate lives, didn't they?

Verecker parked the car outside the house, turned the wheel toward the curb, shoved the selector into Park and pulled the hand brake full on. A runaway on this hill would have been equivalent to driving the car over a cliff.

"Mr. Ryder isn't going to like this," Annie said as she got out.

"Screw Mr. Ryder," Verecker replied.

The man they referred to owned the ground-floor apartment of the house opposite the one Verecker and Annie lived in. He couldn't stand anybody parking in front of his apartment, not even himself. He parked his own car in front of his neighbor's house. Most of the residents in the immediate area found other parking spots rather than face the tirade Ryder would rain down on them, but Verecker maintained that he had a perfect right to park where he liked and wasn't going to be bullied out of it. The last time they'd had a confrontation they'd got into a shouting match, with Verecker telling him to go to hell and Ryder promising to slash his tires for him next time he found his car there. Verecker had replied that for every tire Ryder slashed he'd slash two of his. Annie had finally had to drag him away, telling him not to be so childish, but Verecker had insisted he wasn't going to be outslashed by a dyspeptic old bastard like that.

"I think you park here just to make him mad," Annie said.

22

Verecker said, "If I moved to Oakland I'd still park here."
He let them into the front door of the house.

Annie fumbled with her apartment keys and said, "See you in the morning."

Verecker paused on the bottom step. "Say, er, you want to come up for a drink?" Annie looked at him suspiciously.

"I just thought we could hash over this 747 business. Maybe we could come up with something." He tried to make it sound like all work and no play.

"Thanks, but I have a date."

"Not Laughing boy again—the one with the bloodshot ears?"

Indignant, Annie said, "If you're referring to Frank Golson, he does not have bloodshot ears. In fact, I think they're rather superior to yours."

"I'm sure you think everything of his is superior to mine."

"*Really!* Does it ever occur to you that it's possible for a man and a woman to have a relationship without sex entering into it?"

"Sure, if the man's over ninety and under constant sedation, but even then—"

"Are you telling me it's not possible for a man to admire a woman for her brain?"

"Well," Verecker said doubtfully, "a mad scientist building a monster, maybe."

"Oh, Verecker, be fair. All men don't want all women."

"Of course they don't. Who's got that kind of time?"

"No one I know except you." Annie was getting a little mad. "No doubt the drink you just offered me would be a fast one; you've probably got a date with that Woolworth's check-out girl, what's-her-name."

It was Verecker's turn to be indignant. "Julia Farrel? She is not either a Woolworth's check-out girl. There's a catty remark for you."

"Well, what is she then?"

"She's on the glove counter at Macy's."

23

"Oh, the *glove* counter. How stupid of me."

"As a matter of fact," Verecker said loftily, "they're thinking of making her assistant buyer."

"Listen, I've seen her walk, and believe me, she's not buying, she's selling."

There was a short pause while they glared at each other.

Verecker said, "O.K., don't come up for a drink. Go ahead and have a real swinging time with Frank Golson. I'm sure he's got something great in mind, like a bus ride and a couple of Hershey bars. But please don't wake me up with that 'Oh, Frank, don't' routine at one o'clock in the morning. Let him or don't let him, but keep quiet about it."

"You wouldn't care if I did let him, would you?"

"Who, Golson? He wouldn't know how."

"Ha!" Annie snorted. "On our wedding night it was you who wouldn't come out of the bathroom."

"I've explained that," Verecker said irritably. "I was threading the cord through my pajama pants and I lost the safety pin."

"Oh, why don't you go upstairs and put on a clean shirt? And the shoes with the mirrors. You don't want to keep Our Lady of the Glove Counter waiting."

Verecker stomped up the stairs. "Don't worry, I'm going. And don't come to work in the morning with lipstick on your ear."

Annie looked toward the ceiling and said, "Ooooh," through clenched teeth. She unlocked her door, went through it and slammed it shut. She opened it a second later and hollered up the stairs, "And to think the day I married you was the biggest day of my life."

"It was the dumbest of mine," Verecker called back from the landing.

"Verecker, I still think there's one part of our marriage worth saving."

"What's that?" he asked grudgingly.

"The divorce."

Their doors slammed like a two-gun salute.

24

Seven hours later somebody hammered on Annie's door. A light clicked on inside her apartment and her sleepy voice drifted out into the hall. "Who is it?"

"It's me. Let me in, quickly."

"Verecker, are you gassed again?"

"No, goddamn it. Let me in."

"Do you know what time it is?"

"I know it's getting steadily later."

Annie opened the door and said, "I thought we'd agreed about after-hours visits."

Verecker brushed past her. "This isn't an after-hours visit—not that kind, anyway."

Annie was wearing a pink and cerise negligee, almost see-through, that swirled around her body in soft folds like waves of pink mist.

"Although it might turn into one if you don't put a robe on."

She turned and walked into her bedroom. The pink mist swirled again.

"In fact if you stood in a packing crate it might be even better."

"Pervert," Anne said. She came back in a moment later tying a robe around her. She sat down on the sofa. "Well . . . ?"

Verecker launched right into it, excited about something, his words coming like buckshot. He was wearing jeans and a shirt and old loafers, a glass with an ounce of bourbon waving wildly in his hand. "Do you know where I played golf today?"

"Golf?" Annie's voice had needles in it. "Verecker, if you woke me up to talk about mashie niblicks . . . "

"The Green Hills Country Club," he said, as if it would explain everything.

"Well, they're no snobs."

"Annie, the Green Hills Golf Club is practically right next door to the airport."

"And you couldn't concentrate with all those planes flying around and that's why Rogers beat you. Is that what you woke me up to tell me?"

Verecker closed his eyes; she still hadn't got it. "Rogers' ball," he said, enunciating each syllable, "Rogers' ball. It rolled into a hole with a burnt-out firework in the bottom, remember?"

"Yes, yes," she said tiredly, "and he took a drop and threw a hole-in-one and—"

"I think what I thought were fireworks were really burnt-out flares. I think a small plane landed on that golf course."

Instant silence—the street outside the house, the house itself, the room inside the house where Annie stared at Verecker.

She broke it. Her eyes flickered to the glass in his hand. "Can I fix you some coffee?"

"For crissakes, Annie, I'm not kidding and I'm not bombed. There was an entire row of those holes. And I'll bet you a weekend in Las Vegas there's another row opposite—a makeshift runway."

"Now just a second." She pulled the robe tighter around her, preparing to play the cool, logical advocate. "This afternoon they were rockets let off by kids getting a jump on the Fourth of July. Then you hear about a stolen plane and suddenly they're burnt-out flares left over from some clandestine midnight landing. I'd say your imagination's working overtime."

"And I'd say yours isn't even working." Verecker paced up and down the room, annoyed. "Come on, Annie, think for a second. A small plane lands secretly at night less than a mile from where a 747 that nobody's seen since takes off from. It's got to tie up."

"Maybe. If you're right in assuming a plane did land on that course."

"Look, there were ruts on that fairway—the kind of ruts a small plane might make. I didn't give them a second thought at the time, but I'm giving them all kinds of thoughts right now."

"All right, suppose it was a plane," Annie said. "How do you know it wasn't an emergency landing?"

"With an airport only a few minutes away? You're kidding." He stopped pacing and sank down into the sofa next to her.

26

His voice was quieter now, a tense note creeping into it. "Annie, this could be it. We could be on the edge of a fortune."

"What fortune?"

He put the glass down on a side table, the liquor untouched. "From the insurance company. Those planes are worth millions. If the plane was recovered through information we gave them it'd have to be worth a hundred grand to them."

Annie turned away. "My God. How mercenary can you get? How about the poor people who were kidnapped and their relatives who must be worried sick? Why don't you think about them?"

"I am thinking about them. If we helped find the plane quicker the passengers would be released that much faster, wouldn't they? And the relatives could stop worrying."

"And you could stop worrying because you'd be a hundred thousand dollars richer, is that it?"

Verecker reached for the drink and asked the glass, "What have you got against money suddenly? This afternoon you were waving bills in my face and telling me we needed a truckload. Well, here's our chance."

In a softer voice Annie said, "It just seems like such a shoddy way to get it."

"What's shoddy about it?" He put the glass down and counted off on his fingers. "We'd be helping the passengers, the relatives, the airline, the insurance people—even the FBI."

"Oh, Verecker. You don't really think you're smarter than the FBI, do you?"

"Not smarter, just luckier. Why should the FBI think of checking Green Hills? I stumbled on those flares only because I happened to be playing golf there. Mere chance, that's all."

Annie stood up. If she'd been wearing a watch she would have looked at it. She said patiently, "The first thing you have to do is find out whether or not they really were flares, so the best thing you can do now is go up to bed and check the golf course first thing in the morning."

Verecker stood up, too. "The morning? I was planning to go now—with a flashlight."

27

"If those holes were there today they'll be there tomorrow. Go upstairs and get what's left of a good night's sleep."

She smiled at him and shook her head slowly. Her hair had fallen over one eye, and Verecker reached out and gently took it back off her face. The sweet, warm-woman, fresh-out-of-bed smell came to him, scented bread in a baker's oven. He said, looking down at the pink froth of night dress that showed at the neck of the gown, "The doctor said I should cut out climbing stairs. Says it's bad for my heart." He thought, pink zabaione I could eat with a spoon.

She said, "What you have in mind is worse for your heart."

"Oh, come on, Annie," Verecker said petulantly. "You didn't act like this when we were married."

"That's because we *were* married."

"But you didn't act like it before we were married, either. You always said you believed in premarital sex."

"I still do. It's postmarital sex I don't believe in."

Verecker tried to get through to her. He couldn't understand why she couldn't understand. "But, honestly, we're not kids. We're two mature divorced adults."

"And you know perfectly well why we're divorced."

"Oh, not that again. Besides, you promised to take me for better or for worse."

"Worse I could have lived with, but I draw the line at unspeakable."

Verecker opened his mouth to reply, couldn't think of anything, and closed it with a snap. Annie took advantage of this and steered him toward the door. "Now you've got a big day at the golf course tomorrow and I've got a big day, too—filing unpaid bills. So off you go."

Verecker still couldn't think of anything to say, so instead he stalked to the door, mad. "O.K." he said. "Good *night*."

"And don't slam your door. You'll wake Mrs. Grabowski."

Upstairs, Verecker slammed his door and woke Mrs. Grabowski.

28

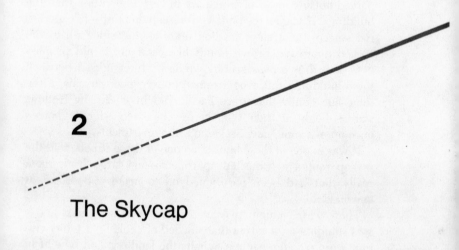

2

The Skycap

It used to be that if you were driving out of the city and down the Peninsula the road you took was the El Camino Real, which was then the main highway to the south. But about fifteen years ago the Bayshore Freeway was built a mile east which cut the driving time from the city to San Bruno by two thirds. This meant that you could get to Los Angeles a lot faster, although most people who live in San Francisco can't see any advantage in getting there at all. The Bayshore runs for only seven or eight miles; Camino runs for about five hundred. It starts on the southern edge of the city and by the time it reaches San Bruno it's already a frantic conglomeration of coffee shops, laundromats, cut-rate supermarkets and used-car lots strung with multicolored plastic bunting, phallic electric signs over the driveways flashing like distress signals. The streets that crisscross the old highway around this section are

pretty much interchangeable—continuous rows of drab apartment houses in sharp contrast to the bright, shiny automobiles
parked outside, most of which are in better condition than the
buildings. If you've seen one you've seen them all—five stories,
red stucco, three steps leading up from the sidewalk to the
arched doorways, brown blinds like cataracts in old people's
eyes, half drawn over grubby windows. Interspersed between
these buildings, tall, wood-framed houses, poor cousins of the
same fine family that grace Pacific Heights and Cow Hollow,
stare sullenly at their twin across the street—family houses
once upon a time, now broken up into apartments.

It was in one of these houses, on one of these streets, that the
skycap rented a furnished apartment—one large front room
really that had been partitioned off to make a bedroom at
one end.

There wasn't much: two fat reupholstered armchairs and a
sofa standing on a carpet that smelled of cooking, a table with
four worn wooden captain's chairs the landlord had bought in
the Mission when the old Star Hotel had closed; a TV set in
the corner that needed rabbit's ears; a black, grainy sideboard
along one wall; two rococo metal lamp stands, each six feet
high, with large brown-tasseled shades shielding two forty-
watt bulbs; a two-feet-square wrought-iron table with a glass
top slotted into the metal flanges; crinkly cream and brown
wallpaper on all four walls. The bathroom was down the hall.
There wasn't any kitchen.

He'd moved in three years ago because the place was only five
minutes' drive from the airport, which meant he could take it
easy on gas and oil for his '60 Olds. He didn't use the car apart
from getting to and from work; he had everything else he needed
within walking distance. Breakfast was coffee and doughnuts at the drugstore on the corner. A hamburger and a malt
from the wagon that came around the airport in the noon hour.
Back to the drugstore for dinner—pot roast, slice of pie, coffee.
There was a movie house a few blocks down Camino if he felt
like it and a bowling alley a little farther on where he usually

went Tuesday nights with
after he was through for t
spent on a bar stool, dawdli
at a local bar called the Stret
Swiss Chalet, and it had b
changed hands a number of ti
had altered the name but left t
it had been bought by an ex-ho
made it but saved enough to buy
embroidered on the decor—gloss
finishes, dated and blown up, por
winners and colored reproductions   .....ury en-
gravings showing elongated thorough   ....uing in profile—
all tacked to the walls on which smiling alpinists in *lederhosen*
and tufted hats scampered up the side of a miniature Matter-
horn. The new owner had kept up his connections with the
track by having what was practically an open line to the
biggest bookie south of the city. Saturdays the place was
crowded and noisy, with everybody in the place lining up
for the phone to get two dollars down. But the rest of the week
it was a quiet neighborhood bar with a steady clientele of
regulars who came in to watch the Giants game. They'd sit
hunched over drinks, looking up at the TV screen, an empty
bar stool between each person the way solitary drinkers seem
to prefer it in America, willing to chat with their neighbor but
happy to remain isolated, as if a man's drinking were not a
pleasure but a problem he had to get over by himself. Now and
then they'd comment on a triple or a called third strike, but, in
the main, they didn't try to compete with the insistent, never-
ending commentary that seemed designed for people who'd
lost the picture and had no hope of ever getting it back.

Apart from a "Hi" when he got there and a "So long" when
he left, the skycap didn't say too much. One of the local
hookers—a girl named Elaine whom he'd go with now and then
—used to call him Old Gabby. Nothing but yak, yak, yak, she'd
say, kidding him. They'd have a few drinks, then go back to

...ard, zipping up her skirt, she'd say she really ...ge him extra, him being black and everything. ...ays laugh when she said it, but he knew she half ... it.

He'd grown up in the East Bay, in Richmond. His father had brought them west in 1943 when they were hiring all the help they could get to build Liberty ships in the newly created shipyard in the Inner Harbor Basin. They'd lived where everybody else had lived who'd come out there to work: in the temporary housing thrown up by the Government. When the war ended and the shipyard closed, his father had been one of the ninety thousand people in the immediate area who were looking for a job. But he was luckier than most; he not only found one, he found a cushy one: driving cars on special order from the Ford plant, which had started up production again, over the Sierras to ranchers in Utah and Nevada and Wyoming. The skycap had been taken along on one of these trips once, to Salt Lake City, when he was nine years old. He'd never forgotten it. He'd sat up in front beside his father in the glossy new Ford, lost in the smell of new carpet, new leather, and the gentle elevator sensation of going up and over the mountains, the car eating up the blue Nevada roads on the other side. They'd stopped in Elko at a noisy Italian restaurant where everybody sat on benches around a long table and ladled out thick soup from steaming tureens and passed around wine and bread and mounds of glistening, garlicky spaghetti, and no one seemed to mind that they were colored. The next day they'd driven across the salt flats on a narrow black river of macadam that flowed straight as an arrow over the dead-white moonscape, the city shimmering on the edge of the lake, a phantom city that never seemed to get any closer. They'd delivered the car and caught the bus back, and his father had said he'd take him again some time. But a month later his father had got up from his chair, walked out of the house and never come back, which had puzzled his nine-year-old son. He'd had a toy once that he'd adored, a kaleidoscope a cousin from back East had given to him. He'd taken it to school and lost it and cried all night, but the next day it didn't seem to matter so much. He could understand how you could lose a toy, but he couldn't understand how the same thing could happen to a father.

His mother had taken him across the bay to San Francisco to a rundown apartment hotel where she got a job scrubbing floors in return for meals, a few dollars and a room at the back. He left school soon after and washed cars for a quarter a time —the truant officers got tired of coming around and eventually let his mother alone. After that there was a succession of similar jobs—years of them—dishwasher, shoeshine boy, supermarket sweeper, anything that required only a pair of hands and was menial enough. Then he heard you could make big money from the tips people gave you for carrying their bags at airports. He took a job as a skycap at the International Airport down the Peninsula, but the tips weren't all that bigger than the ones he got cleaning cars. But he stayed at the job and settled in because a plan for the future had begun forming in his mind. He realized that the one thing this job did that the others didn't was constantly to bring him into contact with people who had money—people who could afford to fly in an airplane all the way across the country—first class, too, a lot of them. And he figured that being close to money was the first step in getting his hands on some. And there was no doubt about it: money was what he needed. Not needed the way you needed a life jacket on a sinking ship, more the way you needed an aspirin to take away a nagging headache. This decision wasn't motivated by greed or acquisitiveness or even boredom, but by the fact that if he was rude to the wrong passenger and lost his job there was always a dirty car or a pile of dirty dishes waiting, or a supermarket floor that wanted sweeping. And he was through cleaning up after people. The thought of jail didn't bother him overmuch; a lifetime of jail or a lifetime of being what he was—to him there didn't seem to be much difference. He was already in a kind of prison anyway.

He knew he'd probably only get one crack at taking money,

so it had better be a good one. There wasn't much point, he reasoned, in knocking over a gas station for two hundred bucks, because in a few weeks' time you'd need another two hundred bucks. And the chances of getting away with a second robbery had to be smaller. The odds had to be with a guy who'd never done a job before, which meant, for the first time in his life, the odds would be with him. He liked the idea of that. The only question was what to steal and how to go about it. If he worked in a bank he'd help himself to some money, wouldn't he? A bank teller was in a perfect position. But he worked at an airport.

He drew the obvious parallel.

It never occurred to him that what he had in mind was fantastic. He simply figured that if he spent enough time on it he'd find a way, and time was just about the only thing he had a lot of.

He told the counterman he'd slipped a disk lifting a heavy bag and would have to quit bowling for a little while. He also settled up his tab at the Stretch. Elaine asked about him a few times, then forgot him. So his social life changed, but not anywhere near as much as his working day. Previously, the only things that had concerned him at the airport were the size of the bags he carried and the size of the tips he got for carrying them. Now he started noticing a whole lot more. His mind became a vacuum cleaner sucking up every piece of information he came across—facts about every big and little operation an airport goes through to get a plane and passengers from one point in the country to another: check-in procedure, air routes, load control, catering, ramp operations, traffic control—everything from what kind of books passengers bought to where the parking-lot guys parked their own cars. And he did it not by asking questions or making himself obvious but by getting all over the airport every chance he got, finding excuses to get behind the counter, into Operations, down onto the ramp.

Nights, he'd grab a bite at the drugstore, go home and stretch out on the sofa and stay that way till the early hours of the morning, smoking his way through a pack of Camels, staring up at the smoke flattening out against the stained ceiling, thinking.

He lived like this for eight months. But at the end of that time he had the solution—a solution plus, as a matter of fact. To make absolutely sure, he spent another two weeks on it, sanding and polishing till it was as smooth and shiny as a beach pebble. Then he paid his first visit to the Stretch in months, called the bookie's number and asked for the boss. The voice on the other end told him he didn't need to talk to the boss if he just wanted to get a bet down, but the skycap said he hadn't called about a bet—he wanted to talk to him about something else.

3

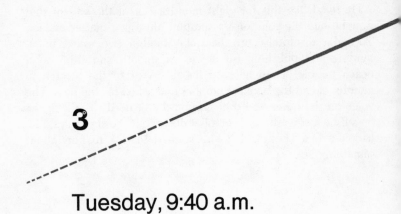

Tuesday, 9:40 a.m.

There was only one lone golfer out this early. Verecker watched him guide his electric buggy around a sand trap and over a hill. He looked like a wheelchair case out getting some fresh air.

Verecker walked past the clubhouse and started down the long green boulevard of the eighteenth fairway, his eyes fixed on the manicured grass. He walked its entire length, almost to the driving tee, then retraced his steps, looking more carefully this time.

The holes and the ruts were gone.

He wondered for a moment if he had the wrong fairway— but Rogers had pipped him on the last hole, and this was the last hole.

A spooky feeling he didn't like started up inside him and slowly began to mushroom.

Away to his left he spotted a man moving fat black hoses around a green. He crossed to him. The man had his back to him, crouching down, his hand buried in the grass. On the green a sprinkler started up, its stiff outstretched arms beginning to move in slow circles, water arcing up from the spigots and spattering down with a wet flopping noise.

"Good morning," Verecker said.

The man turned his head and straightened up, an elderly man with a permanently tanned face, wrinkled like brown paper that had been balled up and smoothed out again. "Howdy."

Verecker had a story all ready. He didn't want to come right out and ask the man about the holes. "Say, you didn't find a spare club in your travels, did you? A five-iron, about halfway down the eighteenth?"

"When did you lose it?"

"Yesterday. I asked up at the clubhouse but nobody handed one in."

The greenkeeper shook his head. "I didn't see anything. A five, eh? We mainly find eight- and nine-irons people leave around the green. How did you come to lose a five—fall out of your bag?" He was looking at Verecker in a funny way.

Verecker shrugged. "Must have just forgotten to put it back. I remember I was having a little trouble trying to dig my ball out of some kind of hole. There was a row of the darn things."

"Oh, those." The wrinkles got deeper. "Craziest thing—some kind of firecrackers in the bottom. I filled 'em in yesterday afternoon."

Verecker relaxed a little; the holes were there and accounted for. The spooky feeling went away. "Firecrackers? You still got them?"

"Naw, threw 'em in the incinerator."

"Oh, no . . ."

"How's that?"

"I mean, how can people do things like that?"

"Whole country's gone mad," the man said.

37

"I seem to remember some ruts, too, in the middle of the fairway."

"Yeah, filled them in, too. Never seen divots like it. Goddamn lady golfers—ruined the game when they let 'em in."

"When did you first notice them, the holes I mean?"

"Oh, people started complaining a few days back, but I've got a man off sick and I couldn't get to it till yesterday." The man finished the sentence with his head cocked to one side, suspicious suddenly. "How come all the questions? You know anything about those holes?"

Verecker denied it with a little laugh. "Not me. My ball rolled into one, as I say. Would've broken par but for that."

The man grunted, unimpressed. He figured sub-par golfers didn't leave clubs scattered all over the course; only duffers and women did that. But then, everybody lied about his score.

Verecker kept at it. "What do you mean, a few days back?" If the man said any other day but Saturday he'd had a long drive for nothing. And Annie would say I told you so. And he could kiss a hundred thousand dollars goodbye. It had to be Saturday; please say Saturday. "Which day exactly?"

"Sunday," the man said.

"Sunday," Verecker repeated in a tiny, defeated voice.

"Or was it Saturday?" the man said thoughtfully.

Verecker closed his eyes and moistened his lips. He was aware of his heart pounding out paradiddles and rim shots and a dry tightness in his throat. He said simply, "Was it Saturday or was it Sunday?"

The man was certain. "It was Saturday. I remember now. We had a tourney here and one of the competitors complained."

"Are you sure they weren't there Friday?"

"Positive. I mowed that fairway Friday for the tourney next day."

Verecker wished he could be as positive; the greenkeeper obviously had a memory like a sieve.

"I still can't see," the greenkeeper said, "why you're so interested in those holes."

"Oh, er, it's just a fixation I have." Verecker started moving off. "Well, thanks for your help; I'll take another look for that club."

The greenkeeper watched him walk back to the other fairway, then bent and turned the sprinkler on harder. Strange young fella, he thought.

The strange young fella moved cautiously up the fairway, head down, like a man afraid of stepping on a land mine. Halfway up on the left-hand side he found what he was looking for. He could see where the greenkeeper had filled the hole in, the three-inch circle slightly greener than the grass around it. He counted off a dozen of them set at ten-yard intervals. He crossed to the other side of the fairway and found the same thing over there, just as he knew he would. Opposite the third set of holes, equidistant between the two rows, the twin ruts had been filled in in the same manner, and twenty feet beyond them another pair, longer and more distinct. As he figured it, the plane had touched down heavily, bounced off, hit again and bounced again, then settled down and completed its runout. He cursed himself for not bring a tape measure, went quickly to a clump of acacia bushes which divided two fairways and came back a few minutes later tearing the yellow pods off a long, thin branch. He snapped a piece off a foot from the end and was left with a dead straight stick. He bent over the ruts and moved the stick between them, measuring the distance as accurately as he could. He did it a second time —and a third to make sure. Finally, he walked back down the fairway doing the land-mine bit again, in the center this time. A hundred feet from the tee he stopped, dropped to his knees and put his face close to a black patch on the grass about the size of a fried egg. Then he straightened up and walked quickly toward the parking lot.

Halfway there he broke into a trot.

"What do you think of that?" Verecker triumphantly threw the branch onto Annie's desk.

39

Annie picked it up and examined it. "Wonderful. We can use it to beat off creditors. What do we need with a stick?"

"That stick, my dear, is going to be worth one hundred grand."

"What is it—early Chippendale?"

Verecker sat on the corner of her desk and told her about the holes and the ruts and what the greenkeeper had said and how he'd used the stick for a ruler.

Annie was still skeptical. "But it's all supposition. After all, the greenkeeper thought they were fireworks, too. Maybe they were."

Verecker admitted it was a tough break, the man burning them. If he'd been able to get hold of just one he could have proved conclusively that they were flares. "However," he said, "at the end of the fairway I found an oil slick, and no double banger I ever heard of leaks oil." He climbed off her desk and laid the stick down on his own. "O.K., pad, pencil and ruler, please."

Annie opened a drawer and handed him a plastic ruler. Verecker carefully measured the stick. He said, "Twenty-three inches and . . . seven sixteenths. You got that? Now the stick went between those ruts three times, so work that out. Then add on . . . " He measured the mark he'd made on the stick. "Add on seventeen and eleven sixteenths. Call it seventeen and three quarters."

Annie calculated swiftly. "I make it a fraction over eighty-eight inches."

"Eighty-eight," Verecker echoed. "Then that's the magic number."

"Why magic?"

"Its going to tell us the name of the guy who landed on that course."

Annie threw her pencil down and snapped the notebook closed. "You're going to find out a man's name from a stick? What are you, an aborigine?"

"You're going to find out his name, and it's simple. You know the plane's wheelbase, right? Eighty-eight inches. So you simply check and find out what kind of plane has a wheelbase of around eighty-eight inches. Let's say it's a Beech Bonanza. O.K., then you check the airports round the Tahoe area and see if a Bonanza landed there sometime Friday night. When you find it you ask for the name of the pilot and we've got our man."

Annie looked bewildered. "But who's going to have that kind of information—and how am I supposed to get it?"

"Call the small-plane dealers for a start. They'll give you the wheelbase measurements. Give them some excuse."

"What kind of excuse?"

"I don't know. Get them interested in your bosom or something."

"How are they going to be interested in my bosom over the telephone?"

"Describe it. You'll think of something."

Annie stopped looking bewildered and started looking doubtful. "What about the rest of it, calling up the airports . . . which airports?"

It was all crystal clear to Verecker. He said patiently, "Call the local FAA and—"

"The local FA what?"

"The Federal Aviation Authority. Don't you know anything?"

"I didn't spend two years in the Air Force like you, you know."

"Hell, I didn't get this stuff from the Air Force; I got it from reading Steve Canyon. Where do you think the Air Force gets it from?"

"Look," Annie asked, "say I call the Federal whatever-you-said and get a list of the airports in the area—what do I tell the airports? I mean apart from letting them know I'm a thirty-six B cup?"

"Tell them you're calling for Phil Rinlaub of Calair. They may not have heard of him, but it'll sound impressive. Ask them to check back through their flight plans for last Friday night—see if they have a Beech Bonanza, or whatever the plane

41

is, that landed later than it should have. The guy must have been overdue, dropping in on a golf course, and he would've had to have given them some excuse—high winds or engine trouble or something. It shouldn't be hard to trace."

"Shouldn't be hard? Come on, Verecker, you know all about these things. Why don't you do the calling?"

Verecker moved to the door. "Because that's what I pay a secretary for."

"That's what you *what* a secretary for?"

"Sweetie, you come up with the right answers to those questions and I'll pay you ten times what I owe you."

"How about in the meantime?"

"In the meantime—" Verecker opened the door—"I'm going to look for an attractive rich widow to defend."

"If you find an attractive widow she'll need defending."

Verecker was halfway out of the office. He came back in, made a fist of one hand and pointed the other at the ceiling. "One of these days, Alice—bang! Zooom!"

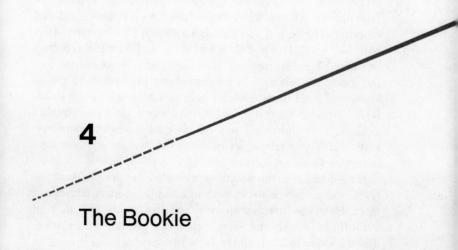

4

The Bookie

It was funny because when he'd first started out he was no different from the people who were now his best customers—a compulsive, small-time, can't-give-it-up horse player. He'd got that way the same as anybody else gets that way—by picking up a few early wins, thinking he'd got the magic touch, going in over his head, losing out and spending the rest of his time trying to get even. He never had regained the magic touch, of course, but then he was smart enough to realize he'd never ever had it, which was why he was taking bets now instead of putting them down. Not that he'd bet foolishly—like picking a horse because he liked the color of the jockey's silks, the way some women do—he'd gone at it very professionally. He'd chosen one track and stuck with it all season, never betting anywhere else. He'd got up at dawn and gone out and watched the horses working out in the early-morning mist and

clocked them through their gallops. He got to know the exercise boys, the stable boys, and found that for a couple of
bucks they'd tell you which horse had got up feeling good that
morning. They'd tell you that horses were like humans—they
had their good days and their bad days, and on a bad day they
just didn't feel like running. He found out a lot of things: that
the jocks, for instance, were just about impossible to get to
know and most times couldn't help you as much as the stable
boys. Owners you could forget; that was a club you couldn't
get into. They didn't talk to anybody except other owners anyway, which was why a lot of them broke even on their own
horses and made a fortune betting everybody else's.

He got to know the people working on the periphery of the
track: the barmen who heard things and the waiters who heard
more. He made friends with everybody he could—nobody kept
a hot tip to himself and everybody had a piece of information.
The trick was to lump all the little bits together, sift through it
and find the one percent that could help you. You never knew
which direction it would come from: sometimes from people
who made their living at the track without working there or
going near a betting window—like the guy who'd photograph
all the horses working out in the morning, go home and develop
the shots and be back at the track in time for the first race. He'd
hang around the grandstand and wait for the happy owner of
a winning horse to emerge, sort through his prints, then go up
to him and tell him he'd just happened to catch Doughboy or
Bold Crusader in full stride that morning and show him the
picture. Without fail the expansive owner, several thousand
dollars richer, would buy the print for ten dollars. Even people
like that knew things.

Going out to the race course every day he got to know everybody anyway—the tipsters, the runners who'd put bets down
for people for a tiny percentage of the take, and the pick-
pockets and con men who lasted only as long as the security
police took to catch up to them—guys who'd tell a mark they

were the track vet. Or stand next to a sucker and yell hello to a jockey during the walk-past and claim he was his brother.

And, of course, like everybody else he never missed the racing columnists and pored over the scratch sheet daily. That was how you got to know almost as much about a horse as its trainer did: how it'd done last time out, what weight it was carrying, whether it liked the mud or not, who its sire and dam were, how it'd done the last couple of weeks, whether it was due for a win this week, who was riding it, who was in the field that could upset it, whether it liked to run from the position it'd drawn, and whether the distance was too short, too long or just right.

He did it all, but the horses still beat him; and he was forced to conclude that if he was going to make his living from thoroughbreds, it wasn't going to be by betting on them. So when he heard from one of the railbirds that Frank Mealey was looking for somebody who knew something about the ponies and was smart and could keep his mouth shut, he applied for the job.

Frank Mealey was just about the biggest book south of the city and one of the smartest. He had a small-appliance repair shop in one of the towns on the Peninsula, a dumpy little store littered with old toasters and broken irons and radios. Upstairs there was a switchboard with ten lines.

Mealey thought of himself as a businessman first and a gambler second, and he ran his business along strict professional lines, as if he had a stockholders' meeting at the end of every month. He always claimed he'd never welsh on a bet and didn't expect anyone else to. If a customer was slow paying he'd send Roger Sam around to remind him. Sam was huge and plodding and weighed three twenty, spoke in a high, soft voice and always kept his hands in his pockets. There wasn't anything in those pockets, but the people he called on weren't going to take a chance, and nine out of ten paid up inside a week. If anyone still held out after a second visit Mealey sold the bet for half

its value to a collection agency who weren't as gentle as Roger
Sam and did have other things in their pockets. It made sense
for Mealey to keep his hands off the customers—the cops
frowned on it for one thing and if somebody got too badly hurt
it brought in another section of the department, which meant
more outstretched palms and less money all around.

He had guts, too. When a police captain of a town a little
farther down the Peninsula had asked for a bigger slice of the
pie than Mealey thought he was entitled to, Mealey had told
him to go to hell; he'd operate under his nose anyway, and if
he didn't like it he'd just have to catch him at it. That's why he
needed an extra man, as he explained to the man who came to
see him about the job—a short, plump, balding guy who'd been
given the O.K. by a track tout.

The job was simple enough—driving for a linen rental service. All he had to do was walk into the washrooms of the bars
and gas stations and launderettes on the list, install a fresh
roller towel, take the old one back to the van and, before it
went off to the laundry, copy down the bets that had been
penciled on it. It was simple and it was good—anybody could
get a bet down just by going in to wash his hands. And the
sweet part of it was that there was nothing in the washroom a
suspicious cop could spot. A customer simply wrote down his
bet, pulled the towel down a couple of times and the evidence
disappeared up inside the metal holder.

So he went to work driving a van for Frank Mealey for one
hundred and twenty dollars a week. But it wasn't long before
he got a raise. He figured out a code to keep track of the bets,
then figured out a better one. Finally, he found he could keep
them all in his head. When his boss found out about that he
took him off the van and made him his assistant.

Two years later he made him his partner.

Ten years later, when Mealey died from a heart attack, he
took over everything—the business, the house in Hillsborough
and the widow inside it.

From then on the business changed. He opened offices in

46

San Mateo, San Carlos, Redwood City and over in the East Bay. As his business grew he installed managers, then a general manager, and thought more and more about retiring. He felt he owed it to himself; he'd come a long way. But when the skycap called and they met and talked, he had to ask himself what was wrong with going a little farther.

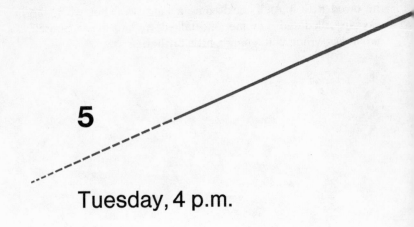

5

Tuesday, 4 p.m.

"Annie? It's me."

"Verecker, where the hell are you? It's four o'clock already."

"Don't yell at me. I'm weak. I've been giving blood."

"Whose blood? Not your own."

"Of course not. I bribed an eighty-seven-year-old grandmother to go in my place."

"Don't lie, Verecker. Since when have you been a blood donor?"

"Since they started serving Pepperidge Farm Tahiti cookies afterwards."

"You're not in any blood clinic. You're half gassed in some Market Street poolroom, aren't you?"

"I am not either."

"Then what's that clicking noise I can hear in the background?"

"My eyes. They keep crossing. Anyway, enough about me; I'm just a cipher. I called to see how you got on."

"It was like pulling teeth. Hold the line for a second." Annie put the phone down, opened a drawer and pulled out her pad and picked up the phone again. "That measurement you took, eighty-eight inches—it seems to fit a couple of planes. The Piper 250 Aztec and the Cessna Super Skymaster."

"Did you check the airports near the lake?"

"Take it easy. I'm getting to it. On Friday night a Piper Aztec landed at Carson City at eight forty-five. A Cessna also landed there two hours earlier. However, a Piper Aztec landed at Truckee just before nine, so you've got three to choose from."

"Did you get their embarkation points?"

Annie flipped another page. "The Carson City plane came from Mexico. The earlier one from Rio Vista. The Truckee flight from Lompoc." There was a long pause. "Verecker, you still there?"

"Yeah. I was just thinking. Mexico, huh?"

"You find that fascinating?"

"Kind of."

"Why?"

"Because I've been asking myself. Why should anybody want to land on a golf course at night anyway?"

"Obviously to keep it a secret."

"Yes, but why?"

"How should I know? Maybe the pilot told his date he was out of gas. What's that got to do with Mexico?"

Verecker said, "What if you had to smuggle something into the country—an unscheduled landing would be a beautiful way of doing it."

"Sure, but in this case what would you be smuggling?"

"The guy that hijacked the plane."

"Verecker, you shouldn't talk about it over the phone."

"Oh, nobody's going to know what I'm talking about. Nobody does any other time."

"Well, speak a little lower, then. Anyway, bring in somebody

49

just for that? It doesn't make sense. One thing this country isn't short of is hijackers."

"Yeah, but they're all amateurs. And with all that dough riding on it maybe whoever pulled this didn't want to risk any slipups. So they brought in a pro—some guy who'd only have to point a gun and any airline captain in the world would know he wasn't kidding. What's the pilot's name?"

"Lee Clarke."

"Lee Clarke . . . Sounds American enough. Just where in Mexico did he fly from?"

"Mazatlan."

"We could call the airport at Mazatlan and find out where he came in from."

"I already did, although I wore the pants out of my Spanish doing it. He flew in from Novato."

"Annie, you're fantastic. Remind me to give you a raise."

There was a long pause and it was Verecker's turn to ask if the other was still on the line.

"Oh sure," Annie replied. "Just a touch of apoplexy, that's all."

Verecker said, "I was about to say, before we were so rudely interrupted by your silence, that if this guy Clarke keeps his plane in Novato he probably lives in Marin somewhere."

"Two sixty-three Johnson Street, Sausalito."

"See, I told you so. Call him and tell him I want to see him, would you? Think up some excuse. Try and make it first thing in the morning."

"Aren't you going to check on the other pilots?"

"What other pilots? You mean Rio Vista and the guy from Lompoc? Why bother? He'd have to fly too far out of his way from Rio Vista. And you don't have to smuggle anybody out of Lompoc; they leave by their own accord. Clarke's the guy we want. I've never been so . . . " The phone bleeped in Annie's ear. There was the sound of a coin dropping and the bleep went away.

"Verecker, this call's costing a fortune."

50

"I've never been so sure of anything in my life."

"But you're always sure. You were certain that Benson was honest and would pay his bill until you got a rude postcard from Brazil."

"At least he cared enough to write."

"And when the Appleby kid broke down and confessed to a packed courtroom and a TV audience of millions you pleaded not guilty."

"O.K., O.K."

"And how about Johnny Richardson? You knew the judge was all set to let him off with a suspended sentence, but after your brilliant summation for the defense he handed him a sixer at San Quentin."

"All right, so I've been a little mistaken now and then. But I'm right about this, Annie. I can feel it in my bones."

"It's probably just rheumatism. Was there anything else?"

"Well, as a matter of fact, I was thinking that, er . . . maybe I should sleep at your apartment tonight so we can get an early start in the morning."

"No thanks. I know what kind of early start you're thinking of."

"Why, Anne Verecker!"

"Sorry if I shocked you. I'll give you breakfast and that's all."

"In bed?"

"Is bed all you ever think of?"

"Of course not. I think of sofas, too."

"Well, think about a cold shower as well. See you in the morning."

"Annie . . . " Verecker's voice was urgent.

"What?"

"You hang up first."

"Idiot," Annie said.

51

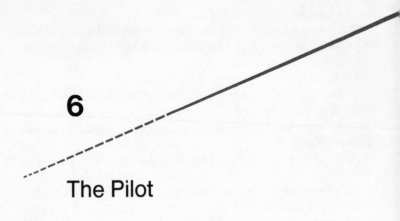

6

The Pilot

When he was seventeen and growing up in a small town in northern Ontario he'd answered an ad in *Popular Mechanics* that said, "You Too Can Have a High Paying Career in the Airlines." There was a picture in the ad showing a smiling pilot waving from the cockpit of a Constellation and palm trees in the background. It turned out to be a come-on for a pricey correspondence course, sent each week from some place in Kansas, that trained you as an airline mechanic at home. He talked his mother into coming up with the down payment and enrolled. He studied by mail, sat for exams by mail and graduated by mail. When he left home and went after a job with an airline in Toronto they told him his diploma wasn't recognized in Canada but agreed to take him on as a trainee. Six months later he knew as much about airplane engines as his boss did.

He stayed with the airline for a couple of years, then quit

when the maintenance chief at the small-plane airport on the Island offered him a better deal. Around about this time the Ontario Goverment came up with a scheme whereby you could learn to fly for free. You paid one hundred dollars for the lessons, and when you got your license the Government refunded your money. So he scraped up the hundred dollars and took lessons. He soloed the third time up, and the instructor said he was a natural.

From then on, flying was all he wanted to do. His first job was piloting a Tiger Moth, towing a sign that urged the crowds at the Canadian National Exhibition to listen to radio CHUM. But that meant a series of long, slow circles at minimum speed, which wasn't his idea of flying.

He liked his next job a lot better: flying for a guy who was in the joy-ride business. But when a blond secretary from Buffalo complained that he'd tried to really take her for a joy ride he'd been bounced out on his ear.

There hadn't been much else around after that, and the summer was running out fast, so he caught the Greyhound to Vancouver and landed a job flying hunters into Big Timber country—loudmouths who talked big, drank themselves blind and secretly prayed to God the guide would know what to do if they ran into the grizzly they were paying him to find.

When winter came and the season was over he moved down to California. He took a one-hour lesson in a helicopter, went for his license next day, leased a 'copter and made money renting out to TV production companies—a lot of money. The word soon got around that he'd get you closer than anybody else—under bridges, on top of waterfalls, wherever you had to go if you wanted a tight shot. He stuck at that just long enough to get five thousand dollars together and bought his first plane—an old Stinson. From that he made money flying sailors, with twenty-four-hour passes and no time to waste, from Long Beach to San Francisco and back. And cut into the seaplane trade flying weekenders from L.A. to Catalina, but he had to give it up when he found out the FAA was onto him.

So he went to work flying tourists legitimately down to a resort in Baja California, to a town that wasn't serviced by a regularly scheduled airline. It was on one of these trips that somebody approached him in Ensenada, where he'd stopped to refuel on his way back, and asked him if he'd be willing to deliver a package for five hundred dollars, no questions asked. He'd jokingly replied that he might consider it for five thousand dollars and without batting an eyelid the man agreed. He'd dropped it in a prearranged spot in the San Pedro Channel a few miles off Avalon, where it had been picked up by a fishing boat. He had no illusions of what it was he was carrying, just as he had no illusions to the way his bank balance had built up after three months of stopping off at Ensenada.

But then something happened.

The man with the package didn't arrive one day, but the narcotics squad did. They stripped him and the plane down to the ground, found nothing and had to apologize. It was obvious to the pilot that the gang had been tipped off and wouldn't be back. Ensenada was over.

He quit the resort, took his money out of the savings and loan and bought a brand-new six-seated Piper Aztec for twenty thousand down. He put it to work right away flying families up to Lake Shasta for houseboat vacations. Then somebody wanted him to come in on a deal in Peru flying dude archaeological expeditions which would try to trace the old Inca roads from the air. But nothing ever came of it.

He hung around San Francisco for a while waiting for something to turn up. Then he saw the ad—a Business Proposition. It was for somebody with his own plane who might be interested in a new, big-money-making enterprise. He was skeptical about it at first—he'd answered ads like that before —but he figured, what the hell, he may as well check into it.

After he'd been interviewed for the third time, and the short, plump, bald guy had finally told him what it was all about, he had to admit it was new. And they certainly weren't kidding about the money being big.

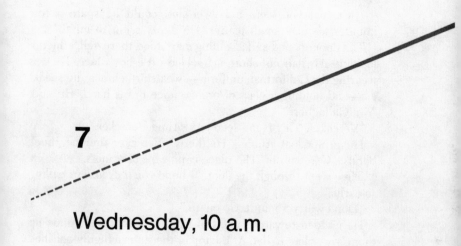

7

Wednesday, 10 a.m.

Two sixty-three Johnson Street looked like two sixty-five
Johnson Street: one of a row of white two-story frame houses
with new picture windows top and bottom and old shingled
turrets sprouting on the roof. It was halfway up the slope of a
steep hill running off Bridgeway, about a quarter mile past the
cutsie-pie section of Sausalito.

Verecker parked behind a cream-colored Pontiac that had
its front wheels pointing straight down the hill, a sure sign of
an out-of-towner. There was a delivery van parked on the other
side of the road and up a bit. It had the words "Kingston Air
Freight" emblazoned on the side panel, red on white, silver
wings with speed lines flowing off the last word. Verecker
looked at it long and hard as they went through a small gate
and up the steps of the house.

He buzzed at the bell opposite a name plate that said "L.

Clarke." "What did you tell him on the phone?" he asked Annie.

"Just that you were a lawyer and could he spare a few minutes about a small matter. He didn't seem to mind."

The door opened and a smiling man stood there, tall, athletic-looking, fair hair cut short, a freckled little-boy's face. He was wearing the Californian uniform—sweatshirt, chinos and sneakers—and holding a glass of orange juice in his hand. He said, "Mr. Gallagher?"

"Verecker. This is my secretary, Anne Verecker."

He grinned at Annie. "Hi there." Verecker and he shook hands. "Come on in. The place is in a bit of a mess."

They went through the door. "I hope you'll excuse us calling so early."

"Don't worry about it. Go on up."

He nodded toward a flight of stairs and followed Annie up them, very close to her. At the top of the stairs a highly polished wooden propeller was mounted on the wall, grainy and honey-colored.

"It's off an old Jenny," Clarke said.

They went up another half flight and onto a landing. "Go in and sit down, why don't you? I've got some coffee on." He waved the glass of orange juice toward an open doorway, then went the other way into a kitchen.

Verecker took Annie's elbow and steered her into a large sunny room that looked as if it had been bought whole from Cost Plus: yellow cane furniture, African-print fabrics, bulky Japanese ashtrays, Indian brass ornaments, rattan mat on the floor. There was a set of do-it-yourself shelves against one wall full of hi-fi and photography magazines and a beautifully made balsa-wood model of a Curtiss Hawk standing on a Chinese chest. Colored-ink drawings of First World War biplanes covered one wall. In the picture window Mount Tamalpais, foggy and green in the distance, was framed like one of the drawings.

They sat down. A voice called from the kitchen, "Be with you in a second."

Cups and saucers clinked and Clarke walked into the room carrying a tray. He handed around coffee and said, "Sorry about the unmatched cups. I'll have to win some more at the movies."

They laughed politely and he bathed them in a big smile. He seemed to be able to turn it up or down like a rheostat.

They sipped their coffee and small-talked for a while, then Verecker said, "Well, as I think Mrs. Verecker explained on the phone, I'm a lawyer. I'm representing a client who claims he has a complaint against you."

Clarke raised his eyebrows. "Oh? What have I done now?" He turned the smile up a fraction and looked over at Annie and kept looking at her. Annie spooned sugar into her almost empty cup.

Verecker said, "You're a flyer, aren't you?"

Clarke waved vaguely at the drawings. "What else?"

"A small plane?"

"Two-fifty Aztec."

"Registration number 4757Q, right?"

"That's me."

"Yes. Well, my client claims you almost killed him last Friday night at Palo Alto."

"He *what?*" The smile went out.

"He says you completely disregarded ground control and taxied out right in front of him just as he was landing."

"He's crazy. I flew Mazatlan–Carson City Friday night. I wasn't within five thousand feet of Palo Alto."

"Uh huh," Verecker mumbled. "And you didn't make any stops along the way?"

"No sir. Flew direct. You can check my flight plan."

"Oh, that won't be necessary. My client obviously got the wrong number, that's all."

"If he was so busy dodging a plane on the deck, how would

57

he have time to get a number?" Clarke said it harshly, then tried to soften it by adding a little laugh at the end.

Verecker kept him company. "To tell you the truth, this particular client is a little erratic. He's a business friend, you know?" The other man nodded understandingly, two businessmen discussing the foibles of another. "But I promised to check it out for him. I'm sorry to have taken up your time."

Verecker glanced at Annie and they got to their feet. Clarke rose with them. He said, "Don't worry about that—sorry I couldn't help you." He lit up the smile again and beamed it at Annie, dropping his eyes to her sweater for a long blatant second. She moved quickly to the door, feeling her clothes practically falling off her.

Verecker followed her to the landing, then asked Clarke, walking beside him, "How's your golf game these days?" He threw it away as if it were just polite, incidental conversation.

"My golf game? I'm a tennis man. Never could see walking after a little ball. Why? Do you play?"

"Oh, I fool around."

"How about you, Mrs. Verecker?"

Annie shook her head and said flatly, "No."

They reached the bottom of the stairs and Clarke held the door open for them.

"Once again," Verecker said, "sorry to have taken up your time."

"No trouble." He pumped Verecker's hand like a college kid. They walked down the steps to the sidewalk.

"Take it easy," he called. The door closed behind them.

They crossed to their car and got in. Verecker noticed that the airline freight truck had gone. He sighed, leaned back on the seat and said, "He wasn't exactly a bundle of nerves, was he?"

"I don't like him," Annie declared.

"Me neither. The guy's in love with himself and wants everybody to see why. Still, he didn't turn a hair over that golf-course line. I was watching him pretty closely."

"He was watching me pretty closely. I think he knows where babies come from."

"Yeah, I saw him. Goddamn it, either he's a sensational actor or we've got the wrong man."

"You want to check the Rio Vista pilot?"

Verecker reached into a pocket. "I'd like to check this first." It was a small cardboard frame with a fold-out easel die-cut into the back. It held a color print of a pretty blonde in what looked like a stewardess' uniform.

"Did you steal that just now?"

"Yep."

"That's not very ethical."

"Neither is stealing a planeload of people."

"You think he's lying then?"

"Impossible to tell, but look at it this way: We go to see a guy we suspect might know something about a twenty-five-million-dollar kidnap. We walk into his living room and the first thing we see is a photograph of a stewardess, obviously his girl. You've got to check on something like that."

"But, after all, he's a pilot. He probably uses a lot of big airports, so it stands to reason he'd know a few stewardesses." Annie squirmed in her seat. "In fact, I'm sure that boy knows most of them."

Verecker studied the print as if he were trying to spot some retouching. He tapped the frame thoughtfully on the steering wheel. "I suppose so. I guess it would make a lot more sense if she were wearing a Calair uniform, which she isn't. Maybe I'm wrong about the guy—I mean he just didn't react—no surprise, no hesitation, just good old California Joe College grinning and slapping people on the backside."

"I thought he was going to—" Annie broke off and clutched Verecker's arm. She was staring at something across the street. He swiveled his head in time to see Clarke taking his front steps two at a time and fumbling at the door of the white Toronado parked outside his house. He jumped into it and took it away, tires screaming, over the curb and down the hill. It

59

barely paused at the stop sign on the corner, turned left and disappeared.

Verecker had the Chev charging down the hill a second later. He went through the stop sign, screeched into the turn and spotted the white car racing along Bridgeway. The highway wasn't far, just around the corner. Verecker knew Clarke was heading for it and he didn't think he'd turn south toward San Francisco; he knew he'd turn north even before the Toronado flashed by the Marin City underpass and melted into the traffic rushing toward the Mill Valley.

Annie said, "He's moving awfully fast for someone who was dawdling over a cup of coffee a minute ago."

Verecker shot the car onto the highway. "I'll bet you a year's alimony he takes the Richmond Bridge."

Annie knew what Verecker was thinking: that Clarke was heading for Tahoe: that he'd take the bridge across the bay to Richmond, then turn up Highway 40 to Sacramento and from there either keep on 40 or switch to 50. Either one would take him straight to the lake.

Verecker had gained a little on the Toronado and was driving in the middle of a bunch of cars spread out on the highway, the Toronado in the lead in the outside lane. They wheeled up a long straight incline and through the Mill Valley cut, around a long bend and down the grade past homes like Monopoly houses curling in waves above Corte Madera.

They zipped under the first Richmond Bridge sign. Clarke was still in the outside lane.

Verecker hit the accelerator and Annie stiffened. "Take it easy, Billy." The needle flicked past 80. "Billy, you're going too fast."

He said, "We can't risk losing him now."

The second bridge sign flashed by. Ahead, Verecker could see the last sign, green and white, coming toward them out of the sky like a leaf blown in the wind and the road forking underneath it. He cried out, "He's going to go by it." But as he said it the Toronado swung across the highway and belted into the turnoff. Verecker hit the brakes, flashed a signal and started to switch lanes but was honked back violently by a car drawing level on his right. There was a string of other cars close behind it and no room to cross between them. When she saw what he had in mind she yelled at him, but he didn't seem to hear. He stamped on the gas pedal, cut right in front of the horrified driver in the inside lane and swerved into the turnoff. The Chev skidded crazily from left to right, straightened itself and continued down the ramp. Slowly, Annie brought her head up from her shoulder where she'd instinctively ducked her face and let out a long shuddering breath. She looked over at Verecker. Apparently he was surprised they were still on the road, too.

They came out at a narrow road that ran under an overpass, past an old cement works and around the edge of a bay. They twisted and turned for a mile, then swerved around a tight corner past a gate like an entrance to a factory, a long, high cyclone fence stretching out beside it, small wooden cottages on a sloping green lawn behind it and, farther back, the immense, cement-dipped edifice of San Quentin. The road joined a large one coming in from San Rafael and became the approach to the bridge.

The Toronado was barreling along in the outside lane. Verecker kept well back of it, in the inside lane, matching the other car's speed. There was nothing to do for four miles but keep the car pointed straight.

It gave Annie time to recover. She had her face turned to the window, watching Tiburon flicker by through the railings and the green-wooded triangle of Angel Island off the point. Ahead, the toll gates appeared. There were two open. Clarke pulled into the one on the left, stopped and stayed stopped. He had his head out of the window talking to the man in the toll booth about something.

Verecker slowed the car to a crawl, but Clarke was still stopped when the Chev eased into the next booth.

Verecker handed the man a dollar bill and tried to sink down into the seat. Annie was leaning forward digging into her hand-bag, her head averted. The man handed him his change. Clarke still hadn't moved; he was arguing with the toll man.

Verecker moved off slowly, his eyes on the rear-view mirror. The long white car rocked back on its haunches, sped away from the gate and flashed by them.

Verecker said, "For a minute there I thought he was trying to be cute."

"Do you think he saw us?" Annie asked.

"We'll know when we get to the highway. If he goes north we're O.K. If he has spotted us he'll probably turn south and make it look good—you know, go into Berkeley and buy a book or something. But if he does that I'll slash my wrists."

Verecker guided the car through the almost palpable reek of an oil refinery, over a series of interchanges and down the long straight street that bisects Richmond. The Toronado was about four cars ahead, mixed up with a jumble of automobiles that had joined the road from residential side streets.

Five minutes later they saw ahead of them, low in the sky, a blur of traffic on an overpass: Highway 40. In front of them, a line of cars waited to make a left turn to drive up onto it. The inside lane moved straight ahead, either to El Cerrito or to the ramp that fed the highway with south-bound traffic. Clarke joined the lane waiting to make a left, and somewhere inside Verecker something started to tingle.

He threw a quick look at Annie. The same thing seemed to be happening to her. She asked quietly, "Do we have enough gas?"

Verecker had already checked. "We'll make it."

There was a break in the oncoming traffic, and the Toronado shot across the road and vanished up the ramp. Verecker followed it a minute later and merged with the traffic on the highway, switched to the outside lane and risked a speeding ticket for a few miles till he had the white car in sight. He shifted to the center lane and sat on 65 the same as Clarke was doing. The lake was four hours away. Again there was nothing to do but stay close and steer the car. And think.

Tires hissed on the pavement and a deeper engine noise came up at them. A Greyhound bus passed them in the outside lane, bullying cars out of its way. It said Reno on the front.

Annie nodded at it. "I figure Nevada."

"Why?"

"Because there's no place you could get a plane down around Tahoe and still stay in California."

"But, as Phil Rinlaub said, what are you going to do with it once you get it down—how do you hide it? It's too big to put in a barn and cover with hay."

"Wait. Let's get the plane down first. Will you grant me you could land it in Nevada somewhere close to the lake—one of the canyon bottoms, maybe—say near Virginia City?"

"Oh, lady. It'd be hard enough in the daytime, but at night . . ."

"But you'll admit it's possible?"

"Grudgingly. And then I'm not a hundred percent sure."

"O.K., so now at least it's on the ground."

"All right, I'll go that far. Now make it disappear."

Annie pressed her teeth into her bottom lip and stared at the glove compartment. "Well, how do you usually hide something?"

Verecker said, "You put it in a locker at the bus station."

"Give me another way."

"Slip it into a magazine and leave it in plain view on top of the coffee table."

Annie worked on her bottom lip again. "Why not?"

"Why not what?"

"People also bury things in their backyard, don't they? Why couldn't they have done that—dug a gigantic hole out there in the desert and covered the plane up?"

Verecker glanced across at her to see if she was kidding. She was dead serious. He said, "Why didn't they build a gigantic magazine and coffee table?"

"Verecker, be sensible."

"*Me* be sensible? Are you seriously proposing somebody snuck out one night, hired the Seabees and dug a hole in the

63

desert big enough to take a 747? Do you know how big they are? As long as a football field. I mean, think of all the equipment you'd need. You're not going to get stuff like that from your local Hertz man."

"But they're always building highways around that area. What if over a period of, say, a week they stole bulldozers and things at night, worked on the hole and put the equipment back at dawn?"

Verecker looked at the roof in mock despair. "Oh boy."

"What do you mean 'Oh boy'?" Annie said sharply. "Answer me properly."

"That's the craziest thing I ever heard."

"Verecker, somebody stole a jumbo and everybody on board —how can anything sound crazy after that? The very idea is crazy. It follows that the solution has to be pretty crazy, too."

"Well, it's my considered opinion, Nutsy, that digging a hole the length and breadth of a football field in a canyon in Nevada—and doing it so no one would notice—is a little too crazy."

Annie was mad. She felt like jamming her foot on the brake and flouncing out of the car. Instead she slammed back in her seat and watched the twin bridges over the Carquinez Straight coming up ahead.

The tires hummed over the steel deck. Below them a miniature white liner was moored to a river wharf. It looked as if it had sailed home from the Celebes fifty years ago and had never gone anywhere since.

The traffic slowed as it approached the toll plaza. Verecker chose a line and moved up on the toll booth, drew level, tossed a coin into the hopper. A bell dinged and the light in front of his left fender changed green. He spurted away, overtook a couple of drivers and settled in three cars back of the Toronado again.

"All right," Annie said, giving it another try, "how about this? It takes off from the airport . . . "

"Granted."

"It flies normally for a while . . . "

"I'll buy it."

"It descends over the lake . . . "

"Right."

"It flies a little farther . . . "

"Yes . . . "

"And lands at an abandoned airport."

"An abandoned airport?" Verecker repeated. "You mean an airport that drinks a lot and sleeps around?"

Annie thought about flouncing out of the car again.

"Come on, Annie. There aren't any abandoned airports in California anymore; they're all housing developments now, or motor race tracks."

"Well, at least I'm coming up with theories, which is more than you're doing."

"Why bother with theories at all? We stick on Clarke's tail we may know the answer in a couple of hours."

"Verecker, you're a romantic. You really think it's going to be that easy? Nobody who's smart enough to steal a 747 is going to be dumb enough to lead two hicks like us straight to it on a bright sunny day. We don't know where Clarke's going; he may have nothing whatsoever to do with this thing. He may be on his way to picket the Government in Sacramento. And a good thing, too."

It was Verecker's turn to be mad. "All right, you want a theory, I'll give you a theory. The gang gets in with this riveter at Mare Island where they've got the mothball fleet. They slip him ten bucks, and one lunch hour he converts one of the aircraft carriers into a submarine. They sail it submerged up the American River to the Sierras. It surfaces, the 747 lands on it, it submerges, goes back the way it came, surfaces in the bay and, cleverly disguised as the *President Roosevelt*, sails out the Golden Gate to Japan."

After that, conversation ceased abruptly.

An hour later, the dome of the state capitol building appeared on the skyline and then the south pylon of the bridge over the river. Sacramento began on the other side in a burst of steel and glass buildings and congested traffic. An overhead sign gave drivers a choice of two ways of getting to the lake: through Roseville on 40, through Placerville on 50.

Clarke took 40.

They followed him through the town, past the mint-green park with the beautiful high palms and through an old section of the city where one or two elegant frame houses had somehow survived. There were a couple of stops for red lights, then the traffic speeded up and poured into the highway running out of town northeast.

After Roseville, the traffic thinned out; at Auburn, the road started to climb toward the Sierras. There was nothing but small towns now, glimpsed off the side of the highway, and signs pointing to the old gold-mining settlements with the improvised names.

Higher still, at a peak in the road, the Sierras sat on the skyline, smoky blue in the distance, wearing white party hats of snow. Then pines began to appear and clumps of ice melting in the ditches beside the road, the grass still hard and moist from the last of the late-spring snows. Ski signs began to multiply and billboards for gambling houses in Nevada. The pines got thicker, whole forests of them—tall green walls flanking both sides of the highway. They passed a huge red garage, barnlike, chimney smoking, its winter signs still offering antifreeze and chains for sale—enormous yellow snow plows parked next to tow trucks and fat-tired jeeps. A-frames popped out underneath the trees, Tyrolean balconies and the inevitable crossed skis above the front doors. A few miles farther on, opposite the old Donner Pass, the road leveled out and started down in a long, sloping glide to the valley below.

"He'll take eighty-nine for sure," Verecker said.

The sign came up pointing to Truckee straight ahead, 89 and Tahoe to the right. Verecker flashed a right turn even before Clarke did.

The road followed a river in a series of gentle twists and turns, past more ski huts and thick forest and green riverbank. There were still three cars between the Chev and the Toronado. In the rear-view mirror Verecker watched a brown Tempest he'd seen off and on since the Richmond Bridge. He'd lost sight of it around Sacramento, and it had turned up again an hour later. He didn't attach any significance to it; lots of people went to the lake, and he knew that if you start about the same time and drive at about the same speed you travel in a kind of unofficial convoy anyway.

While he was thinking about it the car drew level and passed them. Inside were two men and a woman. They looked ordinary enough, although there was something vaguely familiar about the woman.

They swung by the entrance to Squaw Valley, which meant the lake was only ten minutes away. Verecker got the tingling feeling again. Annie could be wrong, he thought. It was often an obvious little detail that proved to be the flaw in the most foolproof plans—like one person following another in broad daylight. Clarke would have assumed they'd driven off when they left his apartment; he could be on his way now to warn the gang that somebody had found out about the plane and the golf course. But wouldn't he have phoned? Not if the passengers were hidden someplace out of the way—some old camp or something where they wouldn't have a telephone. On paper it made sense—a lot of sense.

At Tahoe City the road divided, and Clarke took the right-hand fork toward Emerald Bay. It ran around the rim of the lake—the water only feet away but screened by thick clumps of tall pines and invisible from the road—past a neony bar and the entrance to a lodge, an ugly new church and a motel that looked like a slum in fairyland—tiny wooden cottages, old and run down, nestled in a dell under the trees.

It happened in a flash. One moment Clarke was three cars ahead, the next the Toronado had vanished.

67

Verecker took a chance, hit the gas pedal and passed the cars in front on a bend. The road stretched straight, as empty as a track in the desert.

"Goddamn it," he yelled. He jammed on the brakes, slammed the car into a screeching U-turn and rocketed back up the road.

"How could he do it?" Annie asked. "I didn't see any turnings."

"Neither did I, but there must be one."

They spotted it the next second, an old dirt road, rutted from the winter snows, running off to their left. There was a group of large, cold-looking fieldstone houses tucked away in the damp shadows under the pines, small neat mountains of cordwood stacked beside each one; the chimneys smoked and in two of the houses lights shone from high windows.

There were no cars visible.

Farther on, the road opened into another one, crossing it like a T—a brand-new road that served a small development some builder had carved out of the forest. The road was shaped like a horseshoe, half-built houses flanking both sides. Verecker drove slowly up the section on his left, turned around in the circular dead end and drove slowly back. Most of the garages were just wooden frames and they could see right through them. You couldn't have hidden a wheelbarrow in them, let alone a car. And it would have been impossible to get a car around the back of the houses—the driveways were all piled high with lumber.

"Where the hell is he?" Verecker said through his teeth.

They inched past the bottom of the horseshoe and up the other side. It was the same thing there: a couple of cars parked in the street—neither of them Clarke's—and more see-through houses. And nothing else.

Verecker said disgustedly, "Come on, we're wasting time here," and started to swing the car around.

"What's that? The other side didn't have one." Annie was pointing to a paved driveway at the top of the street that

68

vanished in a belt of pines. Verecker jerked the wheel the other way and headed into it. It curved gently for a little way, then stopped at a high stone gate. Behind the gate a paved parking lot fronted a long one-story building, brand new and glistening with oiled pine, and a taller building behind it. The sign over the gate said, "Knollwood Pines High School," and the man who was sitting underneath it got up out of a chair and moved ponderously forward to meet the car. He was a big man, surly-looking.

"Help you?" He didn't look as though he wanted to.

Verecker said, "I was following a friend of mine and lost him. Thought he might have come up here."

"Nobody's been in here last coupla hours."

"Sure you couldn't have missed him—a white Toronado?"

"No white Toronado." He said it as though Verecker had asked him to cash a personal check.

Verecker fished his wallet out and flashed a five-dollar bill. "Would you mind if we just took a quick look around anyway?"

The man didn't even glance at the money. He said heavily, "Private property, bud."

Verecker saw it wasn't because the money wasn't enough— the guy had orders. He put the money away, backed down the drive, drove down the new road and turned the corner and parked.

"Don't think he liked us," Annie said.

Verecker didn't reply; he was thinking.

She said, "What kind of school has a guard on the gate anyway?"

Verecker scratched the corner of his mouth, which wasn't itchy. "Are schools on vacation right now, do you know?"

"They could be this time of year. Why?"

"Well, if it's vacation time, what were all those cars doing in the parking lot?"

"They could be having a seminar of some kind. Anyway, I didn't see Clarke's car. Did you?"

69

"No, but that doesn't mean it's not there. And frankly, I thought that welcome we got was a little too unfriendly for somebody looking for a lost friend."

"What are you suggesting?"

"Only that an empty school would be a great place to hide people."

"True. But you'd have to get them here from wherever they landed."

"So what's wrong with school buses? There were four of them in that lot." Verecker opened his door. "I'm going back and take a look."

Annie grabbed his arm. "Verecker, that's silly. That guy isn't going to let you in, and he looks like the type to turn nasty."

"I'm sure he's the type to turn nasty. That's why he's not going to see me. I'll get over that wall from the back somewhere."

Annie still had hold of his arm. "Look, it's a thousand-to-one chance I know, but what if the passengers are there? What if the kidnappers see you? They're not going to let you walk out again."

"Then give me twenty minutes. If I'm not back, go for the cops."

"Billy—" she pulled herself closer to him—"for God's sake be careful."

"If you promise to stay in this mood I won't even go." He gently disentangled her hand. "I'll be back," he said.

He slid over the seat and closed the door behind him, walked quickly to the corner and peeked around it. The street was empty. He crossed to the opposite sidewalk and made his way past the half-finished houses to the last one in the road. The driveway leading to the school was on his left. To his right was a high jungle of pines. He moved around sand piles and cement mixers and crept down the side of the house, traversed a cleared space at the back and struck off into the forest. He worked his way through the trees, walking on a soft brown

70

carpet of pine needles, the air sweet and sappy and a little chill. A minute later he found what he thought he'd find. The wall was about six feet high but smooth and tough to get a grip on. The trees grew right up against it as if crowding up to peer over at something they longed to touch. He followed it deeper into the forest and spotted a small pine that butted up against the rough brick. He swung himself into the tree, climbed a few branches and stepped onto the top of the wall. The buildings were only sixty feet away—the long low building and the other one behind it, which looked like a gymnasium now. He couldn't see the guard; the gate was hidden by a clump of trees. He dropped to the ground and ran to a window and cautiously looked inside. It was some kind of kindergarten classroom with maps and plants in pots and bright finger paintings with first names scrawled on them pinned around the walls. The rooms on the other side looked more senior—a chemistry lab, a library, a blackboard covered with smudged algebra equations.

That left only the gym.

He crossed to it quickly. Big glassy windows ran around its walls high above his head. He tried a door. Locked. Above the door was a small window he thought he could reach. He put a foot on the knob and sprang up and grasped the door lintel, hooked his forearms over it and gradually hauled himself up.

A split second before the man grabbed him from behind and wrenched him away he caught a glimpse of something that stayed with him for years: a couple of hundred people lying face down on a basketball court, packed together like sheep.

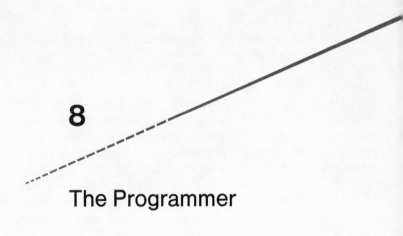

8

The Programmer

His father had assumed that when his son finished school he'd come into the business, learn it from the ground up and eventually take over. But then his father didn't know that his son regarded him as a back-slapping Babbitt—a fat Rotarian with a collection of clichés for a vocabulary and a fund of unfunny, mildly dirty anecdotes that he never tired of telling. He had to live in the same house as his father, but as for working in the same office as well, that was something he didn't have to do and couldn't have stood to do. He knew his mother felt the same way about him. He supposed she'd been attracted to him at first by the confidence he exuded and the recognition that here was a real go-getter, someone who was going to make something of himself and get ahead in life. He supposed that, to a young girl from a poor family, his father must have looked like security with a capital "s." And so it had proved

to be—a large, gadget-filled house overlooking the Presidio,
two cars, a weekend house at Clear Lake, vacations in Hawaii
every year—but once the escape from poverty had been
effected and the new environment embraced and taken for
granted he imagined his mother had become rapidly dis-
enchanted, although he'd never heard her once complain. She
let herself be dragged along to ball games and conventions and
bowling nights and suffered in polite silence the loud business
friends his father constantly brought home for dinner—a
silence which he'd never heard his father remark on. In fact
he wondered if this unperceptive, unfeeling oaf—who he felt
would have greeted the news of a mine disaster with a loud
guffaw and a slap of his thigh—was even aware that his wife
couldn't stand him any more than his son could.

After a couple of years of college he'd gone into the Army.
It was a peacetime army at that point; Korea had just finished
and the genocide hadn't yet started in Vietnam. His father had
said the Army would make a man of him and he'd dreaded
the experience but had been pleasantly surprised. He liked
the Army. For a start, you were just a number, not a person,
so nobody expected you to come on strong with the big handshake and the platitudes. You could live your own life as long
as you lived within the system. The Army fed you, looked after
you, protected you, paid you, clothed you and offered anonym-
ity to a high degree. Everybody dressed the same, looked the
same; personality was a thing that wasn't expected, was dis-
couraged, in fact. He got on O.K. with the other men. He was
tall and slight and no good at sports, but he didn't bother anybody and was always good for a small loan. He usually sold
his leave, preferring to stay in the barracks rather than go into
the small Southern town. The weekends were relaxed in camp.
You never saw much of the officers, who were mainly family
men, and the duty sergeants took it easy on themselves by
taking it easy on everybody else. There was nothing to do in
town except drink and whore it up.

When his stint was over he seriously considered reenlisting

and would have if it hadn't been for his mother. She wrote him every week saying how much she missed him—it was easy enough to read between the lines—and he knew it wouldn't be fair if he escaped from the house and she didn't. So he went back to San Francisco and got a job as a bookkeeper. He started work in one of the biggest insurance companies in town and in this way purposely duplicated his service experience of being just a number on a payroll—one more clerk in a roomful of them—all of them almost as similarly dressed as the clerks were in the Army. The job was a lot like the Army: dull, regimented, protective. If you did your work properly and got in on time nobody bothered you. He could have been reasonably happy if it hadn't been for his home life. After two years away from his father, going back to it all was like a prisoner going back to his cell. He could have moved out, but that would have left his mother to face it all by herself, and he'd already decided he didn't want to do that. The only solution was to get them both out. But he couldn't expect his mother to live in a couple of rooms out in the avenues somewhere. She might not have minded but he would have. He needed money —a lot of money—the kind he could never make as a clerk. So he was more than interested when somebody at the office told him he was leaving to take a course in computer programming. It paid a lot and you got to go anywhere you liked, and you didn't have to be an Einstein, either. He'd taken the course, too, graduated, quit his job and gone to work in the computation center of a bank.

Six months later he got a higher-paying job as a programmer for an airline. The money was a lot better than he'd made at the insurance company, and he was able to save most of it, but at the end of a year it still didn't amount to a hill of beans compared with the money he needed. He was wondering what to do about it when the ad appeared—a double classified in the Situations Vacant. Somebody with a box number was looking for a very special airline computer man; he had to have flair and imagination and had to be ready to make big money. The ad asked for a brief résumé and a letter telling something about yourself. Naturally he'd applied along with just about everybody else in the office, but he and two others were the only ones to get a nibble. They had to call a number and ask for a Mr. Ferguson. When he called, Mr. Ferguson told him they were screening applicants carefully because of the special nature of this job and he could save them both a lot of time by answering one question: Did he have an adventurous spirit? What did he mean by an adventurous spirit? Was he willing to take a risk? They were working on a new computer application that hadn't been ratified by the Government yet. It was only a small legality but there was a chance that, if they were caught operating before approval came through, they might just be prosecuted. On the other hand, the money was commensurate with the risk. Was he interested? He'd said yes.

They'd met the following Saturday at a resturant down the Peninsula. Mr. Ferguson, a short, plump, bald man who chain-smoked cigars, told him that what he had in mind was a little more illegal than he'd made out over the phone, and if he wanted to back out this was the time to say so. He'd asked the bald man about the money and been told that the money wasn't just good; it was unbelievable. It didn't involve anybody getting hurt, did it? No, nobody was going to get hurt. Now was he in? Fine. The man had promptly paid the check, driven him to a house in Hillsborough and explained what it was he wanted him to do.

On the way he told him his name wasn't really Mr. Ferguson but he may as well call him that.

9

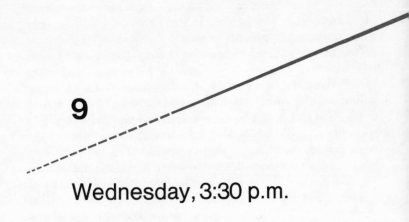

Wednesday, 3:30 p.m.

Verecker found himself with his arm expertly pretzeled up behind his back and a rough hand forcing his jaw back over his shoulder. "Take it easy for crissakes," he yelled. A hard voice told him to shut up. His arm moved up his back half an inch and Verecker went up on his toes.

"Move," the voice commanded.

Verecker couldn't see who was marching him around the side of the building, but the grunted monosyllables and the hamlike hand digging into his jaw gave him a pretty good idea. He couldn't see in front of him either, only to the side, so he was completely unprepared when the hand let go of his face and shoved him stumbling through a door.

The people on the floor were wearing long, white flowing robes, such as a monk might wear, and their faces, raised and staring unseeingly ahead, were painted from chin to forehead in the colors of a nightmare. They were lying on their stomachs, dead still except for their left hands that moved as if they were erasing something written on the floor beside them.

A sound like a plague of giant grasshoppers filled the room— an eerie metal clicking that grated on the ears—and laid underneath it, like felt under a rug, a long, low buzzing rose and fell in quivering waves.

Verecker was standing on a small raised stage at the front of the gym, and the white robes stretched to the end of the room as if he were standing on the edge of a foaming sea.

A sudden movement to his left caught his eye. A single robed figure was standing there, hooded and sinister, his robe covered with shapes worked in sequins—lotus blossoms and birds and fish and sun symbols. The guard shoved Verecker forward again and said to the figure, "Caught him snoopin' around outside."

"Now just a second." Verecker didn't get any further. The hooded man suddenly dropped to his knees and cried, "Praise be. Our prayers have not gone unheard." Then he snarled at the guard, "Fool, do you not recognize the Messiah, descended from the astral plane?"

"Him? He came in a Chevy."

"Release him. The Messiah must not be touched by the uninitiated."

The guard reluctantly let go of Verecker's arm and lumbered toward the door. "Messiah, my ass," he mumbled.

"Master," the hooded man began, "forgive this unseemly welcome."

Verecker coughed and said, "Er, there seems to be some . . ." Again he got no further. The hooded man sprang to his feet, turned to the sea of bodies, raised his arms above his head and roared in a voice that carried to the rafters, "Arise, ye Sons of the Innermost Planet. The prophet walks among us again; come to lead us to our true and rightful place in the world."

The horde of white figures rose as one and let out a great cry. The clicking and humming sound increased.

77

Verecker thought that things were getting out of hand. Whoever these people were they weren't kidnapped airline passengers; he'd apparently strayed into some kind of nut religious service. Clearly, the first thing he had to do was get out of there. He backed slowly toward the door, nodding and smiling. "Sorry to break up your meeting. I, er, got the wrong address." And then, because he felt something of a more religious nature was expected of him, he gave a vague pontifical sign and said, "God is love. Jesus saves . . . er." His smile broadened as he racked his brain. "The wages of sin is death."

The hooded man, obviously some kind of priest, had prosstrated himself again. He didn't appear to be listening. "Bring the prophet to us," he intoned, "so we may sit at his feet and bask in his glow."

Two large robed figures Verecker hadn't noticed standing at the door grasped him gently but very firmly and led him forward. Verecker shook his head and smiled weakly. "You don't understand. I'm just a simple Presbyterian. You've got the wrong prophet."

The priest rose, clapped his hands, and a chair was brought. Verecker was lowered into it, hands still holding him firmly by the arms. He knew there was nothing he could do—just wait and ride it out and get away as soon as he got a chance.

"Let the sacred initiation begin," the priest cried to the ceiling.

A white robe was lowered over Verecker's head and somebody began daubing his face with greasepaint and sponging on some kind of moist, colored clay. He still couldn't believe what was happening to him. In a state of mild shock, he said to the make-up man, "Give me a marvelous mouth, will you?"

The congregation was on its feet now, swaying like bleached grass in a wind. Verecker saw that the clicking noise was coming from some small round metal objects that they held in their left hands and knocked together; and the low buzzing sound was some kind of humming noise they made through their pursed lips. Beside him, one of the priest's helpers was stirring

78

something in a bowl, a foul-smelling mixture the color and consistency of yellow paste. Verecker didn't like the look of it.

Suddenly the priest whirled around and spoke to the far corners of the gym. "This do I ask Thee, O Lord, tell me truly: Who is—" the entire assembly joined in— "the Creator, the first one of Righteousness? Who laid down the path of the sun and the stars? Who is it through whom the moon now waxes, now wanes? All this and more do I wish to know, Wise One."

Verecker said, "Well, for me it used to be Carole Lombard."

The massed chanting hardly paused. "Who holds the earth below and the sky as well from falling? Who created the waters and the plants? Who harnesses the two courses to wind and clouds? Who, O Wise One, is the creator of Good Mind?"

This time there was silence. The echoes faded away and it was as quiet as a tomb.

With a panicky feeling starting inside him Verecker realized they expected an answer. A horrible thought struck him. Up till now they'd been harmless nuts. But what if they turned nasty—what if they denounced him for a dog of a Christian unbeliever or something? Was theirs a peaceful religion that preached love, tolerance and understanding? Or were they the prophet's good soldiers, wild-eyed fanatics who wouldn't hesitate to put blasphemers to the sword? Whoever they were and whatever they believed in he'd been right about one thing: the buses. They'd probably come in on them from Reno. No doubt they'd flown up from Los Angeles—they could only be from Los Angeles. Another horrible thought struck him, more chilling even than the first one: He was alone with two hundred people from Los Angeles! And they were waiting for him to speak, straining forward to catch the wisdom of the ages. He had to stall them and hope for an eclipse.

He was saved from having to say anything when the man who'd been stirring the paste whispered something to the priest. "It is time," the priest cried. "Let the ceremony begin." Apparently that was more important than the answer to the chanted questions. Two robed figures picked up the mixing

79

bowl and poured the contents into what looked to Verecker like a round flat pan covered with some kind of thick, pale, doughy-looking substance.

The priest broke into a singsong chant. "O Zarathustra, O immortal Zoroaster, O ancient Zardusht, Leading Light of Bactria, divine author of the sacred Zend-Avesta, conqueror of the false prophet Mithras, we thank thee for sending thy holy messenger to lead us, your faithful servants, the Sons of the Innermost Planet." The clicking noise increased. "Help him to help us in our eternal struggle with the reviled Ahriman, spirit of evil." The buzzing rose menacingly. "Help him to show us the way to glory in the eyes of the good spirit Ahura-Mazda." The buzzing subsided and the clicking grew louder. "Show him the way to reveal to us the hidden mysteries of the great Gathic Commentaries."

Verecker was watching the two helpers with a horrid fascination. They had just covered the yellow mixture with a layer of the same doughy substance that lay underneath it. It covered the pan completely and dropped evilly over the lip. From the voluminous folds of his sleeve the priest whipped out something that flashed like a dull mirror. The handle was gold, the blade no wider than a scalpel, the edges disappearing into a cold sharpness. Verecker shot to his feet, but two pairs of meaty hands pushed him firmly back into the chair and held him there.

The gymnasium was suddenly dead quiet.

Helpless and frozen with horror, Verecker watched the priest advance toward him. He halted a foot away, made some kind of cabalistic sign in the air, then very carefully ran the knife around the outside of the pan. The excess doughy substance fell away, leaving the pan a perfect circle about eighteen inches across. The priest took it, lifted it high above his head and turned dramatically to the congregation. The clicking noise rose in a metallic crescendo.

"Let the three layers of the holy Hoashyanha," the priest crooned, "symbolize the three golden ages in which we believe. Let it be offered to the prophet who has come amongst us as it was foretold in the sacred Yasnas."

He turned to Verecker, still clamped in the chair, and held the circular object a few inches in front of Verecker's eyes. It looked like a pale, lumpy full moon.

"O son of Fryana, descendant of Kavi Vishtaspa, be one with the divine planet of your birth."

A ghastly realization flooded Verecker's brain. He recoiled in horror, as if he were trying to push his back through the chair. "That's no planet," he began, hysteria rising in him like bubbles in champagne. "That's a custard—" Splat! The priest solemnly pushed the round object into Verecker's horrified face. The clicking ceased and there was a loud, dull thump as if hundreds of bodies had simultaneously slumped to the floor.

Verecker sat quite still for a second, then slowly brought his hands up and peeled the thing off his face. He wiped his eyes clean and blew through his lips like a whinnying horse. He sighed and said fatalistically, "Only in California."

He looked around him. The entire gym was prostrate, the priest, the helpers, his two guards, everybody. Cautiously he got up out of the chair and crept toward the door. He had his hand on it, was turning the knob, when a warning shout struck like a thunderbolt behind him. He pulled the key out of the lock, tore the door open, jumped through it and locked it behind him. A great weight thudded against the other side. Verecker hitched up his cloak and took off over the grass, running frantically for the drive. A second later the door burst off its hinges and a horde of robed figures poured through, the priest in the lead. "Master! Master! The ceremony . . . there's more."

"You eat it," Verecker yelled. He raced down the side of the main building and saw the guard at the gate getting out of his chair. Oh God, Verecker thought, was he going to have trouble with him again? But the big man made no move to stop him in spite of all the shouts to do so. He apparently felt he was only paid to keep people out.

Verecker galloped by him and shouted, "You could have warned me. I thought they were just kidnappers." He pelted down the drive and into the dirt road. The priest seemed to be gaining on him.

Around the corner the Chev was just pulling out from the curb. "Annie! Wait!" The car halted. Verecker pulled open the door and tumbled in. "Get out of here, quick."

The car didn't move. Annie was glued to the wheel, gaping at him.

"Come on," Verecker screamed, "before the ceremony starts again."

Painted men in white robes pounded around the corner. Annie took one look and shot the car away like a drag racer. The car rounded a bend, bucked and swayed over the rutted road and careened into the highway.

Annie looked back and forth between Verecker and the road like somebody watching a fast tennis rally. "Who . . . ? What . . . ?" She swallowed and made a fresh start, enunciating her words with great care. "What happened to you?"

"A bunch of fanatics threw a pie in my face. Keep driving."

"What kind of fanatics?" Again, the careful enunciation.

"Religious ones, of course. Who did you think, the Ladies' Temperance?" He made a sound like "Yeckhh" and wiped his mouth. "Although even they could bake better."

Annie was having trouble taking it all in. She decided to skirt around the edges and work toward the middle. "But the get-up—you look like King Lear."

"I'm way higher than him. I'm Zarathustra's brother-in-law or somebody, descended from the void. A heavenly messenger, no less."

Annie blinked hard. "And that wild-looking bunch that chased us back there?"

"Some of my faster disciples."

"But . . . but how about Clarke? Did you see him?"

"I was too busy being force-fed. The only thing I saw was

82

a couple of hundred Captain Queegs clicking steel balls together and blowing raspberries at me."

Annie thought she'd better come back to that one. She looked doubtfully at the goo on his face. "Religious fanatics, O.K. But why hit you with a custard pie?"

Verecker turned in his seat and regarded her wearily. "I don't know. Maybe they thought it was blueberry."

"I was just about to go for the cops when you got here." She glanced across at him again. "I'm still not sure I shouldn't."

As she spoke a siren wailed behind them.

Verecker whipped his head around, then moaned like a man with a stomach ache. "Oh, Annie . . . *anytime* but now."

"Well, you said to step on it, so I stepped on it."

She pulled the car over onto the side of the road. The policeman wheeled in behind them, the siren dying as if someone had stuck it with a pin. He took off his sunglasses, reached for his book, checked his pen, then laboriously eased himself out of the saddle and moved toward them. Except for his helmet he was dressed entirely in black—big, fat, potbellied black— while his motorcycle, the size of a Volkswagen, was a gleaming pincushion of cylinders, wing mirrors and radio aerials—a suspended explosion of polished metal.

Verecker tried to get underneath the dashboard. Annie had put the top down and he was open to the world.

The cop said to Annie, "Miss, don't you know what the speed limit is in this—" He broke off, looking past her, and said, "Well, hello there. Don't be shy. Come on out." Verecker reluctantly unfolded. "And who are you supposed to be, hmmm?"

Verecker didn't know what else he could do but try and brazen it out. "I am the divine prophet of the Sons of the Innermost Planet, recently descended from the astral plane."

The cop ran his eyes over the long-flowing cloak and the make-up. "Looks more like the daughters of whatever you said."

83

"We're a highly respected, tax-exempt, bona-fide religion with roots dating back to 1952." Verecker told him huffily.

"Uh huh. What's that stuff in your hair?"

"Ectoplasm."

Annie could see that things were in danger of getting out of hand. She smiled sweetly and said, "We stopped a ways back for pie and coffee. He's a messy eater."

The policeman grunted, looked at Verecker for a long second, then asked Annie for her license. He wrote out a ticket, handed it to her and returned the license. "Take it a little easier from now on. And maybe you'd better put the top up." He nodded toward Verecker. "We don't want a traffic jam." He sauntered insolently to the bike, kicked it over, spent an age adjusting his sunglasses, revved the motor loudly, made absolutely sure they were watching and roared off down the road in a series of fast-racing changes.

"Support your local fuzz," Verecker said.

Annie started the car. "Where to now?"

"Home, I guess. But stop at the next gas station so I can get out of this trick-or-treat costume."

They drove in silence for a few miles, Annie bursting to ask a hundred questions but thinking it better to wait, then pulled in at a Chevron ramp. The gas station was empty of cars, and Annie chose the pump nearest the washrooms. Verecker darted around the side and tried the washroom door. It was locked. There was nothing else for it. He couldn't see Annie asking for the key to the men's room. A man with his head in a sack could have seen she didn't qualify. He'd have to ask for it himself. He walked briskly around to the office and said as casually as he could to a uniformed man making out a repair bill, "Say, could I have the key to the washroom?"

The man was wetting the end of a pencil with his tongue. He looked up. The pencil stayed on his tongue. He closed his eyes, opened them again, then very carefully laid the pencil down on the bill. "Men's or ladies'?" he asked.

Verecker made an attempt to turn away manfully and stride

out of the door, but the way the cloak hampered his movements it came off as more of a swish and a sashay. A low, dirty whistle followed him out. He pulled the cloak over his head, balled it up savagely and hurled it to the ground. Most of the goo came off with it, and he might have looked normal but for the paint that tinged his face with an unearthly green glow.

The man at the pump had just finished handing Annie her change and stamps when he caught sight of him. "Boy," he said, "do you get car sick."

"That does it!" Verecker yelled. "That is *it!* Move over," he barked at Annie. He slid in behind the wheel, twisted the ignition key and roared away in a cloud of carbon monoxide. He said, "I'm through with organized religion, do you hear? Through."

"Yes," Annie replied. "There's altogether too much hypocrisy." They drove back to San Francisco at a steady eighty.

10

The Big Baggage Man

Once a year, at the start of the season, all the NFL teams hold a scrimmage at which anybody can go out for the local team. It's mainly to see if the scouts have missed anybody with potential, people they might not know about, like a European emigrant who kicks sixty-yard field goals soccer style, or some big center playing semi-pro whom they could use because their third string broke his leg in the summer. They're non-college men for the most part who didn't have a chance to show their stuff against Stanford or Michigan or Texas. The scrimmage is also held to show that pro football is democratic and everybody has a chance to play.

He'd gone along to Kezar Stadium to try out along with a lot of other guys.

Down in the changing rooms, in the sweat and liniment smell and the nervous dirty jokes, he'd had butterflies pretty badly. If you made the team it was worth a lot of money. Even if you just sat on the bench all season you made like fifteen grand, with a sure offer of a cushy summer job from some local businessman. You couldn't make that kind of money lugging suitcases around all day.

When they'd trotted out onto the field to give the coaches a look, a couple of them had nodded at him and talked among themselves. Good size, they'd said. Six three, two-thirty. And he looked mean and hungry, too. They'd called him over and asked him where he played. He'd told them tight end. Tough position, they'd said. You've got to be able to run, catch and block. Could he do all that? Try me, he'd said. So they'd run a few pass patterns, the third-string quarterback throwing. The passes had come like bullets, a lot harder and faster than he was used to. He'd tried—he'd never tried harder at anything— but he dropped every other pass. He had the moves, they told him, and the speed, but without a pair of hands . . . So he'd gone back to playing with the local semi-pro team, with guys like himself who almost had it but not quite, and swung a pick or greased cars or drove a truck all week and played ball every Saturday for a hundred dollars a game. It was a tough league and there were a lot of injuries, but they went on playing because they could use the money, and there was always a chance at the big time.

Then something happened that changed his prospects. Their coach left when his firm transferred him to another town, and somebody else, a younger man, took over. He'd seen the team play once or twice before but didn't really know the players; all he knew was that the team had a pretty good offense but was hurting on defense. In his first game as coach he'd sent in a play early in the second quarter. It was a fake draw, the pass intended for the big right end. The big man had run his pattern perfectly, but the pass had been overthrown and been picked off by a defensive man, who'd sped down and across the field trying to pick up blockers. Furious, the big man had turned instantly, raced after him, thrown off a couple of blocks, turned on the speed and nailed the ball carrier on the ten-yard line. They'd stalled them there and made them settle for a field-goal attempt that went wide. The new coach had been impressed and asked him after the game if he'd ever played linebacker. He was plenty big enough and if he could run and tackle like that, maybe he could help them more if he played defense. He'd agreed to give it a try.

The following week he'd worked out for a couple of nights at the new position. Saturday they'd had an easy game, and in the last quarter, when they were ahead by seventeen points, the coach had put him in as linebacker.

He was sensational. He grabbed off an interception and ran it back forty yards for a touchdown. He threw the quarterback for a loss of seven and twice broke through to stop the fullback at the line—hard, vicious tackles both. The next Saturday he'd started at linebacker.

He was a natural; he seemed to know what the quarterback was going to do before the quarterback did. If the run was on he'd smell it out, charge into the line at the snap of the ball, go right over blockers and belt the ball carrier to the ground before he'd had a chance to pick up steam. If it was a pass play he knew who was going to get it and was right there. Once the coach had chewed him out for going for the receiver instead of trying to grab off the ball and asked him why he'd done it. "You gotta sting 'em," he'd replied.

A local sports writer had given him a write-up and called him the meanest ball player since Dutchy Klaus, the Green Bay star. He'd also said he was one of the best prospects for the pros the team had ever had. Whether it was the article or just word of mouth he didn't know, but a scout from the Forty-Niners came to take a look at him. He'd liked what he'd seen and told him that this year was out, of course—they already had their squad—but next year they'd really be interested, and if he got any calls from any other clubs to call him first. "The only thing you gotta do is stay healthy," the scout had said. Stay healthy. Two Saturdays later, in a light drizzle on a hard, rutted field, he'd been standing firmly planted on both feet trying to make up his mind. The halfback looked as though he were going to run a sweep but he suspected a halfback toss. He had one eye on the runner and one on the flanker starting down the sideline, so he didn't see the blocker who smashed into his knee. Later, lying in agony on the rubdown table in the unheated changing room, a doctor took one look at his leg and said, "Your football days are over."

After the operation he could walk all right. There was a pronounced limp but nothing that threatened his job; he could still load bags on and off planes. But now he had no prospects of ever doing anything else.

Naturally he jumped at the proposition the skycap put to him. But knee or no knee, he figured he probably would have anyway.

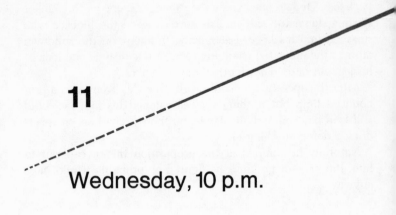

11

Wednesday, 10 p.m.

When they got back to the house Verecker went upstairs, shampooed his hair, scrubbed the paint off his face, dressed, picked up Annie and went out to eat in Chinatown. They went to a small place on Jackson Street, the blazing red and white neon outside almost as big as the restaurant. Verecker ordered seaweed soup, fantail shrimp in their shells, bok choy, rice and a double order of sea snails in garlic sauce.

Annie said, "Religion makes you hungry, I see."

"Look at Buddha," Verecker answered.

"Now that that hair-raising drive has calmed you down and you've got that Cream o' Wheat out of your hair, what do we do now?"

Verecker waved to a waiter, raised his hand to his mouth in a pantomime of drinking and held up two fingers. "Think a little harder than we've been doing."

"What do you mean?"

90

"Well, it's pretty obvious that Clarke gave us the old sliperoo. I don't know when he spotted us. It might have been when we got to Tahoe or at the toll booth at the Richmond Bridge—it could have been anywhere. But you can bet he took us where he wanted to take us before he lost us."

The waiter clunked two bottles of beer down onto the table. He tipped Annie's bottle straight into her glass and got a six-inch head. He reached for Verecker's, but Verecker restrained him and offered to do it himself. "Why don't waiters ever learn to pour beer properly?" he asked when the man had gone away.

Annie reiterated her question. "What did you mean about the school?"

"Not the school so much as the area. Clarke led us to the west side of the lake. The package was mailed from the east side. Now nobody in his right mind would think that a kidnapper would be dumb enough to mail a ransom note from his front door. So you have to look somewhere else. O.K., so maybe Clarke would like us to think we should look west—Tahoe Pines or Homewood, around the area where we lost him. I just think it's a little too obvious." He poured his beer and took a long gulp. "The plane goes off the radar near the lake, the note is mailed from the lake, Clarke leads us to the lake—there's just too much lake. I don't think those passengers are anywhere near it."

"Don't tell me," Annie said in mock surprise, "that you think that plane's in Nevada? What a brilliant idea! I only wish I'd thought of it myself."

Verecker waved a hand in front of him. "All right, all right. So a guy can change his mind. Maybe that plane *is* out there, except if it went off the scope at seven-fifty it could have taken anything up to half an hour to land and get those watches away from the passengers—that makes it eight-twenty. The package was mailed at nine-forty, so it would seem that the plane has to be within a seventy-five-minute drive from the lake. And that just sounds impossible."

91

"Why impossible? You could make it to the lake from those canyons around Virginia City in an hour. Besides, it's more nearly possible than landing *on* the lake, and that's what they would've had to do to get any closer."

The waiter brought the soup and they ate for a while thinking about it.

Verecker paused with a spoonful halfway to his mouth. "On the lake? Why not? They could have rigged up a pontoon bridge maybe."

"The Seabees, you mean?"

"That's right, throw my own material back at me." He picked up his spoon and put it down again. "What am I thinking about, anyway? You couldn't build a pontoon bridge strong enough for a plane that big."

"Maybe they didn't have to," Annie proposed. "Maybe the riveter—the one who converted the carrier—stuck floats on it."

Verecker was gathering himself for a scathing reply when the waiter arrived and busied himself putting down plates of food, chopsticks, mustard and hot sauce and a pot of tea they hadn't ordered. Annie reached for the snails heaped up on a steaming bed of rich brown sauce. She picked one off the top, pried the thin plasticlike lid away from the shell with a toothpick, put the shell in her mouth and sucked. She put the empty shell down on her plate and chewed with a dreamy look on her face. She swallowed, reached for another and said to Verecker, "I would kill for snails in garlic sauce."

They hadn't stopped for lunch and they ate hungrily. Five minutes later, Annie picked up the conversation again. "How about Clarke's girl friend? What do we do about her?"

Verecker reached into his jacket and pulled out the photograph. "Try to find her," he replied, looking at the print.

"And then?"

"Ask her about her boy friend. I don't think he'll tell us anything himself."

"But if Clarke is her boy friend, why should she tell us anything at all? We don't even know if she's involved in this thing. For that matter we still can't be certain Clarke is, either."

"Do you believe that?"

"No, not after today. But I'm only going on intuition."

"Well, I'm only going on ruts on a golf course, but you'll never convince me he isn't in this up to his neck. So it follows that his girl friend, a stewardess, is in on it, too. You couldn't pull a job like this without somebody on the inside."

He passed the photograph over to Annie. A young woman who didn't look much more than twenty-two or-three smiled out at her. She was very striking—good, strong Nordic features with soft lemon-colored hair worn shoulder-length with a fringe over the forehead. Her eyes were slightly elongated, pale blue and misty. Annie couldn't tell from the shot, which was a head to waist, but she got the impression the girl was tall; she could see she had a good bosom. Annie blinked and bit her lip. She said, "You know, she doesn't have to be a stewardess. We're only supposing that."

Verecker took the print from her. "Hey, you're right. She could be a rent-a-car girl, or an airport information lady, something like that. No initials or badges, just a plain blue uniform. No cap, either."

Annie said, "She could be an elevator starter, for that matter."

"No elevator starter ever looked that good. Besides, can you see anybody getting into an elevator, pulling a gun and saying 'Take me to Havana'? No, a girl who looks like that works for an airline. She might be behind a reservations desk downtown, or a check-in counter at the terminal, or she may well be a stewardess, but you're going to have to start at the airport, anyway."

Annie stopped in the act of pouring herself some tea. "*Me* start at the airport?"

"Well, you can't have a man flashing a photograph and asking about a stewardess. What do I say, 'Pardon me, but do you know this girl's number? I'd like to make an obscene phone call'?"

"Well, what am I supposed to say? She's my sister and I've forgotten her name?"

Verecker held out his cup for more tea and sipped at it,

93

frowning. He rested the cup on the table, twisting it in his fingers. He got an idea. "How about that redhead you used to room with—what's her name, Marcia? She's a stewardess."

"So?"

"Borrow one of her uniforms. That way you'd just be one stewardess asking about another. Nothing suspicious about that."

Annie looked doubtful. "I don't know, stewardesses aren't supposed to do that."

"They're not supposed to do a lot of things."

"Don't be catty."

"Just speaking from personal experience."

"And don't brag."

"Look, you'd only need the uniform for a couple of hours. Marcia's a sport."

"Suppose somebody spotted me."

"At an international airport? There are all kinds of uniforms walking around. Nobody's going to notice one extra stewardess."

They settled the check and strolled out of the door onto the sidewalk. They walked around onto Grant and bought ginger-flavored ice creams at a soda counter. Verecker bit into his and said, "Every time I think about quitting this village and moving back to New York I realize that, although I'd be gaining Nathan's hot dogs, I'd be giving up ginger ice cream."

"Life's one big compromise," Annie said.

They walked down to California and rode the cable car up the hill to the Fairmont, got off and switched to the Hyde Street line. It was a clear night, slightly chilly, and they sat outside close together and finished their ice creams. The cable car smelled of yellow brass and polished wood. It rattled and clanked around sudden corners and up long dark hills, the streets quiet but for the clanging of the bell and the snick of the cable under the road, yellow lights winking out in houses as they passed. It was like the last ride of the night at a giant carnival.

When they got back to the house they paused outside Annie's apartment. Annie wanted to know if they shouldn't call Rinlaub and tell him what they'd found out. But Verecker said they hadn't found out that much, certainly nothing the FBI would be interested in. If the greenkeeper hadn't burned those flares that might have been something they could have gone to them with. Without them they were just theorizing. He also wanted to wait and see what the girl in the photograph could tell them. Annie saw the point of this, although she still wasn't crazy about trying to pass herself off as a stewardess. "But," she said, "if I'm going to I'd better get my beauty sleep."

Verecker said innocently, "Do you mind if I bunk on the sofa? After the meal tonight and my religious experience this morning I just couldn't walk up those stairs."

"Then run up," Annie answered, beginning to close her door.

"Well, that's a fine good night for a guy who's taken you to dinner."

"I paid for it."

"But who bought the ginger ice cream, tell me that?"

"See you in the morning," Annie said and closed the door.

Verecker had one last shot at it. "Goddamn it, Annie, how many times have you had the chance to sleep with a messiah before?"

An answering voice came through the door. "We said we'd never talk about our past affairs."

Verecker growled, shook both fists at the ceiling and stomped up the stairs.

"And don't slam your door. You'll wake Mrs. Grabowski," the voice said.

Upstairs, Verecker slammed his door and woke Mrs. Grabowski.

95

12

The Fat Baggage Man

He never got tired of telling whomever he was working the shift with that the only reason they had a job was because the bright boys couldn't figure out a way to replace them. What happens when a passenger gets to the airport? he'd ask. A machine weighs the bags, right? And another machine carries it down to the loading bays, right? And one of them computer machines figures out which bags go on which flight, right? But they couldn't invent a machine to load the bags into the containers. Or to unload them, either. That's why they had to have baggage handlers. So they had their jobs only because the bright boys weren't bright enough. He hadn't thought this up by himself; he'd heard one of the other handlers saying it one day and memorized it, practiced it till he'd got it down, then trotted it out every chance he got. The men he worked with were so used to hearing it nobody even bothered to tell him to

shut up anymore. They'd never taken much notice of him anyway—a fat, roly-poly guy who was just this side of being
simple.

Up till three months ago he'd worked at his uncle's fruit stall
at the Farmers' Market on the south side of town. He hadn't
wanted to give up the job; it suited him fine. He liked farm
life. Everybody said you had to get up too early, but it was
easy to get up early if you knew there was a real farm breakfast
waiting—even on those chilly mornings you got now and then
in the Valley, when your breath made little ghosts in front of
your face and the air went up your nostrils like camphor. He
soon got warm anyway loading up the old Dodge pick-up, and
it was always snug driving into town, just him and his uncle, the
heater on and the radio playing. The best part came when they
got to the market. He'd open up the boxes with a tomahawk,
prying up the nails, popping the wooden slats off and stacking
the fruit in shiny red and green mountains on the stall. He
loved to watch the other farmers arrive, their pick-ups loaded
down with produce, pulling up in front of their stalls, shouting
and calling friendly insults to each other like a fishing fleet
tying up after a good catch. And then the first coffee of the
morning, steaming hot from the snack wagon, and maybe a
couple of doughnuts to go with it.

He would still have had the job, and would have still lived
in the big white farmhouse instead of the rundown apartment
in Bay View, if it hadn't been for the poster. He'd gone into
Santa Clara with one of the farm hands one Saturday to pick
up a few things. He'd waited outside the hardware store for
the farm hand to get through, got tired of waiting and taken a
stroll down the street. He'd stopped outside a small travel
agency. In the window a huge plastic Greyhound bus bore
down on a phalanx of bright-colored easel cards showing
stylized drawings of spinning roulette wheels and coin-gushing
poker machines and impossibly proportioned girls in swimsuits
and cowboy boots. A man was stapling a poster to the felt
backing at the rear of the display. It was a four-color picture

of a dhowlike craft drifting on a sunset sea. Above the sails, written in script on the pink-bellied sky, was the word "Mauritius" and at the bottom of the poster another word in capital letters, "BOAC." He stood on the sidewalk transfixed by it, not believing it. Somewhere on earth there was a place like that? Somebody had taken a camera and photographed paradise.

He walked through the door to the counter. The man came through the curtains behind the window, flashed a professional smile and asked if he could help him. That place in the poster, he'd said, Mauritius—he'd pronounced it Moreetios—was that in Hawaii or someplace? The travel agent had gone out onto the sidewalk to take a look at the poster he'd just tacked up. He'd come back in and said he wasn't sure where it was; he'd just put it up because there was a gap in the display and it was a pretty picture. It wasn't really his line. He specialized in inexpensive weekend bus trips to Tahoe and Reno, and was he interested in one of those? He asked the travel agent what the word meant at the bottom of the poster and the man said he thought it was the name of one of the foreign airlines, which meant that to get to that place, Mauritius, would cost a whole lot more than getting to Reno or Stateline. How much more? The agent had scratched his head and said he could find out for him if he was really serious about it. Yes, he was really serious about it. He'd be in town again next week; he'd come back then.

Normally the travel agent wouldn't have expected a guy like that to return, but he had a feeling about this one, and he was right. The guy was waiting on the doorstep the following Saturday. The travel agent told him he'd called a friend in the business in San Jose. That place he wanted to go to was off the east coast of Africa and it was just about the longest fare you could get: the best part of sixteen hundred bucks round trip. He'd really picked a lulu. Of course, he could do it for 10 percent down and the rest over two years, as long as he had a steady job, a good credit rating and a bank account and all that.

He'd gone home and told his uncle he needed sixteen hundred dollars, and when his uncle had asked why he'd told him there was this place he had to go to and it cost sixteen hundred to get there and back. What was so special about it it cost so much money? It was a long way off. Why did he have to go there, anyway? He couldn't say himself except he'd seen a picture of it and there was an island like a green sail and a boat floating on water that was red from the sun going down. All he knew was he wanted to wade out through the water to that boat. His uncle said he didn't have sixteen hundred dollars for him to go wading.

Two Saturdays running he went back and stood in front of the travel agent's window, staring at the poster. The third Saturday the agent got tired of him hanging around and said that if he was so fired up to go to that place why didn't he get a job with the airlines? You took a vacation you paid only 10 percent of the fare, so instead of sixteen hundred dollars he'd have to come up with only a hundred and sixty.

He'd gone back to the farm and told his uncle, who'd said he'd talk to one of the guys at the market who delivered to the airport and see if they had anything going down there. The delivery man had said, a few days later, that they were always looking for baggage handlers, so his uncle had driven him down to the airport and got him a job.

He found out after he started that the airline he worked for only flew around the country, so that he could get a discount only as far as Chicago or New York or New Orleans, places like that. But he stayed at the job; he figured he could stow away in the baggage compartment in one of those foreign jets if he watched for his chance.

When he told his idea to the man he was working shift with one day, a big surly guy who they said had played some pro ball, the big man had looked at him funnily, as if he were sizing him up, and told him there were better ways of going places than hiding in a baggage hold—like going first class. All you needed was money. And sometimes that was easier to come by than you thought.

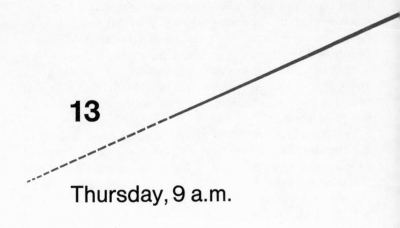

13

Thursday, 9 a.m.

Annie's ex-roommate hadn't been too crazy about being dragged out of bed or lending her a uniform. Annie apologized for the early arrival and told her she wanted the uniform only for a gag; she'd have it back by noon. She'd changed into it, then driven to the airport and parked her car in the short-term parking lot.

She walked across the lot and into the new terminal building and rode up the escalators feeling like the world's biggest fake, expecting any second somebody with braid on his cap to yell "Hey, you." But she got nothing more than a dirty kissing noise from a sailor and a couple of overlong looks from husbands loaded down with suitcases and families.

She walked over acres of cream marble floor and up and down a solid line of check-in desks set against the walls. She checked the insurance girls, the rent-a-car girls, the ground stewardesses, the helicopter and hotel service desks. There were quite a few dark-blue uniforms, but there was nobody who looked like the girl in the picture. But Annie hadn't expected to find her that easily; she knew she could be based anywhere in the country—if she did work for an airline. It was just a uniform; she could be a WAC or a Girl Scout leader. Reluctantly she began showing the picture around. She worked her way down the terminal with no success; then a girl at the Lufthansa desk said she thought she'd ridden out in the limousine with her once and had the idea she was Swedish and why didn't she try SAS; they had navy uniforms like that, in the winter, anyway. But SAS said she didn't work for them, not out of San Francisco, anyway. Maybe L.A.

Annie checked at the remaining desks, got nothing but negatives, left the building and walked over to the old terminal. The first person she asked, one of the ground stewardesses, said sure she knew her; she flew for Alamo, although she hadn't seen her around for some time and maybe she'd been transferred.

The Alamo counter was sandwiched in between two of the domestic giants. It was a small feeder airline that hopped between California, Texas and Mexico, servicing the small towns the big airlines missed. A flight had just gone out and the desk was deserted, the staff still out at the boarding gate. Annie waited, excitement starting to break over her like a slow-rolling wave.

"Can I help you?" somebody asked. A smiling blond man was moving in behind the counter.

"I'm trying to trace this girl." Annie didn't offer a reason and the man didn't seem to expect one. He took the print from her.

"Oh sure. That's Ingrid Arosund. She quit us about a month ago. Nice kid."

She wrote it down. "Ingrid Arosund. Would you have her address?"

"Just a minute." The man moved up the counter and picked up a phone. He spoke into it briefly, waited a few moments, then jotted down something on a slip of paper and hung up. "There you go," he said, handing the note across the counter. "You new around here?"

"Just in from Milwaukee."

"Listen, if you need somebody to show you the sights . . . "

"I'll keep it in mind." The man put his elbows on the counter, cupped his chin in his hands and watched Annie walking away. He let out a low, wistful moan and dragged himself back to his work.

The note said 5821 Scott Street. Annie moved toward a bank of phone booths, intending to call Verecker, but the phones were jammed with semi-hysterical kids who'd evidently come out to welcome some pop group, so she figured she'd call from the other terminal on her way to the car. As she went out of the doors onto the sidewalk an airline limousine pulled into the curb and a stewardess got out. The driver leaned over and told Annie to hop in if she was heading for the other terminal. There were two stewardesses in the back seat and Annie hesitated for a moment but then thanked him and climbed in. She reasoned that if she'd fooled everybody so far, why should she start worrying now? The girls in the back didn't even notice her; they had their heads together, talking about one of the girls who was pregnant and was using up all the sick bags on the morning flights.

When they reached the terminal somebody grabbed her arm before she was halfway out of the car. "Where in heaven's name have you been? You should have been here half an hour ago." A tall angry stewardess was dragging her into the terminal.

"Now just . . . how about taking your hands off me?"

"No sir. Not until you're on board. Operations is throwing a fit." Annie trotted beside her, trying to disentangle her arm. "Look, you don't understand—"

"You're the one who doesn't understand. When you're on stand-by you're on stand-by and not screwing on the sundeck with your boy friend."

102

It suddenly occurred to Annie that the woman's uniform was exactly the same as the one she'd borrowed from Marcia just over an hour ago. Oh, God! And she'd been worried about not passing for the real thing. The worst part was she didn't know what she could do about it. If she told the truth and said she was just a legal secretary in a borrowed uniform she'd get Marcia fired for sure. It was a dilemma she didn't have much time to think about. A man in a uniform picked them up as they jogged through the doors, grasped Annie's free elbow and ran alongside them. Annie felt as if she were being deported.

"Really!" the man said prissily. "You'd stay by your phone if you thought Paul Newman was calling. We've been trying to get you for ages."

"O.K.," the stewardess said, "I've been through all that." She clearly didn't like him.

"But it's outrageous," he said. Annie got the impression he would have stamped his foot if he hadn't been running.

They dog-trotted through the departure gate, down the walkway and into the jet. The man released her arm and stepped back outside. "Simply outrageous."

The door was slammed shut, the engines revved and the plane rolled away from the terminal. This is insane, Annie thought to herself. It had to be some kind of bad dream: too many sea snails in garlic sauce. She'd wake up in a minute to hear Verecker calling through the door.

"Stow your handbag and see if the customers are tucked in." That wasn't Verecker; he didn't say things like that. "And don't forget to smile." It was for real—she was a stewardess on a plane.

Zombie-like, she walked to the rear of the jet and found a cupboard for her handbag. She knew she was going to have to fake it. If they suspected she wasn't a stewardess they'd want to know where she'd got her uniform. Hey, she could say she was a writer for a women's magazine getting the inside dope. Oh? Where did you get the uniform? A stowaway then, with a new wrinkle. Whose uniform? All right, she was really George Plimpton in drag. The uniform—she was definitely going to have to fake it.

She walked to the end of the Economy section and back to the galley. "All comfy cozy," she said to the tall girl she supposed was the senior stewardess.

"Then what's that guy doing?" The stewardess nodded toward a man standing up in his seat prodding a coat into the shelf above his head. "Go and check his belt."

Annie raised her eyebrows but went down the aisle, spoke to the man and came back. "He says it's a Hickok, seven ninety-five at Macy's."

"His seat belt." The stewardess pronounced the words very carefully.

Annie went back down the aisle. Now that the man was sitting down he was having trouble figuring out which way the belt went through the clasp. Annie couldn't figure it either and, rather than call for help, she improvised.

The aircraft had reached the end of the runway and turned and stopped. The engines roared and Annie saw the stewardesses diving for the empty seats. She jumped into one herself and tried to strap herself in; seat belts had always given her problems. She looked up. The tall stewardess was sitting opposite watching in fascination. "Don't lift it, just push it," she said. "Did you take a correspondence course or something?"

The engine noise rose a notch, the plane shook slightly, the brakes were released and the jet bounded forward down the runway. The stewardess leaned across the aisle. "Stop clutching the seat rests and open your eyes. What are the passengers going to think?"

"Sorry, it's just that flying makes me nervous."

"You're joking. Why did you take a job like this?"

"Why? Oh, I, er, like the hats."

The plane lifted off the strip and rushed into the air. There was a hollow grinding noise and a long thud as the undercarriage folded into the fuselage.

"What the hell was that?" Annie asked a little old lady sitting next to her.

Five minutes later the stewardess unfastened her seat belt and told Annie to see if they'd lost any passengers. Annie went down the aisle, briskly efficient, trying to smile like a stewardess. She looked as though she were exposing her teeth for an X ray.

A man touched her elbow and said, "Oh, miss, what time do we get there?"

It dawned on her suddenly she didn't even know where they were going. "What time do we get where?" she asked anxiously.

"Hawaii," the man answered, a little surprised.

"*Hawaii?*"

Several passengers looked around.

"Yeah," the man said, "how long does it take?"

"Oh, God," Annie moaned, "it must take hours. Hawaii," she said despondently, looking at the man but speaking to herself. "It couldn't be L.A. That would have been asking too much."

"L.A.?" the man said, alarm in his voice. "They told me gate five."

"What's the matter?" the woman next to him asked.

"This plane's going to Los Angeles," he sobbed. "I'm on the wrong plane."

"Los Angeles?" the woman cried.

"Now just a second, everybody," Annie began.

"We're going to Los Angeles," the woman told a man craning in his seat.

"Goddamn it," the man said, waving a briefcase, "I've got an important meeting in Honolulu. This could mean the end of my career."

Two rows down a worried woman shouted, "Korea! I heard them say something about Korea."

A teenager grabbed Annie's arm. "Is it true we're going to Korea?"

"It better not be," she replied. "Hawaii's bad enough."

A man behind her announced to his row, "She says Hawaii's socked in. We're turning back."

105

A stewardess coming up the aisle was met by a barrage of questions, backed off and fled through the First Class curtains. A minute later the cabin microphones crackled and a voice a full octave lower than anybody else's started to speak. "Ah, ladies and gentlemen, this is your captain speaking. It's been brought to my attention that there's some kind of, ah, rumor going around back there that we're not going to Hawaii."

"We're not going to Hawaii," a woman confirmed to her husband. She'd known something was wrong all along.

The captain was continuing. "I don't know how that rumor started, but it's completely unfounded, I can assure you. We'll be landing at Honolulu International in approximately four and one half hours, so just relax and enjoy your flight. Thank you." The mike clicked off, then clicked back on again. "Oh, and as for the gentleman who should be on the L.A. flight, as soon as we get to Honolulu, why, we'll get you on the first plane going east."

"They distinctly told me gate five," a voice said.

Annie went back to the galley and was joined by the stewardess who'd gone to see the captain. "I've never seen anything like it in my life," she said to Annie. "It swept through the cabin like a brush fire."

The senior girl coming up caught the tail end of the conversation and glanced at Annie, who shook her head in baffled wonder and said, "It's amazing. All they had to do was ask one of us."

Another stewardess arrived. "Hey, the craziest thing," she said. "One of the passengers had his seat belt tied around him and knotted in front in a neat bow."

The senior girl looked at Annie again. "Probably just a show-off," Annie said.

The senior girl went on looking for a long second, then clapped her hands. "Come on, we'd better get moving. We're way behind. And seeing you're the reason we're late you can do the cabin announcements."

"The cabin announcements," Annie repeated dully.

106

"And without reading them. Let's see what they taught you in that correspondence course." She thrust a hand mike at Annie, who took it as if it were a dead fish. Then she picked up a yellow life jacket and walked halfway down the aisle and stood there looking at Annie expectantly. There was another girl with a life jacket farther down the plane near First Class.

"Good night!" Annie said under her breath; this had to be it. She thought of turning herself in and wondered miserably what the penalty was for impersonating a stewardess. Then she thought of Marcia again and knew she'd have to have a shot at it. It shouldn't be that difficult. She'd heard it lots of times; she'd just have to try and remember. "Ladies and gentlemen," she said into the mike. The senior girl was gesturing to her, pointing to her ear and shaking her head. Annie clicked a button on the mike. "Ladies and gentlemen—" the senior girl nodded—"as we'll probably be passing over water during our flight . . . "

"Probably?" a man said to his wife.

"You see?" she answered smugly. "I told you we were going to Los Angeles."

". . . you'll want to know how to use your life jacket in the event that we—in the event that you have to use your life jacket. Not that we think there's much chance of that," Annie hurried on, trying to smooth it over. "Heavens, it's been ages since we had a crash, which must be bad news for all those people who took out flight insurance." She gave a soprano trill to illustrate that she was only joking. The senior stewardess had a terrible fixed grin on her face that looked as if it had been slipped over her head when she wasn't looking. She put the life jacket on and pointedly held up the tapes.

"See? You just slip it on and tie it the way the stewardess is doing. Then you, er, um . . . " The girl held up a toggle and made a little jerking motion. "Then you pull that little toggle and it inflates automatically."

The stewardess indicated the toggle again, pointed down at her feet and shook her head. "And er, er . . . " It suddenly came

107

to her with a rush. "And for God's sake don't inflate it in the cabin or you'll never make it out the door. Wait till you're in the water before you do that."

The senior girl looked as though she were having a painful splinter removed. She opened her eyes, which had squinched shut at Annie's last line, and resignedly held up the little silver whistle hanging from a cord.

"And the whistle"—what the hell was the whistle for?—"er, that's so you can attract passing liners."

The stewardess had her eyes closed again. She was pointing at the bulkheads over the seats. A voice whispered uncertainly over the cabin speakers, "No smoking? Fasten seat belts?" Annie couldn't make out what she was pointing at. The girl brought a finger up to rub her eye and mouthed the word "Oxygen" behind her hand.

"I can't hear you," the speakers said.

The stewardess coughed and said loudly to her foot, "Oxygen masks."

"Oh yes," the speakers said gaily. "And before you jump into the water don't forget your oxygen masks." Annie wondered if that didn't sound a bit grim, so to compensate for it she finished with "Now just sit back and enjoy the flight. And remember, nothing's going to happen."

The stewardess marched up the aisle and took the mike from her as if she were defusing a bomb. "Well, *that* should keep them off the trains," she said. "You know, with all that you forgot to point out the emergency exits, which I assumed you were building up to. Now we'll have to do it as a special announcement." She shook her head doubtfully. "They may stampede. You've already convinced them we're hurtling toward the ocean in a power dive."

Annie said defensively, "I thought I broke it to them pretty gently."

"You're not supposed to break anything to them. Boy, have you got a lot to learn. Here." She held out a pad and pencil. "Go and take drink orders. I'm sure the customers could use a couple."

Annie moved down the plane and a stewardess from First Class came up to the senior girl. "Who was that on the mike, Dracula's daughter?"

"A new kid. A last-minute replacement."

"Last minute's right," the other girl answered. "I had passengers saying their beads."

"Would you care for a cocktail before lunch?" Annie asked the first person in the first row.

"Certainly not," a woman snapped. "He's only thirteen."

"Oh, really? Big for his age."

"He's five foot one."

"Well, he sits tall," Annie replied.

"Did you say lunch?" the woman asked.

"Lunch," Annie confirmed. She thought, It's ten now and we won't be landing till around two. Of course they'll serve lunch.

An elderly man sitting in the window seat said, "Are we having steak? I can't eat steak."

Annie told him she'd check. She went back to the galley, where a stewardess was pouring orange juice into a paper cup. "One of the passengers wants to know if we're having steak for lunch."

Had she seen who was asking, the stewardess would probably never have answered, "Tell him we've only got lobster. What else on the champagne flight?"

Gee, Annie thought, walking back, champagne and lobster in Economy class. I must find out the name of this airline.

"You're in luck. It's lobster today," she told the elderly man.

The woman next to him lit up. "Lobster? Then I won't be needing this." She handed over a small cardboard box. "That's the box lunch I bought at the airport," she explained. "Would you take care of it for me?"

Somebody in the opposite row asked, "Are we getting lunch?"

"Lobster," Annie answered.

"Then you can have mine, too."

By the time she got back to the galley she had eight boxes cradled in her arms. She was throwing them under the counter

109

when the senior stewardess arrived, paled and asked her what she thought she was doing now.

Annie laughed. "A bunch of first-timers down there brought their own lunch. You should have seen their faces when I told them they were having lobster."

The stewardess started to say, "You told them they were having lobster?" but got only as far as "You told" before her vocal cords froze.

Annie took one look at her horrified face and began to get that old feeling. "You mean we're not having lobster? One of the girls said this was the champagne flight."

The senior girl recovered her voice. "Sweetie, we call it that for a gag. This is the budget special—a hundred bucks each way and bring your own salami. You have to be a VIP to get coffee. You better return those sandwiches before they start on the upholstery."

Annie thought, I promised them lobster Thermidor and instead I'm going to have to serve them their own sandwiches. Now would be a good time to turn myself in. She thought of Marcia again, sighed deeply, piled the boxes in her arms and went back down the aisle. "Sorry, folks, I made a boo-boo. There's no lobster." A collective moan went up. "It's just as well," Annie told them. "There's no 'l' in the month." She read off the top of the first box. "Now, who's the corned beef on rye?"

"Over here," somebody said.

"Egg salad on whole wheat?"

"That's me."

"Miss," somebody called, "I had a tuna on a roll."

"Just a second, sir, I'll get to you as soon as I can. Egg and onion on whole wheat?"

"Right here."

"Ham on white?"

"Ham on white," somebody claimed.

"Hey," a man said, "this isn't egg salad on whole wheat; it's egg and onion on whole wheat."

"Oh. Would the egg salad on whole wheat please swap with the egg and onion on whole wheat?"

"I'm still waiting for my tuna on a roll."

"Tuna on a roll," Annie called, handing over the box. "Roast beef no mustard?"

"That's mine," a woman said, "but I'll swap it for a ham and Swiss no dressing."

"Would anyone like to swap a ham and Swiss no dressing for a roast beef no mustard? No takers? Sorry. Now, who gets the—yeckhh!—nuts and wheat germ on date loaf?" There was a deep silence. "Nuts and wheat germ on date loaf, anybody?" Nobody moved. "Cowards," Annie said.

"Mommy," a small boy whined, "my apple's bruised."

His mother said accusingly to Annie, "It wasn't bruised before you took it away."

Annie swapped it for the apple in the unclaimed box. "Everybody happy now? Good."

She moved toward the galley wondering why they hadn't torn her to pieces. Just before she reached it a hand stopped her and an indignant voice said, "I didn't get my lunch."

"Oh, you must be the nuts and wheat germ on date loaf."

"I am no such thing," a pinch-faced matron told her. "I'd just like lunch like those people got."

"They brought theirs on board," Annie explained.

"I distinctly saw you carry them down the aisle from the galley."

Annie was getting a little passenger-weary. "Didn't you distinctly see me carry them *up* the aisle before that?"

"No, I did not," the woman declared, making it clear she thought Annie was lying.

"Well, if you don't want nuts and wheat germ on date loaf, how about a bruised apple?"

The woman sucked in her breath and let it out with a shocked "Oh!" Then she said, "I'm hungry. I demand you do something about it."

Annie leaned toward her and said conspiratorially, "I'll tell

111

you what. I'll have the captain call ahead to Hawaii and arrange to have a coconut waiting for you when we land."

She tried again for the galley.

She didn't make it.

A young mother with two struggling four-year-olds smiled at her wearily and asked what the chances were of getting somebody in the front seat to swap with her. Annie promised to check. One of the front seats was occupied by a man with his leg in a stiff cast. A teenage girl and a middle-aged man and woman sat on the other side. There was a pet pack at the couple's feet and the woman was leaning over it, crooning to it. The man, a real dyspeptic, was saying, "Don't bother her. She's fine, I tell you. You'll only upset her." The teenager, clearly not their child, was reading a book.

Annie said, "Pardon me, but there's a lady with two children who'd really appreciate it if you'd trade seats with her, so the kids can run around up here."

The woman, fat and dumpy, sniffed. "I'm sorry but Queenie hates to fly anywhere else."

"How can she tell in a box?"

"She knows where she is better than you or I. She has it up here." The woman tapped a finger against her temple.

Annie said, "Well, how would she like to have it up here down there a few rows?"

"I'm not stirring from this seat. I paid for it. It's mine. If people aren't prepared to take proper care of children they shouldn't have any in the first place."

The teenage girl told Annie she'd be glad to swap. Annie said thanks but she needed two seats. She thought for a moment, then asked the couple if she could see their tickets: just a routine check. The man unzipped a plastic case and grudgingly handed them over. She promised to return them in a minute, walked back up the aisle, got the young mother's tickets and took them all into the galley. She peeled off the numbered seat stickers, swapped them over and returned the tickets. She went up to the senior girl and said casually,

"Couple in the front row claim they've been sat in the wrong seats." Then she locked herself in the washroom.

Three minutes later she emerged to hear the senior girl complaining to another stewardess, "What a battle! I could have moved the seats with less trouble than the dog."

The other girl looked mystified. "This is the craziest flight. There must be a jinx on board."

They both turned and looked hard at Annie.

Annie opened her eyes wide and said innocently, "Maybe we hit an albatross."

A buzzer sounded in the galley. The senior girl said, "Whoops, captain wants his tomato juice." She opened a can, poured the juice into a glass and handed it to Annie. "Take this down to him, will you? He's heard about you, but I think he feels we're putting him on."

Annie moved down the plane, knocked on the cabin door and went in. "Good morning, everybody. This is for the captain."

"That'd be me." He looked like an airline captain—close-cropped silver-gray hair, hawklike profile, large green Polaroid sunglasses. The co-pilot, flying the plane, kept his eyes straight ahead. The engineer gazed at Annie like a thirsty man looking at a glass of beer. He said, "Hello there. You new around here?" He smoothed his hair back and hoped she'd notice the crow's feet at his eyes and put it down to the effect of years of peering through the limitless stratosphere.

She flashed a smile. "Just started today."

The captain accepted the tomato juice and said, "I heard about the life-jacket demo, although I don't believe it. That bit about the passing liners . . ."

"Yes. Well, see you in Hawaii." Annie made a fast exit.

She walked back through the First Class section; it was an oasis of calm compared with Economy. It was only half full and just about everybody seemed to be having an after-lunch nap. In the center of the aisle was a serving trolley loaded with shapely liquor bottles and florid cigar boxes. The tray under-

113

neath was littered with corks and red-and-white-centered wine-glasses. On top of the trolley Annie noticed a clear plastic cover shielding half a plump chicken garnished with asparagus and mayonnaise. She looked at the chicken, looked at the snoozing passengers, picked up a carving knife and split the chicken in half. She shared the chicken and asparagus on two plates, grabbed up napkins, knives and forks, stepped through the curtains and thrust the food at the two four-year-olds. "Just don't tell anybody," she said out of the side of her mouth.

She went back to the galley.

"Right," the senior stewardess said. "Give the captain his lunch and you can take a breather. He likes to eat last of all."

"Where do I find the captain's . . . ?" Annie froze in mid-sentence, a stupefying possibility occurring to her.

"It's on the First Class trolley."

"On the First Class trolley," Annie repeated like somebody under hypnosis.

"You remember where First Class is, don't you?"

"In front of the propellers," Annie replied, still in shock.

"In front of the propellers," the stewardess said to the cup-board above her head.

Annie eyed the washroom. No, that would be the coward's way out. She squared her shoulders, picked up something from the counter and walked forward the way she imagined Marie Antoinette and Mata Hari had once walked forward to the roll of drums, her mouth firm and her head high. She held the pose all the way to the cabin door, where she collapsed like a jelly. She went in. "Oh, er, Captain . . . Captain, I'm afraid we didn't save you any chicken."

In his deep bass the captain said, "Never mind. I'll take a steak."

"We didn't save you any steak, either."

"Bring me a lobster then."

"There's definitely no lobster."

"No lobster either?" The captain's voice had climbed a notch. "Well, what have we got? Prime ribs, lamb chops, what?"

114

Slowly, torturously, Annie took her hand from behind her back and held out a cardboard box. "Nuts and wheat germ on date loaf."

"What?" This time it was a high contralto.

Annie, her eyes shut tight as if expecting a blow, decided she may as well go all the way. In a tiny, trembling voice she said, "With a bruised apple."

The Late Show was just starting when Verecker got up to answer the bell and found his secretary leaning exhaustedly against the door, her head pillowed on the frame.

"Annie! Where the hell have you been all day?"

She stumbled into the room and collapsed into a chair. "Hawaii."

"I could believe it. You look as though you walked all the way."

"I damned near did. I've been up and down that aisle today more times than Barbara Hutton." She eased off her shoes and sat back with a luxurious groan.

Verecker opened his mouth, but it was a few seconds before words came. "You don't really mean . . . you're not trying to tell me . . . But—but how? Did you get carried away with the role or something?"

"*It* carried me away. One minute I was on my way to call you, the next I was serving coffee, tea or booze thousands of feet in the air."

"You, a stewardess," Verecker said in disbelief. "I just can't get over it."

"Neither could anybody else. On the return flight we hit some turbulence and I went green. A passenger had to get me a glass of water."

"You mean coming back? Weren't you used to it by then?"

A pained expression crossed Annie's face. "That was worse still. I had to announce the life-jacket drill on the flight out and made such a hash of it they put me on the practical part coming back. I pulled too hard on the silly toggle and in-

115

flated the damn thing. They had to cut me loose with a cheese knife."

"It could have been worse," Verecker suggested. "It could have been the Tokyo–Sydney flight."

"Please! They would've had to ship my feet back under a flag."

Verecker said, "I guess I'll have to check on the girl then."

Tiredly, Annie reached into her handbag and handed him a slip of paper. She said, "I got that much done before I was shanghaied."

"Annie, you're a marvel. Ingrid Arosund, 5821 Scott Street. Pacific Heights, probably. Is she a stewardess?"

"She was until a month ago. She quit."

"Who was she with?"

"Alamo."

"Alamo. Well, isn't that interesting." Verecker tapped his teeth with the folded note. "Annie, I think this is beginning to look like something."

"I don't see anything but little black spots."

"Look, Clarke flew from Mexico and the girl's with an airline that flies to Mexico—or was until she quit. And the fact that she quit is interesting in itself."

"Why?" Annie asked. "If I were a stewardess the first thing I'd *do* is quit."

Verecker bent over her. "Really beat, huh?"

"I'm dead. If I could get out of this chair I'd go downstairs and go to bed."

"No sense walking all that way," Verecker said suavely, lowering himself onto the arm of her chair. "Now that you're here you may as well stay."

Painfully, Annie dragged herself to her feet. "Verecker, even a goat doesn't try as often as you do. Anyway, I wouldn't be much use to you; I'd probably fall asleep halfway through."

Verecker made an understanding gesture. "Well, under the circumstances I wouldn't be offended."

"You wouldn't be offended if I ate an apple halfway through."

"Thank you very much," Verecker said, terribly, terribly hurt.

Annie shuffled to the door, her shoes dangling from her fingers. "See you in the morning, Ace. Around three in the afternoon." She went down the stairs to her door.

Verecker appeared at the top of the landing. "I thought stewardesses were supposed to be easy," he called down.

"They're not easy," the reply came back. "They're just too tired to care. And don't slam the door."

Upstairs, Mrs. Grabowski paused in the middle of putting the last curler in her hair. She looked down at the floor, surprised, then said to her dog, Lulu, "He was early tonight."

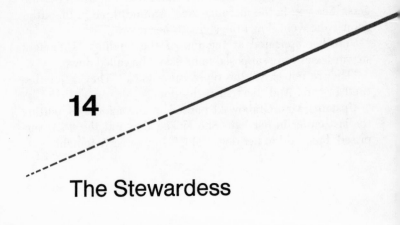

14

The Stewardess

Two months and a few days before her tenth birthday the man who'd come to fix the TV had looked up from the receipt he was writing, run his eyes over her yellow hair and angel face and said smilingly to her mother, "You're going to have trouble with that one." Her mother had laughed; she was getting used to people commenting on her daughter—one of those little girls nature gets ready early, the features all set to form quickly into loveliness.

By the time she was thirteen her father was surprised to find her suddenly a young woman, and faintly embarrassed by it, although it was good for business: She waited tables at her parents' restaurant. That was in Solvang, the town the Danish settlers—those who'd decided to go all the way west—had gone to to become acclimated among their own folk before battling the unfamiliar language and customs of America. The surprising thing about Solvang, forty miles north of Santa Barbara, was that, in spite of the sailing windmills and the umbrellaed outdoor cafés the Chamber of Commerce had built for the tourists, it had still remained authentic—full of strong-faced, big-boned people from Odense and Arhus and Copenhagen who once had intended to stay for only a month. The restaurant had started with her mother baking cakes and selling them to the tourists from a bench outside the house. Then she'd offered tiny spicy meat balls and chilled cucumber salad and told anyone who wanted to eat sitting down to go in and use the dining-room table. She'd finally moved everything inside, had the living room built out almost to the street, added tables and chairs, and wrote up a menu each day. A lot of the people who got out of cars and stopped for lunch stayed for dinner, surprised by the wonderful food and the sweet, icy red wine, the beautiful room with the porcelain birds over the fireplace, and the lovely young waitress who served them.

When she was fifteen a late diner who'd been unable to find accommodation for the night had been put up in the spare room. When he'd come into her bed in the small hours of the morning she'd been too frightened to call out. And the next time something like that had happened she hadn't tried to call out.

It didn't take long for the news to get around that the waitress at the Three Crowns knew what was good for her, and if her mother wondered at the sudden predominance of young men who came to eat at the restaurant in whispering pairs she certainly didn't connect it with her daughter.

A few years later when her father caught her naked on the sofa with a man twice her age he'd told her to get dressed and packed, then he'd given her a hundred dollars and two heavy-handed slaps in the face and advised her not to come back. Her brother had thrown the man out with a broken jaw.

She'd taken the bus to Los Angeles, to Hollywood. The first person she spoke to when she got there, a pretty dark-haired girl who served her a hamburger in a drugstore, told her that a girl with her looks should try to get a screen test—she was

119

having one herself next week. The girl was from Laramie, Wyoming. Her name was Pat Harris, but her screen name was going to be Angela Evans. Pat got her a job in the drugstore waiting tables and took her home to her boarding house for the night. The next day they pooled their money and rented a small flat in a pink Spanish Colonial apartment house on Fountain Avenue. Pat said she knew a few people in the movie business and could introduce her. She'd won a Miss Rodeo title back home, and the big prize had been two weeks in Hollywood and a screen test. She'd got the trip all right—she hadn't gone back —but somehow the test had never come off, even though, she confided, she'd had to sleep with a lot of different men who'd said they were working on it. But there was this assistant producer at Columbia who was going to get her a test for sure, and maybe he could get her one, too.

The assistant producer took one look at the long blond hair and the figure and claimed that getting her a test would be easy —the studios were crying out for Swedish types. He'd just have to get to know her a little better so he could sell her to his boss. Two weeks afterward she found out that the assistant producer was a grip at KTTV. A woman who sometimes came into the drugstore for lunch tipped her off. She said she'd seen him pick her up a few times in his convertible and she thought she should know that he was famous around town for the big-producer act. She was an older woman, still pretty but a little faded, a manicurist in the plush barbershop around the corner on Hollywood Boulevard. The woman had asked her where she was from and when she told her the woman had nodded her head and smiled and asked if she could stand a little advice. She'd told her that what she was doing, running around after screen tests and waiting tables, hoping to be discovered, well, it just didn't work that way anymore. You had to be able to act these days; you had to have credentials. Once upon a time all a girl had to do was look sexy and hold a flaming torch while the tuxedoed star tap-danced down a marble staircase; but they didn't make pictures like that anymore, so they didn't need girls like that anymore. Besides, Hollywood was mainly TV now. If she couldn't act or dance a pretty girl like her would do better to try modeling. If she was interested she knew an agency that was always after fresh faces.

When she related what the woman had said her roommate had claimed it was just sour grapes. And as for the fake producer, she wasn't seeing him anymore anyway. She'd met an agent who was going to get her a couple of lines in Skolsky's column. As a matter of fact she was going to Vegas with the agent for the weekend and maybe she wouldn't be back.

As it turned out she didn't come back. She had her things sent for the following Monday. But that was O.K. The modeling job was really something and inside a month she was earning five times what she'd been earning at the drugstore.

She worked at it for two years, going all the way from posing in swimsuits on a goose-pimply winter beach to getting fat TV residuals for admiring foaming glasses of beer. She was one of the top models on the Coast, but she had sense enough to realize that in something as faddy as the modeling business nobody stayed on top for long; and not having any idea of what else she could do, she decided on a simple course of action: She would marry a rich man. She knew the men she met in her job didn't qualify—lighting cameramen, faggy art directors, agency VPs and ad managers. She needed a job that brought her into contact with millionaires. It didn't take her long to think of becoming a stewardess, with one of those airlines that flew between Houston and Dallas and the banks in San Francisco. She'd read somewhere that the average stewardess worked only fourteen months before she left to get married, because most men thought they made the best wives—a pretty girl mixing them drinks, bringing them pillows, cooking their food—it was easy to see why.

She quit the model agency, gave up her apartment and went to San Francisco, where the airline she was after snapped her up like a shot.

Six weeks later she started flying. And exactly twelve days

121

after that her plans went haywire. She met a pilot in the coffee shop, a guy who flew people up to Shasta for houseboat vacations, and she made a big mistake: She fell in love. She compounded the mistake by telling him. When he accused her one day of not caring for him she'd told him he was out of his mind; she was crazy about him, do anything for him. He'd smiled then and drawn her close, kissed her nose and her eyes and said into her hair, "Of course you would, baby. That's what I'm counting on."

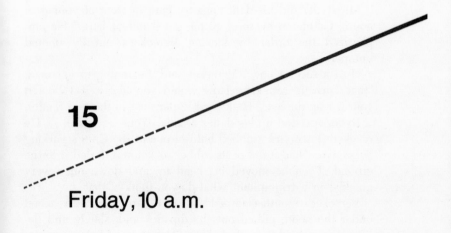

15

Friday, 10 a.m.

Verecker knocked on the door. "Annie? I'll see you out at the car. I want to check the plugs."

A sleepy voice said, "Grummmph."

He went out into the street, crossed to his car and lifted the hood. He noted with glee that he'd beaten Ryder out of his regular parking spot and forced him to park a few feet in front of him. Verecker noticed the dents in his front bumper where Ryder had backed into his Chev, probably on purpose, the bastard, Verecker thought.

He was leaning over examining them when somebody beside him said, "Get that heap out of here or I'll have it towed away."

Verecker straightened up. "Mr. Ryder, I wish you'd back up a little more carefully. Look at that bumper."

Mr. Ryder, a short, wiry little man, did a dance on the sidewalk and shook his fists like a character in a comic strip. "Next time I'll rip the thing off. Get it out of here!"

"Now listen, Ryder, we've been through all this before. This is a public street and I'm allowed to park anywhere I please."

Mr. Ryder did his dance again. "Park in front of your own house. Goddamn eyesore, go on, get it out of here." He emphasized the order by kicking Verecker's already dented bumper.

"Just a second now," Verecker said, beginning to get mad, "that's private property. How would you like it if I booted your car up the ass?" He kicked Ryder's car in the rear fender.

Ryder speeded up his dance a trifle. "You . . . you . . . " He reached down and grabbed hold of one of the Chev's parking lights, wrenched it out of its rubber socket and hurled it to the ground. Then he moved his head up and down once, very quickly, in a triumphant what-do-you-think-of-that.

Verecker's mouth clamped shut in a hard line. He reached under the hood, pulled out the dipstick and, slowly and deliberately, wiped it on Ryder's tie. Then *he* nodded in a what-do-you-think-of-that. Ryder watched it happening in a trance of disbelief. His face changed from red to eggplant and he spluttered like a kettle coming to the boil. He reached in under the hood as Verecker had done, twisted off the radiator cap, marched two steps to his left and hurled it at the Chev's windshield. There was a loud popping noise and a tinkling of glass.

Verecker stared at the shattered windshield, his mouth as wide as the hole in the glass, his hands spread in front of his chest as if expecting to catch a medicine ball. He whirled around and advanced on Ryder's car like a mad robot out to destroy the world. He paused momentarily, searched wildly for a vulnerable spot, wrapped his hands around a wing mirror and, as if he were stirring a giant cauldron, worked it around and around itself until it snapped off. He marched back, hurled it like a metal gauntlet at Ryder's feet, then kicked it.

A thought struck him: a wing mirror for a windshield? He was being short-changed. He put a shoe onto the tail pipe that protruded from Ryder's car, stepped off the ground, balanced his full weight on it and busted it loose from its clamp. Then he looked victoriously at Ryder and made an elaborate pantomime of dusting off his hands.

Ryder was about to have apoplexy when a voice said sharply, "Verecker! Cut out the Laurel and Hardy. You'll get arrested for littering." Annie had crossed the street and was regarding them as though they were two naughty little boys.

Verecker appealed loudly. "Will you look at what this nut's done?"

"I'll have it wrecked and towed away," Ryder screamed.

Annie steered her boss into his car. "I'll see a lawyer about this," Verecker yelled.

Ryder danced up and down on the sidewalk. "Park it there again I'll slash your tires, ya hear me? I'll slash 'em."

They left him on that note and drove around the corner to the Chinese garage.

"I want it back by tonight," Verecker snapped at a man in a white coat.

The man walked around the car scribbling on a clipboard. He said, "Shattered windshield and broken front parking light. Do you always drive with the hood up?"

"It looks sportier that way," Annie answered.

Verecker grabbed her arm and they started toward the street.

"Hey!" the man called after them. "Where's your radiator cap?"

"On the back seat."

"Wow!" The man scratched his ear with his pencil. "Worst case of overheating I ever heard of."

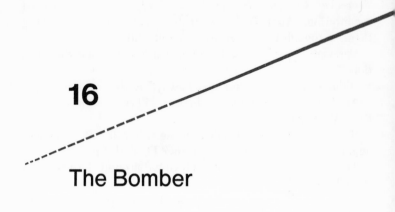

16

The Bomber

He'd worked for the same firm, in the same office, in the same building for twenty-seven years. He'd changed his desk three times, when people had left, moving over from the wall to the center desk to the window, the way permanent patients in a hospital ward change beds when somebody dies. He'd been late for work exactly three times, once when there was a fire in the apartment block, once when a streetcar came off the tracks and once when a cinder had blown into his eye and he'd spent the morning in the Out Patient. He didn't drink and he didn't smoke. He bought a new suit every five years, new shoes every two. He lived by himself in the Mission, an area that was a little seedy in parts but, as he told himself, economical and the best climate in San Francisco. He had a small life-insurance policy and a tidy little bank balance he'd built up steadily over the years. Every night he ate his dinner in Chinatown in the same restaurant, a large, cavernous place with red vinyl seats around the walls and a partition running down the middle of the room that divided off miniature booths for two. He usually shared one of these with someone who was there for the same reason he was—because he lived alone, hated to cook, and because Chinese food was excellent value for the money. After dinner he'd puff up the hill to Stockton, then walk through the tunnel and around to Union Square, where he'd sit for a while if it was a nice night, watching the electric frenzy of the neons and listening to the cable cars clanging up Powell Street behind him. If it was raining or cold he'd go straight to the streetcar on Market and go home and watch television if there was a play on, or read one of the library books he'd borrowed—biographies of famous men mostly. On weekends he pursued a hobby most people would have thought a little strange: He watched clouds. He'd get out of bed early Saturday morning and check the weather. If it was a still day with the sky a faultless ocean of blue, he'd be just as disappointed as if it were rainy or foggy. The best days were sunny and windy with a good cloud mass building up in the west. Then he'd dress quickly, walk around to Mission Park and sit for hours looking up at the sky, watching the beautiful pristine forms shifting in an endless variety of shapes and patterns—cumulus like fat, bulky kites, bowling along majestically; whispy commas of high-flying cirrus, delicate white brush strokes on a blue canvas. Now and then he'd take the Greyhound up to Shasta—"Big Sky" country, they called it—long, flat stretching plains with half the world's sky arcing overhead, no smokestacks, no refineries, no factories. No airplanes. Small planes, maybe. But no huge, screaming passenger jets that ruthlessly tore through the clouds and fouled them with a stinking, cloying, solid trail of kerosene. They raped the clouds, those planes, spoiled their spotless purity, crushed their soft, elegant shapes. They wounded the sky, brutally, heedlessly—slashed across it at hundreds of miles an hour and left a long, white, slow-healing scar. He'd written to the airlines about it—many times. No one had ever answered.

127

He'd written letters to the newspaper; they hadn't run one of them. He'd had handbills printed, even taken classified ads, which were very expensive. He'd tried phoning an airline and been put on to a smooth-voiced man who seemed very under-standing and said they'd see to it right away. But they hadn't. They'd ignored his calls just as they'd ignored his letters. But he didn't think they'd ignore his last letter. He'd told them bluntly and very firmly that if they didn't stop this horrendous thing they were doing he'd be forced to take drastic action. Very drastic indeed.

PART TWO

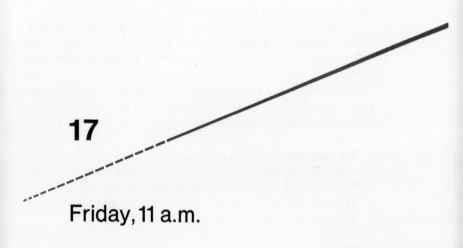

17

Friday, 11 a.m.

It was one of those houses that are snapped up by anybody with a little money and rebuilt inside. Five more bathrooms go in, five more kitchens, several walls are knocked down and several put up, and presto—six nice little apartments that bring in a nice little amount each month. It was painted a smart buff color, the window frames and the gingerbread under the eaves picked out in white, and situated diagonally opposite a small hilly park topped with tennis courts.

They went through a little wire gate and up the steps and examined the names under the buttons on the mailbox. Ingrid Arosund lived in apartment 3B.

Verecker pushed the button and they waited.

No answer.

He pushed it again—longer this time.

Nothing.

There was a plastic name tag that said "Manager Rear Apartment." They walked around the front of the house, up the drive and into a cement-paved backyard.

A small white dog tied to a kennel barked at them crazily.

There were two apartments. The first one looked empty; the door to the other one hung open and a tuneless humming drifted out.

Verecker pressed the bell and the humming stopped. Somebody moved in the darkened living room and came into the light—an elderly woman with a blue rinse and a flowered smock.

"Hi," she chirped. The smile on her face seemed to have been carved there in perpetual memory of a joke heard long ago.

Verecker said, "Good morning. Is the manager in?"

"He's my son," the woman said, not answering the question.

"Yes, but is he in?"

"Who?"

Uh oh, Annie thought, we've got one.

"Your son, the manager," Verecker said.

"My son, the manager," the woman chorused. "That's very good." She laughed like a flute in the upper register. Then her face changed quickly to a serious, confidential expression and she leaned forward and said, "He's only the manager part time, you know. He has another job. I wanted him to be a dentist but do you think he'd listen? No. He wanted glamor, excitement, bright lights."

"What is he?" Annie asked.

"A surveyor."

Verecker said, "Sometimes there's just no holding them."

The woman asked if they'd come about the vacant apartment. "No, we're trying to get in touch with Miss Arosund."

"Ingrid? She's in three B. Just ring and go on up."

"She's not there," Verecker said, "and we were wondering—"

"Of course she's there. She was just talking to me a second

132

ago from her window." The woman jabbed her finger toward the ceiling.

"Maybe she stepped out," Annie suggested.

The woman reached up behind the door and jingled a bunch of keys in the air. "Let's take a look, why don't we?"

The three of them walked around and back down the drive. Verecker tried a little probing. "She's a stewardess, isn't she?"

"That's right. We've got a couple of them in the house—lots of them around this area." The woman frowned, remembering something. "Although maybe Ingrid's doing something else now. I don't see her wearing her uniform much."

She chose a key and opened the front door. There was a red-carpeted hall with two doors leading off to apartments on either side. Stairs rose straight ahead of them, framed balloon prints on the flock wallpaper.

"Nice place," Annie said.

"The owner's no penny-pincher, I'll tell you." They started up the stairs. "If something needs fixing he fixes it, pronto."

They reached the landing. There were two doors with numbers on them; the stairs continued up a flight.

The manager's mother knocked lightly on the door. "Ingrid, some folks to see you."

Music came out to them, thin and tinny, muffled, as if a radio were playing face down on the floor. "She gets too hungry for dinner at eight . . . "

The woman knocked louder. "Ingrid? You there?"

". . . the theater but never comes late . . . "

"That's funny." She put a key in the door and opened it a few inches. "I don't know what . . ." She poked her head around the door and called the girl's name again, then pushed the door all the way open and they stepped hesitantly inside.

Tiny electric feet pitter-pattered up Verecker's spine. There was a quivering tension in the room; the air seemed stretched like the skin of a balloon about to burst. They took it all in slowly—a purple raffia mat, a flower-print sofa against one

133

wall, a long bookcase full of old stone bottles sprouting paper flowers, a portable phonograph on the floor, a glass-topped coffee table, four director's chairs set around a circular table in an alcove in the corner.

"Maybe she's in the bedroom," the woman said and walked to the end of the room and turned into a little hall. "Ingrid? You decent?"

They waited.

She came back. "Well, isn't that the darnedest thing. Bathroom's empty, too."

Verecker crossed the floor and went up the step into a raised kitchen. The radio was standing on the counter half covered by a towel that looked as if it had fallen off the drying rack above. The song had ended and a man was talking about detergent. A cup of coffee steamed on the sink, the liquid still swirling slightly around the spoon standing in it.

Annie came into the kitchen, the woman behind her. "Maybe she's upstairs," Annie suggested.

"Nope. They're at work."

"Well, she might have gone for sugar for her coffee. Is there a store handy?"

"Just around the corner."

Verecker opened the cupboards above the sink and peeked inside. Then he did the same with the refrigerator. "She's got milk and she's got sugar. So what made her leave so fast she didn't have time for coffee?"

The woman moved to the window. "There's her car down there, so she can't have gone far."

"Which is hers?"

"The white Corvair."

The apartment was a rear one, although, because it was built on a wing of the house, it faced the street. The apartment next door, a front one, extended to the left. Verecker looked out of the window at the car. Then his glance fell on the side window of the other apartment. Not six feet away from him a girl was lying stretched out on a bed, mouth slightly open, eyes closed, hair tumbled over the sheet. Her bare shoulders were half in, half out of a blue blanket that covered the rest of her body.

Verecker froze and said quietly, "I think I've found Ingrid Arosund."

Annie made for the window but Verecker stepped in front of her. "Don't," he said.

"What are you two . . . " The woman pushed by Verecker and pressed her face to the glass. "Why, that's not Ingrid, that's Sue Abernathy next door. She works late, sleeps through the morning." She looked at Verecker disdainfully, suspecting a peeping Tom.

Annie expelled a great sigh of relief. "Really, Verecker, must you be so dramatic?" She peeked through the window. "That girl looks nothing like Ingrid Arosund, anyway."

Shamefaced, Verecker said, "I suppose not. Got carried away, I guess. Sorry, folks."

"Oh, stop it," Annie said. She turned to the woman. "When Ingrid returns would you have her call us?" She handed the woman a card.

"Sure, sure. I'll tell my son when he gets back." She went over and switched off the radio. "No sense in wasting power," she said.

They went out of the apartment and down the stairs. She opened the door for them. "I'll have my son call you," she repeated. She wasn't chirping anymore and she seemed suddenly anxious for them to leave.

They crossed to Annie's Volkswagen. Annie didn't use it much, but it came in handy whenever Verecker had a fight with Mr. Ryder. They pulled away from the curb and headed downtown.

"Verecker," she began, "please get your facts straight before you scare the life out of me again."

"It was a reasonable conclusion. She looked dead after all."

"Don't you know the difference between a live woman and a dead one?"

"Not when they're lying on a bed."

135

"You're bad, do you know that? You're really bad."

Verecker shrugged. "You know, if Ingrid Arosund had turned out to be dead at least it would have made sense. It would have explained that spooky apartment. It was like the Marie Celeste in there."

Annie rubbed her arms, cold all of a sudden. "It was awful, wasn't it? As if she'd been dematerialized, or spirited away."

They stopped for a red light. Verecker watched the people crossing in front of the car, coming out of a supermarket loaded down with brown paper bags. "There was something that crazy lady said that rang a bell, you know? One of those things that triggers something in the back of your mind."

The light changed. Annie said, "You mean about there being more than one stewardess in the house?"

"No, it wasn't that. I don't think that means anything. It was something else. It'll come to me."

They climbed the steep slope of Clay Street where it peaks toward Nob Hill and stayed in low gear to go down the other side. The road fell away like a ski jump, and the bay stretched in front of them like a monster wide-screen projection.

They left the car at the underground garage and walked along Kearney. Annie suggested that if the girl turned out to be a dead end they should go to Rinlaub with what they had. Verecker argued against this, pointing out that what they had wasn't much, and Annie accused him of thinking only of the reward and not about the kidnapped passengers. He denied this but compromised by agreeing at least to talk to Rinlaub to see if there had been any new developments. Annie reminded him that for all they knew the plane and the people might have already been found, but Verecker told her that if that had happened they would have heard from Rinlaub.

When they reached the office Verecker called the woman on Scott Street and asked if Ingrid Arosund had returned. The woman told him she had but she'd gone away again, for a few days this time, and she hadn't said where. She'd given Ingrid his card and the message to call him. Verecker thanked her and hung up, then called Rinlaub and made a date for lunch.

He pushed the phone aside and said dismally to Annie, "Well, that's the ball game, I guess. Called on account of lack of evidence. The girl's gone off I don't know where and with her goes any chance of finding out something more about Clarke."

He was bitterly disappointed and it showed. Annie said gently, "You gave it a good try, Billy. But we couldn't really have expected to come up with something the FBI couldn't. It would have been plain dumb luck."

"Finding those flare holes on the golf course was plain dumb luck—the kind the FBI didn't have and I did."

"Then maybe we've had our quota. The best thing to do is to tell Phil Rinlaub everything and let him and the authorities take it from there."

Verecker didn't answer. He went over the window and watched the dentist moving around his office.

Annie said, "We've got half an hour before lunch. Why don't you call Peter Stone?" She walked to him and handed him a letter. "It came in this morning's mail. He says he's snowed under and could you handle a couple of clients for him. It would pay the rent for a while."

Verecker took the letter and scanned it. "Sure, why not?" he said tonelessly. "Get him on the phone, would you?" His voice was as flat as a pancake.

Annie dialed a number, spoke briefly into the phone and handed it over.

"Hi, Peter, how are you? . . . Fine. . . . Sure, I'd be delighted. We're pretty slow here right now. . . . No, nothing much, just a—"

His voice stopped as if a gag had been rammed into his mouth. The phone came slowly away from his ear. "Much," he said under his breath, as if he'd never heard the word before. He jammed the phone to his mouth and gabbled into it. "Pete,

I'll call you back. Gotta go." He slammed the phone down. "Annie, I remember what it was that woman said this morning, the thing that was bugging me. When we were going up to the apartment I asked her if Ingrid was a stewardess, remember?" He was talking excitedly, pacing up and down, punching his fist into the palm of his hand. "She said that maybe Ingrid had got some other job because she hadn't seen her wearing her uniform much. Much, Annie. She didn't say 'at all' or 'anymore'; she said she hadn't seen her wearing it much. Which sounds like she's worn it since she quit her job."

"Hey," Annie said softly. Then she seemed to read Verecker's mind. She grabbed her pad, flipped through it quickly and dialed a number.

Verecker snatched up the extension and listened to the phone ringing at the other end. "C'mon, c'mon," he said to it.

"Hello?" a voice said on the wire.

"Hello. It's William Verecker again. Look, I'm sorry to bother you a second time, but it's about something you said this morning. Remember telling me you hadn't seen Ingrid wearing her uniform much? . . . Yes, that's right. She wore it recently though, didn't she? . . . Fine. Now, ma'am, this is very important. Can you tell me the last time you saw her wearing it?" There was a pause. "You're absolutely sure of that? About what time was this? . . . I see. Thank you. Thank you very much. You've been awfully helpful. . . . Yes. Goodbye." He replaced the phone very precisely, then swung a fist through the air and cried, "Yeah!"

Annie said, "Last Friday?"

"Of course last Friday. She remembers because that's her bridge afternoon. The girl was coming out as she was coming in. She says she always gets home from bridge around five. Around five, Annie. That plane left at seven-fifteen."

"You think she was on that plane?"

"I'm sure she was on that plane. I don't know why. I mean I can't imagine what she did, but she's part of it. She's got to be."

"It's starting to look like something," Annie said.

"It's starting to look like a hundred thousand dollars."

"But you're still going to tell Rinlaub, aren't you?"

"Are you kidding? Tell him now, just when we've got a real solid tie-up? No sir. This is the closest I'll ever get to that kind of money. I'm not just going to give it away."

Annie leaned back on the desk and folded her arms. "Verecker, I've got an awful feeling it's going to be the toughest hundred thousand dollars you ever earned."

"Come on," he said, "let's go and see and if Phil Rinlaub knows anything more."

On the way to the restaurant Annie said, "You know, that funny lady, the manager's mother, she's a pretty observant old bird."

"What do you mean?"

"Well, she knew which day it was, what time it was and what Ingrid Arosund was wearing. And it didn't sound like she had to think about it."

"But she explained why it stuck in her memory."

"All the same . . . "

"I don't know what you're getting at, but she's even more observant than you think."

"How's that?"

"She told me the girl was carrying a flight bag, too, and wearing a topcoat over her uniform. Hell, she even noticed what she didn't have on."

"What?"

"Her hat. She said the girl wasn't wearing it."

"Uh huh."

"What do you mean, 'Uh huh'?"

"Nothing," Annie said thoughtfully. "But like you say, she's even more observant than I thought."

18

The Bomber Again

He gave them a week; then, to be scrupulously fair, another week.

No reply came.

He realized with great regret that there was only one course open to him now—to demonstrate vividly that he meant what he'd said in his letters. He knew what he needed; it was just a case of gathering the materials.

Like all good generals—and he considered himself the general in his one-man war against the airlines—he knew that to fight an enemy successfully you had to know as much about him as he knew about himself. Consequently there wasn't a book about the airlines he hadn't pored over, fact as well as fiction, or a news release in the newspaper he hadn't pounced on. He studied manuals on aircraft maintenance and airport design, tomes on air-crash detection, magazine articles on air safety, even teach-yourself-to-fly books. He had an expert's knowledge of every new weapon the enemy came up with—the airbus, the jumbo jet, the SST and the stretched versions that were already on the drawing boards. There wasn't a hijack incident or a bomb scare he didn't know about—and in detail. He also had subscriptions to half a dozen aviation magazines, and it was from one of these, with its unabashed weapons advertisements, that he read a report of terrorist airline bombings. It went into great detail on the kind of bombs they used, how they made them and how they timed them to explode.

The dynamite and the blasting cap were the hard parts. Everything else he could buy.

He'd read that there was a lot of big construction going on at Yosemite. They were blasting a tunnel. It would be a pleasant trip; there was some lovely sky over Yosemite.

He rented a car one Saturday, crossed the Bay Bridge and drove sedately past Livermore and through Tracy and then ate sandwiches in the pretty green park in Manteca. He drove on through the southern edge of the Gold Country where the signposts pointed to towns with names he'd always loved— Jenny Lind, Cooperopolis, Priest, China Camp, Hetch Hetchy Junction. The road wound through high green pine forests five thousand feet into the Sierras, flattened out for a hundred yards at the entrance to the national park, then tumbled with a whoosh down into the valley. He took the turnoff to Tuolumne Meadows and followed a road out into the sides of slate-gray, hard-rock mountains, past lakes as still as the sky, large black rocks breaking the surface like whales coming up to breathe.

He checked in at a lodge, all tailored lawns and great flag-stone fireplaces and an army of bellhops still wearing the old-style uniforms. It was expensive but nice. And besides, it was only for one night.

He walked into the village and bought a flashlight and an ax, just another camper. He put them in the trunk of his car and went back to the lodge for dinner.

Afterward, when it was good and dark, he drove to the con-

struction site. He hid the car under some trees, took the ax
and the flashlight and walked up a mud road rutted by the
bulldozers and heavy trucks that were parked on its edge. In
the darkness they looked like antediluvian monsters mired in
a swamp.

The explosives shed had a single large padlock protecting it.
He swung the ax twice, three times, smashing into the wood
just above the hasp, and pried it loose from the door. It took
him only a few moments to grab what he wanted, then he hid
behind a truck when the night watchman came running. He
saw a beam playing over the busted lock, heard the watchman
curse, then ducked back when the beam flashed around like a
searchlight. The finger of yellow light slid underneath the truck
reaching for him, almost touching his shoes. He stood very still.
The beam slowly circled the trees to his left. He heard footsteps sloshing away from him.

He waited a few moments, then walked quickly back to his
car, stowed everything but the ax in the trunk and drove back
the way he'd come.

A mile later a car with a screaming siren came out of the
night toward him. When it had disappeared he stopped, got
out, hurled the ax into the forest and drove back to his lodge.

Sunday he returned to San Francisco. Monday he bought a
watch, a medium-priced, waterproof watch. Tuesday he bought
a twist drill. Wednesday he bought a roll of masking tape and
a transistor battery. Thursday he bought a pair of white overalls
from a disposal store on Market Street. Thursday night he sat
down at his kitchen table, moved a lamp onto it and began
to work.

First he made doubly sure the watch had completely run
down. He shook it hard, he shook it gently. He laid it down, he
held it up. He poked it and prodded it and put his ear to it.
There wasn't a single tick and the hands were dead still. Using
a nail file, he pried off the crystal and gently removed the
sweep hand and the minute hand. Then he opened the back of
the watch and examined the works closely, turning the watch

over and over, front and back. He selected a spot just above the brand name, picked up the twist drill, fitted an incredibly fine corkscrew bit and painstakingly bored a hole through the face. He picked up a pin, snipped it in half with pliers and worked it snugly into the hole.

He took his glasses off, pinched the bridge of his nose between his fingers and massaged for a minute. Then he replaced his glasses, blinked his eyes back into focus and reached for a cardboard box.

Two sticks of dynamite lay in it.

He tore off a long strip of masking tape, picked up the sticks and bound them tightly together. Then he wired up the blasting cap and the dynamite and connected the battery. He worked quickly, his hands steady. He knew there was no danger as long as he did things correctly and efficiently—the way he'd always done things.

There was only one more operation: wiring up the pin and the hour hand. For a moment he was tempted to leave it till morning. What, if by some freak, the watch started ticking, the hand moving around the dial, closer and closer to the pin until— But that was ridiculous. The watch wouldn't run until it was wound.

He bent over the table again. He picked up the pliers and pinched one of the wires tight around the pin protruding from the back of the watch. Then he carefully moved the hour hand till it was pointing at seven—it was easier to attach the wire at that position—slipped the hair-thin wire around the gold hand and pinched it tight. The first time the hand wouldn't move on the face, wouldn't clear it. He did it again and moved the hand experimentally back and forth a fraction. It worked. But with cold shock washing over him he saw that the watch had started.

He calmed down. Pretty sensitive watch, he thought to himself. Just a finger on the winder button and a slight jog of the mainspring had been enough to set it going.

He let it go, fascinated to see how long it would run. One

143

minute. Two minutes. Three. What if it didn't stop? he thought for a second time. What if it went right on ticking? And what if he just sat there watching it, the way he was sitting there watching it now, until it was too late? But there was no chance of that; all he had to do to defuse it was disconnect one little wire. Besides, it couldn't run for five hours, not without winding, and he'd only jogged it. It was impossible.

There, it had stopped now.

He put his ear to it.

Tick, tick, tick, tick.

This was crazy. He'd give it a few more minutes, then disconnect the wire. Amazing how just by moving the button slightly he'd set it going again. Must be a pretty good watch, better than he thought. Shame it was going to be blown to bits. Damn good watch; just jogged it and it's still going. Hard to tell by the hour hand, though. Looked like it was stopping now. No, by golly, still going. Must be beautifully balanced. Knew it wouldn't let me down. Bet it could run for another hour if I let it, maybe more. Look at it go now—wait a second, it *had* stopped. Well, what do you know about that? Not such a great watch after all. Should have paid more money. It ran for, let's see, only seven minutes? Seemed longer. Still, not bad for just one little jog. Wonder how long it would run with just one little wind? Better not touch it. Finish up now. Big day tomorrow.

He scraped his chair back, got up, yawned, turned the lamp off and went into his bedroom. He changed into his pajamas and got into bed. He wondered if there was anything he hadn't thought of and convinced himself there wasn't.

He turned over and closed his eyes. He didn't have any trouble dropping off to sleep. But he would have if he'd known that when he'd turned the lamp off in the kitchen his leg had bumped the table.

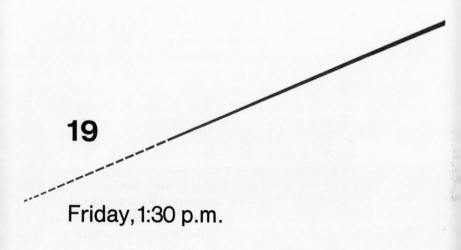

19

Friday, 1:30 p.m.

Maria's was crowded, bustling and noisy as always, the tables packed solid with people eating as if they were leaving for a prison camp the next day. It had once been a Chinese restaurant, one of the few that had spilled over Broadway into Little Italy, but while the restaurant had been willing to cross the boundary of Chinatown the Chinese hadn't. And there was no tourist trade because they wanted to eat Chinese food in Chinatown, not in North Beach, which their guidebooks maintained was strictly spaghetti territory. So the owner had moved back to Pacific Street and sold the restaurant, fittings and all, to an Italian; so now the restaurant looked like a *trattoria* in Shanghai. There was a row of semi-private pagoda-shaped booths running along one wall, while painted on the opposite wall, rearing dramatically over the tables, a fiery, ceiling-high Vesuvius rained scalding ashes down upon a gondola floating on the Grand Canal several feet away. There was a kitchen at the far end of the room and a tiny bar near the door sheltered by a red canopy with dragons rampant on it.

They found Phil Rinlaub tucked away in one of the booths. "Don't I know you from someplace?" Verecker said.

Rinlaub got up and shook his hand. "Hello, Bill. Nice to see you, Annie."

"Hello there."

They sat down. Verecker said, "I thought this would be a good place to talk. No one will hear us; it'll be tough to hear each other."

Rinlaub smiled. "I haven't been here for years."

"Still the best value in town," Verecker declared. "They give you a meal a greyhound couldn't jump over."

A large smiling woman appeared at the door.

"Vincey! Sneaking up on the customers now, eh? This is Vincey," Verecker told Rinlaub. "World's champion waitress. Whatcha got that's really great today, Vincey?"

The woman beamed at him and rattled off a list of dishes. "I got minestrone, spaghetti, ravioli. I got roast lamb, roast veal, pot roast, veal kidney, chicken cacciatore. I got spinach, I got cauliflower, I got roast potatoes."

Annie winced. "I couldn't just have banana yoghurt and a Ry-Krisp, could I?"

"She'll take ravioli and the roast veal," Verecker told the waitress.

Rinlaub said he'd have the same.

"Make it three, Vincey," Verecker said.

"A little spinach with the meat? C'mon now," the woman coaxed.

"Sure, bring it all. And a large bottle of your best watered-down vino. And how about an alcoholic beverage while we wait?" He looked at Rinlaub. "You still drink vodka martinis?"

"Today I could use two."

"Four in three glasses," Verecker ordered.

"I fix it for you special," the woman said, moving away.

146

Verecker leaned across and confided to his friend, "I'd marry her if I weren't just getting over a painful divorce."

Annie sniffed.

They chatted about incidentals till the drinks arrived, Rinlaub took a long sip of his, then another, and said, "God bless booze."

Verecker noted the bags under Rinlaub's eyes, the suit that needed pressing and the shirt that didn't look clean. "Phil, you look as though you've been sleeping in a chair. No progress, huh?"

The other man said, "Not that we haven't been trying. You know, this is the first time I've sat down for lunch since I saw you. I shouldn't really be here now. I should be back at my desk waiting for the phone to ring."

"There's nothing new at all?"

"Nothing we can make any sense of. Yesterday an FBI man prowling around Kennedy Airport just happened to take a look in the unclaimed-baggage room. He found a suitcase that was ticketed for Flight 422."

"You mean *the* flight?"

Rinlaub nodded. "A baggage checker said it had been on the carousel Saturday night and most of Sunday and, being unclaimed, he'd taken if off and stored it. When we checked back at this end one of the girls at the Calair counter remembered it. It had missed Friday night's flight somehow and been put on the first plane to New York next morning."

"Did it tell you anything?" Annie asked.

Rinlaub sighed. "All it did was hand us another riddle." He swirled the liquid in his glass, picked out the lemon twist and sucked. "It was a cheap brown cloth and vinyl bag, no initials, no name, nothing. And you know what they found inside? This is the crazy part—five new house bricks."

"What?"

"Wrapped in an old bath towel."

Annie said, "But that doesn't make sense. Why take house bricks on board a plane?"

147

"You figure it," Rinlaub invited.

"I'm going to have to come back to that one."

Verecker didn't comment on the suitcase but instead asked if they'd found out anything more about the passengers.

"Oh, we got calls from a dozen more relatives, not that it helped us much."

"But still no sign of the plane?"

"Not even a gum wrapper. Wouldn't you think that half the law-enforcement agencies of two states plus a task force of Federal men could find a three-hundred-ton jet? It's hardly what you'd call a needle in a haystack. It's driving everybody crazy." He lifted the glass to his mouth again and the ice cubes clinked against his teeth. "Look at that." He held up his empty glass. "I never drank that fast before this thing happened." He waved away Verecker's offer of a refill.

Annie asked him if they'd learned anything significant about the passengers they knew of—any connection between them, for instance.

"Businessmen mainly. Some vacationers, a couple of soldiers —although, strangely enough, there is a connection. Three of the items that were mailed to us belong to men who are members of the same club."

Verecker said, "You're kidding. Which one?"

"The Montgomery. It's a health club. Lots of brokers, advertising men use it."

"Well, Christ, man—"

Rinlaub had both hands up. "Now before you think you've solved it, let me tell you the FBI went over that club up, down and sideways. They're convinced it's just a coincidence."

"Coincidence?" Verecker looked at Rinlaub as if he were out of his mind.

"Sure, and not much of a one at that. It's one of the biggest clubs in town. Even some of the local FBI men belong to it. Hell, my brother-in-law belongs to it."

Verecker looked disappointed. "Really checked it out, huh?"

"Top and bottom."

The waitress arrived with the food. She put heaped plates down on the table and stood over them with a spoon and a large glass bowl. "A little cheese?" she suggested. Annie tried to refuse. "Take a little," the woman urged with a do-it-for-Mama look and lashed it out all around. She brought an un-labeled liter bottle of red wine and short thick glasses.

Rinlaub poured some wine and asked if they'd had any bright ideas.

Verecker held out his glass and shot a glance at Annie. She flicked her eyes at him briefly and inspected her plate. "Noth-ing much," he said offhandedly.

They started on the food. After a minute Rinlaub dabbed his mouth with his napkin and said, "I was kind of hoping you'd have a few ideas."

Verecker hesitated. "Well, of course I have a couple of theories . . . " He felt Annie watching him stonily. "But nothing I think you'd be interested in."

"Listen, at this stage I'd be interested in what a carnival swami had to say."

Verecker couldn't see how he could get out of telling him now, not with Annie's eyes boring into his conscience. He tried to laugh it off. "Oh, it's mostly supposition and a couple of wild guesses. I seriously doubt—"

"There a Mr. Winelobe here?" The waitress was standing at the door.

"You mean Rinlaub?"

She nodded her head toward the bar. "Telephone."

"Excuse me." Rinlaub got up. "That could only be the office. I told them I'd be here." He left the booth.

Verecker grinned weakly at Annie. "Saved by the bell."

"You can't not tell him now. The poor guy's a wreck," she said.

Verecker looked miserable. "Yeah, I guess so." He poured himself another glass of wine and sat dolefully sipping it. He started to suggest something, saw the concrete look on her face and thought better of it.

149

Rinlaub came back in a hurry. "Gotta go," he said quickly. "Thanks for the lunch. Sorry I have to rush."

"Whoa, hold on now." Verecker grabbed his sleeve. "You can't just leave us like that. That phone call, it was something important, wasn't it?"

Rinlaub said, "I have to go, Bill."

"Not without telling us. We'll go crazy wondering."

Rinlaub looked at him for a long moment. "O.K. But if this ever—"

"It won't, don't worry."

"Those items that came in the mail, the watches . . ."

"Yeah . . ."

"One of them belongs to a guy named Harcourt. His wife identified it. She called an hour ago and wanted to take another look at it. She says it's exactly the same as her husband's, except it's not her husband's. She says it's a fake."

The first thing he did when he got up was to go out to the kitchen and check the watch. The hand was still midway between seven and eight. Remembering, he felt embarrassed about last night; he'd lost control briefly, been hypnotized by his own fears. That wasn't like him at all. Still, he rationalized, it had been late and he'd been tired and under quite a strain, although it must have been more imagined than real. Now, in the bright, clear morning light, the device lying on the table seemed no more threatening than the lamp standing next to it. He spread a newspaper over it. Nobody would come into the apartment through the day, but better to be safe than sorry.

He ate a leisurely breakfast, showered, shaved, dressed and left for the office. On his lunch hour he brought a large portable radio, then, from a small grocer, a case of toilet rolls. He took all this back to his apartment and returned to work.

At 2:30 he told his boss he felt ill and went home. He sat down at the kitchen table and started. First he took off the back of the radio and removed all the components till he was left with just the hollow plastic case. Then cautiously, careful not to disturb the wires, he lifted the watch a fraction, took the winder button between thumb and forefinger and began to twist it back and forth with slow, precise movements. He wound the watch for a good thirty seconds and checked to see if it was running all right. Then, holding it rock-steady, he pulled the winder button out. The flight left at 7:15, in about four hours' time. It was 3:20 now. The charge would explode just before twelve. He set the watch on the dot of seven, clicked the button back in and stopped and thought for a moment. That gave it only five hours; it would detonate less than an hour after the plane took off. It wouldn't get far—over the Sierras maybe. But what if there was a delay on the ground? It wouldn't be very sporting not to hit a bird on the wing. He pulled the winder button out again. No, he thought, he was being foolish, getting nervous again. If there was a delay it'd be only ten, fifteen minutes. He put his hands in his lap and waited till he'd calmed down. He reached for the bottom half of the radio case and laid the bomb gently inside. He taped the dynamite and the blasting cap to the case and the battery next to it, taping the wires, too. Then he taped the watch by its band over and to the right of the dynamite. It all looked secure. He clicked the top half of the case into position and held the whole thing up by its handle. He permitted himself a tiny smile. Unless you tried to play it you wouldn't know it wasn't a radio. He lifted the case of toilet rolls onto the table, opened it and removed four of the rolls. He stowed the bomb in the vacant space, fetched the overalls from his bedroom, folded them flat and laid them on top of the plastic case. He turned the box flaps in on themselves, wrapped the box in brown paper and tied it with string, then left the apartment, got a cab downtown and caught the bus to the airport. It was just 4:00 by the depot clock.

The terminal was crowded with people getting a jump on the weekend, and he had to go all the way to the end of the building before he found an empty men's room. He chose a

151

booth and locked the door, ripped away the paper and string and pulled out the overalls. He slipped them on over his suit. He balled up the wrappings, unlocked the door, crossed the floor and stuffed them into the waste bin. He went back for the box and made sure the rolls were covering the plastic case. If anybody should happen to poke around inside he wouldn't find anything except a radio, and a radio could be explained away. As he was leaving a man coming into the washroom held the door open for him.

He carried the box cradled in his arms out into the terminal, the brand name showing in splashy blue type. Nobody gave him a second look—a guy from the washroom supply company —why should they? He glanced at the arrivals board and noted the gate number of the flight that had just arrived from New York. A Calair flight. A 747. That was the type of plane he'd chosen. They cost millions, he knew. The airline wouldn't like losing a plane like that.

He moved toward the departure gates, rode the moving stairway down the long corridor and walked to a gate that wasn't in use. He went down the stairs and out onto the ramp. A hundred yards away the 747 had just finished unloading. It was surrounded by fuel trucks and catering vans and cleaning units. He walked toward the rear stairs. People in white uniforms just like his own were going up and coming down. He started up the stairs holding the box in front of him like a Mayan priest ascending a stepped pyramid with an offering for the sun. Inside, the jet was full of people sweeping, wiping, vacuuming, replacing—just as he knew it would be. It was all working the way he thought it would. He felt supremely confident.

He moved down the aisle and climbed the carpeted staircase spiraling up into the First Class lounge. There was a long curving banquette at one end, winged armchairs against the wall, high-backed foam benches down the middle, then a door leading to the flight deck. He went though it and into the pilots' toilet, closed the door and slid the knob across, locking it. He saw that it had already been serviced, which he'd been counting on—fresh towels, new cakes of soap. He bent down, took hold of the waste receptacle under the washbasin and eased it out of its slot. He reached for the radio case, stood it upright inside the receptacle and wedged it firmly against the side with a couple of toilet rolls squeezed against it end to end. He shook the receptacle experimentally. The radio case didn't budge. He fitted it back into its slot again, slid it back under the basin, unlocked the door and went out into the lounge.

Nobody.

He smiled. Everything had been so simple.

Walking back across the ramp, he instinctively looked up above him. A single perfect cloud was sailing across the sky like a puff of white cotton candy.

It made him feel very, very happy.

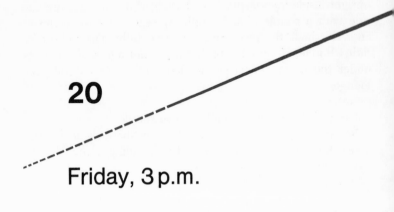

20

Friday, 3 p.m.

When they got back to the office Annie asked Verecker if he wanted her to get Peter Stone back about that free-lance job. He told her not yet. Annie said in that case she might as well earn her nonexistent salary by tackling the files. She pulled out a pile of old correspondence and fussed around at a filing cabinet. Verecker sat at his desk doodling on a scribble pad. Outside the door the elevator sighed open and footsteps clicked away down the corridor. Down in the street a motor bike left a green light behind, disturbing the soft, persistent hum of the traffic. There wasn't a sound inside the office except the rustle of papers and the metallic bump of the cabinet sliding in and out.

It finally got on Annie's nerves. "I still think you should have told him."

"I was about to when that phone call interrupted us. Afterwards I didn't have time."

"You could have made time," she said reproachfully. She resumed her filing.

Verecker tore off a page of doodles and started on a fresh sheet. Silence oozed out of the walls again and filled the room. Annie banged a drawer and drove it away. She picked up another carbon, frowned at it, sorted back and forth through the files, finally threw the paper down on her desk. She slammed the filing cabinet closed. "It's no good. I just can't concentrate with you thinking like that."

"You're the one who's making all the noise. You're banging around there like a panel heater."

"So how do you figure it?"

"So how do I figure what?"

Annie appealed to the heavens. "The house bricks, the fake watch. You're not going to try and tell me you've been sitting there thinking the thoughts of Spiro Agnew, are you?"

"Oh, God knows about the house bricks."

"Aren't you even going to hazard a guess, have a stab at it?"

"What do you want me to say—that I think the bag belongs to a salesman for a building-supply firm? How should I know who it belongs to?"

"It may be important, that's all. For all we know it could be the key to the whole thing."

Verecker made a great show of rolling his eyes. "Oh, Annie, come on. A suitcase full of bricks is supposed to tell us where the plane and the passengers are? This isn't Don Winslow tracking down a Japanese spy ring. There's probably some perfectly simple explanation."

"Like what, for instance?"

Verecker threw up his hands. "I don't know. This is California, after all; people do strange things. Maybe they're somebody's pets."

"You're not seriously suggesting somebody keeps pet bricks, are you?"

155

"Why not? I had a pet rock when I was a kid."

"You had a pet rock? What did you call it?"

"Arnold."

Annie looked at him sideways. "Are you sure that wasn't *your* suitcase they found?" There was a minute of injured silence, then Annie said, "O.K., let me try then. The bag is weighed in at the airline counter and its weight, I remember from my brief career in the clouds, is recorded on the passenger's ticket. Now maybe the owner was planning on bringing something back from New York and didn't want it to show in case anybody checked the records later. So he filled the suitcase with something that weighed about the same as whatever it was he was planning on bringing back."

"Not bad, not bad at all. But in that case it doesn't have anything to do with the kidnapping, seeing the guy expected to reach New York."

"And because they're not going to pay a hundred thousand dollars for anything else, you're only interested in a theory that does have something to do with it, right?"

"Well, I sure as hell don't give a damn for anybody who fondles a brick behind the ears."

Annie was mad. "Verecker, *you* could use a brick behind the ears. Here I am batting my brains out trying to think of something and you're sitting there sneering. Why are you so dull all of a sudden? How do you know that that suitcase isn't a plant—that the kidnappers meant it to be found?"

Verecker had his hand over his eyes as if he were blocking out a terrible sight. "Please, I'm only a simple lawyer and not strong."

Annie had all her sails set and wasn't stopping for anybody. "Maybe we're supposed to have discovered something by now —some weak link the gang was aware of but was unable to do anything about. Maybe this suitcase is supposed to make everybody jump to the wrong conclusion."

"What conclusion?" Verecker asked from behind his hand.

"The only one we can think of is that somebody was trying for Best of Breed at the National House Brick Show."

"Then we've missed something, that's all. Something blatantly obvious."

"Good God, we've already got a plane that lands on a golf course, a Mexican hijacker, a pilot who takes us two hundred miles just to give us the shaft, a disappearing stewardess, a bag of bricks and a fake watch and she says we've missed something."

Annie flounced across the room and threw herself into her chair. "All right, mastermind, this time you make a suggestion and I'll do the hysterical-laughter bit."

Verecker shifted in his chair, brooding about something. He said quietly, "What I have to suggest I don't think you're going to find all that funny. I want to check out a few things before I tell you. I'm probably wrong. I hope to Christ I am."

The Montgomery Club was located above an insurance company in a small office building in Pine Street. Verecker pushed through the glass doors and rode the elevator to the top floor. He emerged into a little vestibule that opened into a large, carpeted room full of overstuffed armchairs and tables stacked with magazines. There was a snack counter at one end, deserted except for one man hunched over a sandwich, a pool table to the left of that in a room by itself and, on his immediate left, a small glassed-in office. A man sat at a desk inside the office shuffling through some forms. In a row above him were framed publicity stills of crew-cut footballers fending off invisible tacklers and wishing him the best of luck in big, scrawly handwriting at the same time.

The man looked up and caught Verecker studying them. "We got a lot of ball players in the club." He got to his feet, a big, gentle-looking man. "Can I help you?"

"I hope so. My name's Verecker. I'm a lawyer." He held out a card, which the man took and nodded over. "I'm trying to

157

trace a client of mine. I handled a matter for him about five years ago."

"What's his name?"

"That's the trouble." Verecker squeezed out an embarrassed smile. "I don't know. I can't remember and my files are no help. I had a temporary girl in a month back who straightened them out before I could stop her. But I do recall he belonged to this club."

The man looked back at the card, said noncommittally, "All you know about him is his club."

"I know it sounds funny . . . "

"What does he look like?"

"Oh, ordinary. You know."

"Do you know what he does?"

"I think he's with one of the brokerage houses."

The man smiled. "We've got a million of them."

Verecker thought for a second, then said, "If I could take a quick look at your membership list I might just recognize the name."

"We don't make our list available as a rule—to protect the members against junk mail, things like that."

Verecker held up a hand and said with a fast laugh, "Oh, don't get me wrong. I'm not going to photograph it secretly or anything. It's just the one name I need."

The man hesitated.

"You'd really be helping me out," Verecker added, trying to smile winningly.

"Just the one name, eh?"

"That's all."

"Hold on a moment." The man pulled open a bottom drawer and leafed through a book Verecker couldn't see, although he guessed it was a phone directory. The man had put Verecker's card down on top of the desk. He stopped turning pages, checked the card, checked the book again, grunted and shut the drawer. "O.K.," he said, pointing to a filing cabinet. "The old membership lists are in the bottom section. They go back about five years. The current list is in the top. Try it first. The guy you're after may still be a member."

"I really appreciate it," Verecker told him. He crossed to the cabinet, slid open a drawer and began rifling through a thinly sliced loaf of yellow cards.

Straight away a name jumped out at him as if it had been fashioned in neon tubing. "Well, what do you know."

"Find it?"

"Yes, I think I might have." He jotted down the name and address. He was busting to get back and talk to Annie, but he went through the rest of the cards to make it look good.

He shut the drawer and turned around. "Thanks a lot. You've been very helpful." Moving toward the door, he said, "I really must get up here one of these days. I could stand a little work-out."

The man said, "Sure, come along. We've got a nice club here."

Verecker waved and went out into the lobby and jabbed the elevator button as if he were ashing out a cigar.

"I was at the Montgomery Club."

"And?"

"And I still have the theory I had before I went up there."

"Which is?"

"I don't think you're going to like it."

"I'm sure I'll loathe it but I'd still like to hear it."

Verecker said, "First answer me a question. If one of those watches is a fake, isn't it possible the other could be?"

"It's possible," Annie conceded, "although Phil didn't mention anything about them."

"They're probably rechecking them now. My point is we can't swear that Albrecht's cuff links are the real McCoy either, even though they appear to be."

"Granted."

"So it's perfectly possible that all those items could be fakes. You buy it?"

"Theoretically, yes."

"Fine. Then let's assume, for argument's sake, that they are all fakes. The question then becomes, how was it done?"

"And the solution?"

Verecker gazed at a diploma on the wall, patting his thoughts into a neat, even pile. He dealt them out like playing cards. "Let's assume the brain behind all this knows some of these people. Say he knows them in a club, for instance."

"One guess which club."

"Wait. He finds out one day that two of them are flying to New York to a convention or something."

"Rinlaub didn't tell us that."

"There are probably lots of things he didn't tell us. I'm not saying it happened; I'm simply saying it could have happened."

"Go on."

"Let's suppose that a third member of the club is going to New York around the same time, finds out the other two are going as well, so decides to join them on the same flight— three local boys going to the Big Apple together. The brain finds out about this and sees his chance. Over the next couple of days he gets into these guys' lockers while they're playing squash, photographs their watches in detail and has duplicates made up—duplicates good enough to fool everybody."

"Except one woman," Annie interjected.

"Except one woman, right."

"O.K., but how about the other people—Albrecht, for example? He's not a member of the club, is he?"

"No, he's not. But it wouldn't have been too hard to find out the names of a few more people traveling on the same flight. I mean the guy could have called the airline and said he was checking to see if his secretary had booked him on Flight 422 to New York, the name's Smith, Brown, Jones, whatever."

Annie swiveled on her seat, mulling it over. She said, "Or

if he knew the right computer man he could get a complete list, isn't that right?"

"Absolutely." Verecker sat up straighter. "That's good thinking. Sure, supplied with names and addresses, he merely picks two easy-to-get-into apartments—street-level ones like Albrecht's—and does the photographic bit again."

"All right, say I go along with all that for the moment. Why is this guy doing it? What's his racket? If he's got the passengers, why mail fake things when he can mail the real ones?"

"Because he can't mail the real ones."

"Are you trying to tell me those people aren't really missing?"

Verecker picked up a pencil and started doodling again. When he replied he kept his eyes on the pad in front of him. "They're missing, all right. But maybe they're not kidnapped." His voice softened. "Maybe they're all dead."

He put the pencil down and flicked it gently with his finger. It rolled to the end of the desk, hung on the lip for an instant, then clattered to the floor. In the silence it sounded like a gun going off.

Annie let her breath out slowly. "How?"

Verecker spoke rapidly. "Clarke flies the hijacker up from Mexico and lands him on the golf course. The guy boards the jet. Right after takeoff he sticks a gun in the pilot's neck and gives him a new course—one that heads them right for the lake. He ties up the co-pilot and the flight engineer. He orders the plane down to a couple of thousand feet—it's all high-level radar, so it goes off the scope—and has the plane slowed down to just above stall speed. He forces the captain to set the automatic pilot, then he clobbers the captain, puts a three-minute time bomb in his lap, goes out into the plane waving the gun and grabs the parachute somebody's hidden under a seat for him—a cleaner or a baggage handler, maybe—and bails out. Sixty seconds later the bomb goes off and the plane falls into Desolation Valley a few miles southwest of the lake. Clarke, meanwhile, is headed toward Carson City. He lands, drives to the lake and leaves the fake watches and things all neatly wrapped on the postmaster's front steps in Glenbrook, making damn sure, of course, that the time is noted. And that's how they hide three hundred and sixty people and a jumbo jet—they're spread all over Desolation Valley, nothing but lakes, mountains and forest—not even a dirt road in."

Annie crossed her arms over her body as if an icy draught had blown into the room. She turned her face away. "That's horrible. I just can't believe anybody would kill so many people—it's a massacre."

Verecker said, "The ransom is twenty-five million dollars. To be callous, that's something like thirty thousand a head. People kill people for the change in their pockets."

"But, something like that . . . it couldn't happen. It's just too monstrous."

"Wouldn't you say kidnapping three hundred and sixty people was pretty monstrous, too? And that happened."

Annie was silent. A minute later she said, "The terrible part is, the more I think about it the more plausible it becomes."

Verecker reached inside his jacket, took out a folded piece of paper and laid it on his desk. "I'm afraid I've got something that makes it even more plausible." She watched his hands smoothing the paper out. "When I went up to the Montgomery I got a look at the membership list. A guy named Nils Arosund belongs to that club."

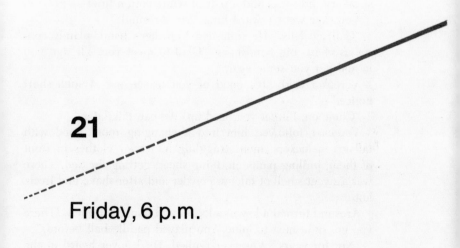

21

Friday, 6 p.m.

Verecker leaned over the manager's desk. "Hello again. Mr. Arosund's expecting me."

"Hi. He told me he had a guest coming. I didn't know it was you. Why didn't you tell me you knew Nils? I'll tell him you're here."

Verecker followed him out of the office and into the lounge. The man disappeared through a door and Verecker strolled over to watch two men shooting pool, a tall, wiry-haired man and a short man with an enormous barrel chest. The tall man missed his shot and left his opponent with an easy set-up. The fat man pounced on the white ball before it had even stopped rolling, sawed his cue through his hands a couple of times, shot, missed and thumped his cue on the floor.

"Mr. Verecker?" A man stood in the doorway grinning at him, a very large man, blond, mid-twenties, Brylcreemed hair, heavy frame plaited with muscles, the stomach sucked in to make it appear even flatter than it was. He was dressed in sneakers and socks and a pair of white cotton briefs.

Verecker went toward him. "Mr. Arosund?"

"Call me Nils." He squashed Verecker's hand, plainly conscious of his big handshake. "Glad to meet you. I'll sign you in and get you some gear."

Verecker said, "It's good of you to see me at such short notice."

"Come on, I'll get you fixed up. We can talk later."

Verecker followed him into a changing room lined with tall green lockers, men struggling into their clothes in front of them, pulling pants on, tying shoes, getting dressed. There was a sweet smell of talcum powder and after-shave and fresh, hot towels.

Arosund turned a key in a locker and banged it open. "There you go, right next to mine. You played paddle ball before?"

"Not for years," Verecker replied. He'd never heard of the game.

"I'll spot you twelve points then. You bring sneakers?"

"No, I, er . . . "

"Forget it. We'll borrow a pair. I'll get your shorts." He went away and came back a minute later with a towel and a pair of briefs like the ones he was wearing. "Thirty-four O.K.?"

"Thanks. It used to be thirty-two." Verecker started to get out of his clothes.

Arosund said, "I thought this would be as good a place as any to talk. We'll play a couple of games, maybe work out a little afterwards, then you can tell me what's on your mind. I do a lot of business up here—I can think better when I'm relaxed." As he talked he rolled his head on his neck and shifted his shoulders as if trying to arrange his muscles into a more comfortable position.

"It's nothing much. Just checking out something for a client," Verecker said. He put his shoes and socks into the locker and slipped on the white trunks. Arosund slammed the door shut, tried to turn the key, couldn't, and opened and slammed the door twice in succession. He appeared to enjoy doing it, the way a child likes to beat a tin drum. He seemed to Verecker like a big man who was sorry he wasn't bigger, his movements forced and heavy, putting too much strength behind a simple operation like closing a locker door, as if he thought he could belt it into submission.

He slammed the door a third time, wrenched the key around and handed it to Verecker. "You keep this with you. Let's go down here." He led the way into a corridor, past a recessed room in which men lay stretched out on benches, blue ultra-violet light flaring in the goggles covering their eyes. They looked like dead World War I aviators awaiting identification. Arosund led him into a narrow room pungent with a stale, rubbery odor. Verecker saw why: Half the wall was taken up by a long, high rack of pigeonholes stuffed with sneakers and bunched-up socks. Next to it dozens of rackets hung upside down. They were smaller than tennis rackets with short, stubby handles, plastic name tags bonded onto their frames.

Arosund ran his eyes over them and grabbed one. "You can borrow Frank Keeling's. Now let's get some sneakers for you." He pulled out a pair of scruffy tennis shoes and thrust them at Verecker.

"You sure the owner won't mind?"

"Nah, everybody borrows. Go ahead."

Verecker sat on a bench and put them on. They were a little big in the toes but they fitted well enough. The big man led the way out into the corridor past a green-tiled shower room over to a group of men clustered around a window in an interior wall. From behind the wall came the thwack of rackets and the thump of feet moving around.

"Hi, Charlie, how they hangin'?" Arosund called, his voice too loud in the small corridor.

A man looked up and said, "Why, it's the always dangerous Nils Arosund." The group around him chuckled.

"Up yours, too," Arosund replied, although he seemed

165

pleased by the greeting. He pushed past them to the window on the other side of the door that led into the court and shoved up against a fat man standing wrapped in a towel. The fat man went away, annoyed. "Come on over and take a look," Arosund called.

Verecker excused himself past the first group of men and Arosund matter-of-factly shouldered somebody else out of the way to make room for him. Verecker peered through the window. Inside, two men stood on a wooden floor enclosed by flat white walls and a high white ceiling. They were both panting, shiny with perspiration. The man in the right-hand court took a deep breath and moved into position. He bounced a small blue ball behind a red line painted on the floor and with a quick, wristy slicing movement of his racket served the ball hard against the front wall. His opponent belted it back a little too high, and the server, his racket loosely held at his side, watched the ball flying toward him, swiveled his body around it like a matador releasing a bull and with silky grace moved to play it as it hit behind the red line and bounced off the back wall. He waited till the last second, swung his racket, caught the ball a few inches from the floor and sent it winging up the court like a bullet. It hit the left-side wall low down, slanted in and died a quick death against the front wall—an unreturnable shot.

Verecker said, "He's played before."

"That's Chuck Merridew, number two in the club," Arosund informed him.

"You mean there's somebody better than him?"

"Jesse Quinlan, an Aussie. Belts the cover off the ball. Not what you'd call a big man"—he moved his shoulders again—"but strong, you know? Got a wrist on him like iron."

"How do you rate?" Verecker asked, running his eyes over the muscle play.

Arosund modestly concentrated on the thin leather glove he was pulling onto his right hand. "Oh, not that high. Ten or twelve, maybe."

There was an explosion of hoots from the other window.

"Nuff outa you guys," the big man called. He grinned at Verecker. "They're always kiddin' around."

Inside on the court the club's number-two player put away another winner and walked back to serve. Arosund frowned and said, "Those guys should be through by now." He thumped on the window. "Hey! What's the score?" he yelled. The players ignored him. He thumped harder. "The score, what's the goddamn score?"

One of the players pointed to his opponent and back to himself and mouthed, "Two three." The group at the other window laughed.

"Bullshit," Arosund roared. He said to Verecker, "Too many goddamn comedians in this club." Verecker grinned uncomfortably and began to suspect that Arosund might not be the man he was after. He'd expected somebody slick and smooth. This guy seemed all wrong. He probably wasn't even related to the stewardess. The whole thing was a big fat waste of time.

He was about to say he was sorry but he had a migraine coming on when the door to the court opened and the players came through.

" 'Bout time," Arosund said in fake indignation. "Guys having a picnic party in there."

Verecker followed his host onto the court and as he went through the door one of the players gave him a funny smile and said, "Good luck." He wondered what he meant by it.

He found out a second later. Arosund slammed the door behind him, picked up the little rubber ball lying on the court and hit it a tremendous wallop, his racket following through inches from Verecker's eyebrow. The ball rocketed back to him and Arosund slashed at it again. Instead of using the controlled, wristy strokes the two previous players had displayed the big man swung at the ball as if he were beating a rug. The ball flew at Verecker, who made for it, then ducked at the last moment as a racket knifed through the air over his head.

167

"Aren't we supposed to take it in turns?" Verecker asked from the wall.

"When we start playing. Right now we're just warming up. But say when you're ready."

"Ready," Verecker said. He figured the sooner he got off the court the more chance he'd have of walking off under his own steam. "It's nine up, isn't it?" he asked, not too hopefully.

"Twenty-one," the other man replied. "You wanna rally for serve?"

"You take it."

Arosund beamed at him. "Hey, you're a sport." He bounced the ball and slashed at it. It pinged off the front wall, zoomed back at Verecker, who had his back turned, adjusting the wrist cord on his racket, and caught him a stinging blow between the shoulder blades.

The big man crowed with delight. "One nothing," he said.

They exchanged courts, Verecker trying to rub at the red welt forming and wondering how he could get out of there— a malaria attack? Amnesia? He doubted whether Arosund would have heard of either of them.

Arosund got set to serve again. He stopped and looked over at Verecker huddled against the wall as far away from the other man's scimitar racket as he could get. "What're you standing there for?"

"Weak backhand." Verecker grinned.

Arosund served and Verecker swung and caught the ball on the wood of his racket. The ball arced through the air, flopped against the front wall and bounced short, an easy put-away. Verecker expected Arosund to pounce on the ball and leave it a heap of charred, smoking rubber. But instead he was standing in the back court rooted to the spot. Verecker imagined the walnut-sized brain signaling frantically to sluggish nerves buried deep in overdeveloped muscles. The message finally made it, for with a strangled cry Arosund launched himself down the court yards too late to make a shot and crashed into the wall with a terrible bone-jarring thump.

"*Son of a bitch!*" he roared. "Nothing against you," he said quickly to Verecker. "That's a damn good short game you've got there. I just get mad at myself, that's all." He snatched up the ball and swatted it angrily. It flew off his racket at a crazy angle and struck Verecker between the eyes. "Your serve," he said. Unlike Verecker, he didn't seem to have noticed where the ball had gone.

Verecker steadied himself against the wall and waited for his vision to clear. He walked after the ball and had trouble picking it up; he couldn't seem to uncross his eyes. He moved back groggily and served.

"Fault," Arosund called. "Try it again."

The second serve went in somehow and with a tremendous wind-up Arosund hacked at the ball like a Crusader in a religious frenzy. He missed it completely; the racket flew out of his glove, struck the side wall first, bounced off and chopped Verecker behind the ear.

"Watch the ball, ya dummy," Arosund yelled. "Nothing against you," he explained. "I always talk to myself in a game. Kind of encouragement, you know?" He became aware of Verecker's body stretched out on the floor. He frowned. "Hey, no resting. You'll never get into shape that way."

Verecker pushed himself to his feet and stood there swaying gently. "Maybe you weren't ready for that one," he said to a point six inches to the side of Arosund's head. "I'll take it over."

Arosund's face lit up. "Say, thanks. I didn't even see it coming."

As fuzzy as he was it was obvious to Verecker that the fastest way of getting off the court was to let Arosund win every point. It was now pretty clear what that guy outside had meant when he'd called him "the always dangerous Nils Arosund." The man was a killer. And this was the guy he'd suspected of slipping like a shadow into other people's lockers. How wrong could he be?

He managed to get through the remainder of the game

169

without suffering anything more than a split finger, and when Arosund smashed the final point the big man couldn't believe it.

"I did it! Twenty-one nothing. My first ever. Great game," he said, pumping Verecker's hand, "great game."

They went out of the door into the corridor and toweled off. The big man was still crowing about it. "No kidding, you're pretty tricky. I mean, twenty-one nothing—like they say, the score gave no indication of the game."

"Right," Verecker agreed, dabbing at his finger. He looked at his face in the mirror. He had an ugly red welt on his forehead the size of a doorknob.

Arosund squinted at it. "What did you do to your face?"

Verecker let out a long sigh. "Too much candy, I guess."

"C'mon, let's take a workout." Arosund led the way through a door into an area that looked like a gym-equipment showroom—rowing machines, horizontal bars, dumbbells on racks, weights on pulleys around the walls. It was empty except for one man skipping at the end of the room and breathing noisily through his nose. Arosund strode to a row of exercycles, swung a leg over the nearest one and started pedaling. Reluctantly, Verecker joined him.

"O.K., what did you have in mind?" Arosund asked, sawing the towel back and forth over his shoulders.

"Convalescence," Verecker was tempted to reply. Instead he said, "Oh, it's just a minor legal matter. It probably could have been cleared up on the phone." He knew he had to give some excuse for being there, and he was in no condition to bolt for the door. The story he'd handed Clarke had worked pretty well; he decided to try it in a different version. He told the big man that his client claimed that he, Arosund, had run over his foot in Petaluma the day before yesterday and driven off without stopping. The client had taken his number, checked with the licensing bureau and obtained his name through them. Arosund told Verecker his client was out of his mind; he hadn't been near Petaluma in years. Who has? Verecker wondered. He told Arosund his client was obviously mistaken.

"Goddamn right he's mistaken. If your client's trying to pin something on somebody, he's chosen the wrong patsy."

"Well, I thought it was something like that," Verecker soothed. "Sorry to take up your time."

"Forget it," Arosund said magnanimously. He got off the cycle, climbed up on a long padded bench and stretched out full length. "Try this. It's great for your gut." He hooked his feet under a wide canvas strap, cupped his hands behind his head and raised himself to a sitting position. He lowered himself flat again and repeated the action quickly a dozen times. "Thirty of these a day you'll be in shape in no time."

Verecker winced. "I think I'll sit this one out." He leaned against a bench and wondered if it was worth mentioning the stewardess. He thought he may as well give it a try. "Arosund," he mumbled thoughtfully. "That's a Swedish name, isn't it?"

"Danish," the other man said, still pumping up and down.

"Danish, huh? Funny thing, I know a girl by that name, a stewardess, Ingrid Arosund. No relation, I suppose?"

The big man paused for a fraction of a second halfway through his exercise, then continued as if nothing had happened. He pulled his feet from under the strap and swung his legs over the table. He toweled his face slowly, looking at Verecker. "Ingrid's my sister."

"No kidding? I've been trying to get hold of her, but she's not answering her phone. Any idea where she is?"

Arosund went on toweling his face. "No idea." His manner had changed somehow—he was quieter, more contained, as if he were trying to make up his mind about something.

"What a shame. I would have liked to have said hello."

Arosund eased himself off the table. His eyes swept the gym. The skipping man had left them on their own. He walked across the floor to a piece of apparatus against the wall and stood looking down at it. Softly, over his shoulder, he said, "C'mere."

Verecker went over, looked at the apparatus. "Oh, I don't think I could handle it."

"Go ahead. Try it." It was a thick bar weighted at either

171

end with circular iron disks and suspended three feet off the ground by two supports. It was encased in a heavy metal frame in which the bar could slide up and down. There was a small rubber mat on the floor directly underneath it.

"No, really. It looks too—"

"Try it." This time it was more of a command than an invitation.

Verecker shrugged and said, "What do I do?"

"Sit down underneath it." Verecker sat down. "Now lie on your back and put the soles of your feet under the bar. That's it. Now you see those supports? Twist them out of the way."

Verecker did as he was directed and the bar pressed down on his feet, pushing his knees onto his chest. Verecker pushed with his legs and the bar rose up the frame. "Wow, I can really feel it in the thighs."

There was a pile of matched weights by the side of the press. Arosund bent and picked up two heavy ones, round metal disks with a hole through the center, and slipped them onto the ends of the bar.

Verecker grunted. "Take it easy. I can hardly budge it now."

Arosund didn't appear to hear him. His face a stone mask, he reached for two more weights.

"Hey, I'm not kidding. What are you doing?" Verecker pushed up hard against the iron bar. He couldn't raise it an inch. He was pinned to the floor as effectively as if a truck had rolled on him. "For crissakes, will you cut it out," he gasped.

Arosund threaded the weights onto the bar and the floor tried to climb through Verecker's back. His brain raced. The man was crazy, insane. What the hell was he playing at? The madman was reaching for another weight. Why the hell— with a sickening shock he saw how Arosund was holding the metal disks—balancing them between his open palm and his gloved hand. *He wasn't touching them with his fingers.*

A river of sudden fear coursed through him and burst out of his body as a million tiny bubbles of sweat. Arosund would pass it off as an accident. His guest said he'd work out a few

172

minutes longer—unfamiliar with the equipment—must have trapped himself—unable to hear his cries in the shower—a tragic thing.

Verecker went through a moment of pure, unadulterated blind panic. He thrust up against the bar with everything he had, his neck crimson, knotted, his legs quivering blocks of wood. It was like trying to push through the ceiling of a bank vault.

"Listen . . . Arosund . . . "

The man looked down at him as though he were a not quite dead animal he had to finish off. He bent down for the last two weights, huge ones almost as big as bicycle wheels. He tipped one on its side and grunted to lift it.

Verecker tried to call out, but the cry gurgled away to nothing in his throat as the weight went onto the end of the bar. His thighs mashed down onto his chest. For a long, long second he fought against the agony in his legs and back, then forgot it as the last crushing weight was slotted onto the bar. The air whooshed out of his lungs as if sucked away by a whirlwind. His chest refused to expand; he couldn't breathe. The ceiling swam through the stinging sweat in his eyes, shimmering like waves of heat. His heart thumped. There was a dull distant sound of surf in his ears.

He was suffocating; he was going to die.

The ceiling turned red, then darkened to black. The pressure on his chest seemed to lessen slightly—his senses dimming? It grew lighter still. He felt rather than heard a heavy thump near him, as if a lead weight had hit the floor. There was another. The pressure lightened again.

The 10,000-ton freighter that had sunk onto his chest lifted off his body and floated upward. Oxygen crept into his lungs. The bar that had been crushing the soles of his feet went away.

His legs uncurled and the pain forced his eyes open. He rolled over onto his side in a foetal position, breathing in great oceans of air. The sea roar in his ears died and was replaced by a high voice split up into words. "O.K.? You O.K., mister?"

In front of his eyes was a white pillar that separated into

173

two thinner ones. The voice was coming from above his head. He moved his head slightly. The pillars were a pair of pants, above the pants a belt and a shirt with something written on it.

Verecker put out his hands and the man grasped him under the arms and gently helped him to his feet. He cried out, his body marbled with pain.

"Lean on me. We'll get you into the hot room."

They moved across the gym, down a corridor and into a shower room. The man opened a door and heat gushed out in a cloud of thin steam. Verecker felt himself lowered into a deck chair. Soft fingers of warmth reached for him, soaked into his trembling muscles. He gave himself up to it, his eyes closed, his head back, arms dangling by his sides.

The pain began to ebb.

He opened his eyes and looked at the man standing over him. He looked like an ex-fighter—flattened nose, swollen eyebrows, high, sloping shoulders. The lettering on his shirt read "Montgomery."

The man asked him how he was feeling.

Verecker closed his eyes again. "I'll live."

"Get a little more heat, then take a hot shower, a cold one after. Think you can make it by yourself?" Verecker nodded. "O.K. Don't want to rush you, but we're closing soon."

He heard the slap of shoes moving over the wet floor. The door opened and closed. Tentatively, Verecker reached a hand behind his back and massaged his spine. He found it hard to understand why a few vertebrae weren't crushed. Bit by bit he eased himself out of the chair, hobbled out of the room and stepped into the shower, sneakers and all. He couldn't have taken them off for a million dollars. The hot water pounded down on his neck, soothing him; the quivering went away. He tried straightening up. A thousand knives stabbed him; straightening up would have to come later. He changed the water from hot to cold for a fast sixty seconds, then stepped out of the shower stall and picked up a large white towel from

174

the stack on a bench. He wrapped it around his waist, put another around his shoulders and went out into the corridor and back down it to the locker room.

There was no sign of Arosund.

The man who'd helped him into the hot room was waiting there dressed in street clothes. He said, "I found your key out in the gym. I opened your locker for you."

"Thanks."

"Dress yourself O.K.?"

"If you could just help me with the sneakers."

Verecker sat down on a bench and the man slipped them off his feet. He dried himself and started to dress. It was a slow, painful operation. When he got to his shoes he had to ask the attendant for help again. The man eased one of them on and bent over it, lacing it, and said, "He's a bad one to get on the wrong side of."

"Who?"

"Mr. Arosund."

Verecker was surprised. "How did you know it was Arosund trapped me under that thing?"

"He told me to go in and get you out."

"He *told* you? I thought you just happened to—I thought the guy was really trying to kill me."

The man started on the other shoe. "Oh no. He plays rough but not that bad. But he was sure mad at you."

Verecker couldn't see how it added up. Had Arosund realized he'd let him win that silly game on purpose? Would that make him mad enough almost to kill him? It couldn't be that. Besides, his manner had changed when he'd mentioned his sister. Maybe he was telling him to stay away. "What exactly did he say to you?"

The man helped him into his jacket, looking a little embarrassed. "I don't like to—"

"Tell me," Verecker demanded.

"You mean word for word?"

"Word for word."

175

"Well—" the man brushed an invisible speck of dust off Verecker's lapel—"he said to go in and let that son of a bitch Clarke up off the floor."

Annie opened the door to find Verecker bent over at a twenty-degree angle. "Some health club," she said. "Look at you. You're down to five feet six. What happened to you, anyway?"

Verecker hobbled in and lowered himself onto the sofa like a man balancing a glass of acid on his head. "Don't ask."

"Don't ask? The guy comes on like Igor the mad hunchback and I'm not supposed to ask? You shouldn't have tried to touch your toes with your elbows."

"Lady, the position I was in I could have touched my toes with my ears."

"Did you meet Arosund?"

"Oh yes. Yes, you could safely say I met Nils Arosund."

"Get anything from him?"

"A couple of things."

"What?"

"A double hernia."

"Huh?"

"By the time he got through you could have fitted me neatly onto a bowling-ball display."

Verecker told her what had happened. When he'd finished Annie said, "But why would he do a thing like that?"

He closed his eyes and shook his head in disgust. "The clown somehow got it into his skull that I was Lee Clarke, the boy pilot."

"Oh, no!"

"Ingrid Arosund is his sister like I figured, and it was when I got around to her that he started getting violent. The only thing I can think of is that he's heard about Clarke, assumed that his sister had run out on him and that I, or Clarke rather, had come to try to find out where she was from big brother."

"Apparently he didn't like what he'd heard."

"Apparently. I wasn't exactly welcomed to the family with

176

open arms. But," Verecker said painfully, "I should have given him a better excuse for being there."

"Do you still think he's connected with the hijack?"

"Jesus, no. The man's an oaf. He can't even get into his own locker, let alone anybody else's. Anyway, I'm discarding the 'all dead' theory. Nobody in his right mind would bail out over Desolation Valley. Especially at night. Besides, if Arosund was connected I'd probably still be under that damn press."

Annie said, "Well, thank God for that. That Desolation Valley bit was the ghastliest idea I've ever heard of."

"But a logical one. And it still leaves the fake watch unexplained."

"So where do we go from here?"

Verecker shifted stiffly on the sofa, eased his shoes off with his feet and inched his legs up, groaning. "I don't know. Give up, I guess."

"You sound like you need a drink."

"Oh, please. A nice, tall, frosty glass of gin."

Annie went toward the kitchen. "I'll check the cellar." She was back a few minutes later with a pitcherful of martinis and poured one for Verecker, who tossed it off and held out his glass for a refill.

They sipped their drinks, silent. Annie said, "Look. Let's give it one more try."

"I don't know, Annie. I've had a pie thrown in my face, I've been rolled into a ball, and for what? We're no closer to the fat reward. We're just taking a beating."

"But we've come this far. To give up now—"

"How far have we come, tell me that? We've found a pilot who may or may not have landed a plane on a golf course and his girl friend who wore her stewardess uniform when she wasn't supposed to. Fake watches, suitcases full of bricks— it's like a ladder with all the rungs missing. It's pointless having a bunch of ifs and maybes if you can't put them all together and we haven't been able to do that."

Annie said, "Maybe the mistake we've made is to concentrate

177

on people. Why don't we sit down and really try to figure out where the plane is?"

"We tried. We didn't get anywhere."

"Let's try harder. Come on, Billy, one more time. If we bomb out, then we'll shelve it for good."

"You're a glutton for punishment, you know that? And I'm the one who gets the punishment."

"Really. You didn't flap your wings all the way to Hawaii like I did."

"And you weren't just flattened like a cartoon cat." Verecker blew out his cheeks. "O.K. One more try. But this is it."

"Right," Annie said crisply. "Let's figure out where that jet is. They've hidden it someplace and what one person has hidden another can find."

"That's true, my sweet, but don't forget they had ages to think of a great hiding place. We've had only a few days."

"Then we'll have to be that much smarter, that's all. Let's put ourselves in their place. If we'd stolen that place, where would we have hidden it? Come on, give me something creative."

"Stuffed it and put it on display at Sutro's Museum."

"Listen, cut out the wisecracks and think of it this way. It's a jumbo jet. A jumbo is an elephant. Now if you'd stolen a priceless elephant, what would you do to keep it a secret?"

"I'd change its license plates and spray it a different color."

"The license plates?" Annie jumped to her feet, excited. "Verecker, you don't know it but you're being bright. They landed it in Nevada, painted out the Calair name and changed it to some other airline's. Then they flew on to New York."

Verecker was completely negative.

"Why? What's wrong with it?"

"About forty-nine things for a start, the biggest being that TWA or whoever would be extremely surprised to find they suddenly had an extra 747 in their fleet. What do they tell the FAA—they found it under a cabbage leaf? And what do they do with the passengers once they get to New York? I think my Sutro's idea is more plausible than that."

"All right, it was just a suggestion."

"A pretty naïve one, too."

"Yes, but it had style," Annie said, getting the last word. She rattled the ice in her glass to scare away the gloomy silence that was threatening to move in. Then she asked another question. "How else would you disguise it?"

"The jet or the jumbo?"

"The elephant."

"Put him in a circus parade, take him to a Republican convention . . . "

Annie flopped back in the chair. "We're getting nowhere like this."

Verecker said, "Then let's stop looking for lost elephants and start looking for airplanes."

"O.K., airplanes. I still think my idea of it landing in a Nevada canyon's a good one."

Tiredly Verecker said, "We've been through that and we decided a 747 was too big to disguise as a diner."

Annie got up and moved across the room. "I still think they could have buried it." She went out into the kitchen and started rattling pots and pans. Verecker stared thoughtfully at the ceiling and didn't say another word till Annie called him for dinner thirty minutes later.

He ate in a trance, his eye boring a hole in the salt cellar. After five minutes of this Annie said, "I'm not crazy about cooking, but if it's appreciated like this it all makes it worthwhile."

Verecker put down a fork. "You know, I don't buy your theory of landing in a canyon, but there's nothing to stop a plane landing on one of those Nevada backroads. There's very little traffic on them and the surface would be strong enough."

"But you don't buy digging a hole and burying it."

"It would be patently impossible to dig a hole that big and keep it a secret."

"But what if the hole was already there?"

"You mean some kind of excavation? They'd still have to

179

fill it in to cover the plane up." He poured the melted ice water in the pitcher into his glass and had it raised halfway to his mouth when he set it down fast, as if he'd spotted a bug in it. He held the glass at arm's length and stared at it, then looked up at Annie, a slow smile starting at the corners of his mouth. "Water," he said. "They covered that plane with water. They sank it in a lake."

After a long second she said in a half whisper, spacing her words, "That . . . is . . . it, Verecker. That . . . is . . . it!"

Verecker's hand dived into his pocket and came out with a key chain. "There's a map of Nevada upstairs on my desk."

It took her only a minute. She bounded back inside the door, pushed the dishes to one side and spread the map out on the table. "Pyramid Lake," she said, stabbing at the map. "Or Walker Lake. They've both got highways on either side."

"No, too far from Tahoe. It's got to be within a ninety-minute drive."

"Spooners Lake," Annie cried, stabbing again. "Just a few miles from Glenbrook."

"There's only a dirt road going by it; they'd be crazy to try landing on something like that. They'd blow-out for sure. Same goes for Marlette Lake. This is the only place—Washoe Lake." His finger rested on a blue teardrop northeast of Tahoe. "You've got a paved road running right into it, straight as a string for two miles. And it's off the highway, so nobody's likely to be traveling on it at night. Look at that. It's about ten miles from Carson City and less than twenty-five from Glenbrook. It's perfect." He got up and limped up and down the room. He was so excited he forgot his strained muscles. "It's at the bottom of that lake, Annie—a little waterlogged but otherwise a jumbo jet in one piece."

"How do you figure they put it there?"

"They could have built a raft—two big ones—planks and oil drums. They land the jet and get the people off, then taxi it along the road, down a boat ramp onto a raft. They float the other raft under the tail, lash the whole thing together

180

and tow it out into the middle of the lake. Then they simply sink the rafts and, bingo, a 747 vanishes."

"We'll drive up first thing in the morning," Annie said, her eyes alight.

"What's wrong with tonight? We could stay at a motel and start looking that much earlier tomorrow."

"No sir. I'm not going to a motel with you."

Verecker looked sour. "Oh, don't worry about your virginity. With a back like I've got, believe me, you're safe."

"Uh-unh. One look at a coin-operated coffee machine and a bathroom sealed for your protection and you're sure to make a miraculous recovery."

"My dear girl, a few hours ago I was folded up like a Chinese fan and permanently pressed. I'm in no shape to perform. Hell, it would even hurt to smoke afterwards."

"We'll go up first thing in the morning," Annie told him, prodding him toward the door. "I'll wake you at six."

He put a hand to his back and winced. "Honestly, I don't think I could make those stairs tonight. Why don't I just sleep here on the sofa? I wouldn't be any trouble. You'd just have to throw a blanket over me."

"And a net. Keep moving."

"You call this moving? I'm walking like a ceremonial police horse."

"Well, don't throw a shoe climbing the stairs."

"I don't know what you're scared of. I don't even have enough strength to slam the door tonight."

"You damn well better slam it," Annie told him indignantly. "I don't want Mrs. Grabowski to think I'm promiscuous."

It was hours before he got to sleep. He ran it over in his mind, filling in the hazy patches. They could have lit the road with headlights from cars; that plus the plane's own lights would have been enough for a landing. The nearest town was miles away—nobody would have heard them or seen them. They would have switched off the cabin and navigation lights anyway. They'd landed and taxied down the road to the lake, taken out any kind of gate, if there was one, and replaced it later. With a wingspan like that they might have had to chop down a few trees. Still, who'd notice it? Washoe Lake was hardly overrun—a few fishermen, that's all. They'd unloaded the passengers—probably keeping them in tents back in the forest—then run the plane down the boat ramp. With that double undercarriage it wouldn't have been too hard. They could have raked the path, got rid of any rocks, smoothed it out, then eased the plane into the water and lashed it to the rafts. The idea of using rafts had come off the top of his head, but now that he thought about it he was certain they'd done it that way. If you bought the lake you had to buy the rafts. They could have built them at night, kept them hidden through the day—no problem. Once afloat with the plane lashed to them a couple of ski boats with big Mercury outboards could have towed the rafts over the water. For that matter, the plane could have moved under its own power, like a seaplane. In the middle of the lake they'd cut the lashings, punctured the drums; the plane had filled up and sunk to the bottom like a tin can in the sea. Then they'd rounded up the floating planks and in half an hour the lake would have been as still as glass again. What a colossal idea! And to prove they were right he and Annie wouldn't even have to get their feet wet, just find some sign—a hastily repaired fence or tire marks in the sand—call the FBI, get a couple of divers up there, and, a few months later, collect a check from a grateful insurance company. If it hadn't been for his aching back he would have got out of bed and clicked his heels.

But, as it turned out, there was no reason to call the FBI next morning. When they arrived at Washoe Lake it was a jumping, bustling hive of activity.

The FBI was already there.

There was nothing on the front page, nothing on the inside pages, nothing in the Stop Press. There was nothing in the other paper, either. He turned on the television, switched on the radio. Nobody was saying anything about an air disaster. Impossible—either they were keeping it quiet or . . . or something had gone wrong. But he'd done everything so carefully, the components were all carefully chosen, they'd cost him a lot of money. Maybe somebody had found it before takeoff. But there was no report of that, either. They would have reported a thing like that. It was a great disappointment—embarrassing, too, after the letter he'd written. They'd never take him seriously now. They were probably still laughing over his letter and the empty threat. Why hadn't the bomb worked? Something wrong with the dynamite? Unlikely. The battery? It was brand new. The watch wasn't new—could it have been the watch, could it have stopped? But he'd wound it. He distinctly remembered: He'd wound it, then set it, then reset it. *Reset it!* He remembered, good Lord he remembered! He'd pulled out the winder button to reset it; he couldn't be sure if he'd pushed it back in. It wouldn't have affected an ordinary watch, but he'd bought a waterproof watch, a sealed watch. It would be too much of a strain for the mainspring; it would slow down and stop. That's what had happened—a little thing like forgetting to push in the winder button—that's why there were no flaming headlines. A tiny fraction of an inch; that had been the difference. The bomb hadn't worked and it wasn't going to.

The hand had frozen an hour and fourteen minutes away from the metal pin. The tape holding the silent watch had begun to peel, gradually releasing its grip on the flat, shiny plastic of the radio case. One end of it slowly peeled back, the weight of the watch enough to loosen the sticky underside and drag it down farther and farther. It hung for a moment on a last elastic strand of gum, then came away, the watch dangling a fraction closer to the bottom of the case. It hung there for some time, held by a stubborn two inches of sticky brown paper that had been pressed harder than its other end. Then

183

a corner bubbled and raised its head in slow motion, like an insect under a microscope. Its body followed bit by bit. The watch fell only two inches. It landed on its side, on the winder button. The button plunged into its slot and the mainspring, nudged by the fall, went back to doing what a man eight thousand miles away in Switzerland had designed it to do.

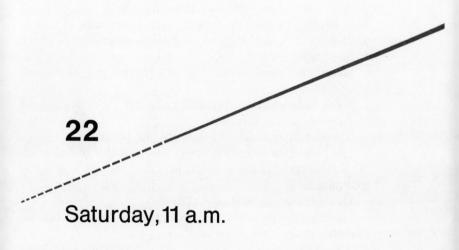

22

Saturday, 11 a.m.

Verecker slowed the car and pulled into the side of the road. A highway patrolman walked over to them. "I'm sorry, you'll have to keep moving. Police business."

Verecker handed a card out of the window. "Would you see if Phil Rinlaub from Calair's here? He knows me."

The patrolman looked at the card. "Rinlaub? Just a minute." He went toward a group of men who were huddled together a hundred feet away on the edge of the lake. Looking out at it, Verecker judged it to be about three miles long and two miles across at its widest point, the northern end tapering in to some kind of swamp. It was swarming with small boats moving in slow circles, as if their rudders were all broken. On the far side of the lake two larger boats were trolling up and down two hundred feet apart with what looked like a net of chains stretched between them, the high Sierra sun flashing on the chains where they disappeared into the water. Spread out on the southern rim of the lake, where Verecker had parked, was a jumble of official-looking trucks and vans and cars, equipment piled up around them. Everybody seemed to be looking for something, and Verecker and Annie didn't have to guess what it was.

Mournfully, Verecker said, "What were you going to do with your share?"

Annie looked just as crestfallen as he did. "Visit Disneyland and put the rest in the bank."

"I wasn't going to let it change my life, either."

The patrolman crunched across the shoulder of the road. "O.K.," he said. "Leave your car here and see the man in the gray topcoat."

They got out and started walking.

The man the patrolman had pointed out detached himself from the group. "Mr. Verecker?"

"Good morning. This is my secretary, Mrs. Verecker." They exchanged greetings. The man said, "You helped us identify a pair of cuff links, didn't you?"

"That's right. They belong to a client of mine, Klaus Albrecht." The man nodded—thinning hair, compact athletic frame. Verecker thought he looked about forty-five. He hadn't introduced himself but he had to be FBI—the conservative clothes, the polite but not really friendly manner, it all fitted.

"Phil isn't here right now," he said. "If he were I'd give him hell. I don't mind so much his telling you about the plane—and I'm assuming he has—but he shouldn't have told you about the bags."

Bags? Verecker thought. Did he mean the bag with the bricks? Was there more than one? Better play dumb. "What bags?"

The man had been wearing a slight professional smile. It shrank a little. "Come on. Why else would you be here?" Verecker told him. The man said, "Mr. Verecker, we could use you in the Bureau. We've been thinking on exactly the same lines, only we thought of it one day ahead of you. Late last night we found six pieces of baggage. We've been dragging ever since."

"Bags from the flight?"

"That's right. And we found seventy-three more early this morning."

Verecker whistled.

"They were lying in a hundred feet of water about a quarter mile out. We've sent them to the lab, but we don't expect to learn much—water's tough on prints, et cetera."

Annie said, "That's only seventy-nine bags. Shouldn't there be more than that?"

"There should be an entire Economy Class more than that. The only bags we found are ticketed for the First Class."

"Do you think they're still on the plane?" Verecker asked.

"We'll be able to answer that if we find the plane." He looked out toward the lake. "We'll know by sundown if it's there or not."

Verecker got the impression that he wasn't holding out much hope. He asked if it would be all right if they hung around for a while and the man told him it was O.K. with him, but he was relying on their discretion to keep quiet about everything when they got back to town. Then he excused himself and rejoined the group he'd left.

Out on the lake the two big boats had turned at the northern end and were beginning another sweep, two hundred feet closer to the far bank. The sun had slid behind a long cloud and a myriad tiny gray flags waved on the water as a chill wind from the Washoe Mountains rippled the surface of the lake. Around the rocky edges black-suited divers broke the surface, vanished again, webbed feet clutching at the sky like drowning hands.

Annie shivered and Verecker steered her back to the car. Inside she huddled in her coat. "Can you imagine what kind of an eerie sight it would be to come across an airliner on the bottom of a lake? It would be just a dark form at first and

187

then it would take shape and you'd see it, wings and the engines, lying on its side in the mud."

Verecker said, "I remember when I was a kid an old Martin Mariner cracked up landing in the bay. They refloated it and left it overnight on one of the local boat slips. Another kid and I went over it at six o'clock the next morning. I'll never forget that smell. It was covered inside with green slime. It had been under for only about eight hours, but it stank like a rotting fish head. I remember we stole some glucose cubes and ate a couple. Then we were sick."

An hour passed, then another. They watched the boats' slow progress uncomprehendingly. There was a three-hundred-ton airliner down there with a tail as high as a five-story building. Why didn't those chains grab it, wrap around the massive wings, drag against two hundred and thirty feet of fuselage? The boats sailed placidly on, apparently dragging against nothing more solid than cold, clear lake water.

Impatiently, Verecker clicked the radio on, twisted the red tuner across the dial, found nothing he wanted and clicked it off again. "If the plane's in the lake," he said, "what is the First Class baggage doing on its own?"

"If the plane's not in the lake, what is it doing on its own?" Annie replied.

A long time later Verecker said, "I figure they've got two more sweeps left." The sun was lower in the sky, glowing pink, its thin heat switched off for the night. The wind whipped up again, swaying the pines around the shore, sending a dark tremor across the water toward the boats trolling on the opposite bank. They sailed through the miniature squall undisturbed, moving on as if powered by engines built by a super race. They turned for their last run, the far boat no more than a hundred feet from the rocks. The divers were out of the water now, standing with the rest of the men in quiet groups, everybody looking across the lake, everybody expecting any moment a shout, a shrilling whistle, a triumphant yell of discovery. The minutes lengthened into an hour. The boats wheeled at the top of the lake, swung around in tight formation for the final sweep. The chains dragged through the depths, scoring the mud, blackening the water.

About halfway down the boats faltered slightly. There was an instant of suspended time; the wind dropped, the pines stood as still as the men on the shore, the lake itself seemed quivering and motionless at the same time, like an animal spotted by a hunter.

The boats continued, the chains brushing over a submerged rock.

Three quarters of a mile to go; half a mile.

The boats sailed on, smoothly, serenely. The lake was empty.

Verecker started the car, backed up and drove back the way they'd come, both of them content to keep their disappointed thoughts to themselves. They stopped in Carson City. They hadn't eaten since early morning, but neither of them seemed to have much appetite, so they passed up a restaurant and settled for drinks and a bowl of chili in a bar got up to look like an 1860 saloon.

The drinks bucked Annie up a little, although they didn't do a thing for her boss. She said, "There's no chance they could have . . . No, of course not. If they could find bags they could certainly find an airplane. Bags but no plane—it's crazy." Verecker said nothing; she went on. "And why only First Class? Do you think they split the passengers up?" Again she answered her own question. "Maybe they found it easier to handle two groups. But in that case why divide them by classes? Why not straight down the middle?"

"What does it matter?" Verecker asked. "It's too late anyway. Monday morning the airline will get the second note and then it's all over. We said we'd have one more try. O.K., so we had it. All we can do now is wait to read all about it in the newspapers like everybody else."

"If it ever makes the newpapers."

"Whether it does or not it's all over for me. Tomorrow I'm going to sleep late and Monday I'm going to call Peter Stone and see if he still needs a hand on that brief."

"Well, thank heavens for that. Maybe we should have done that days ago."

"Maybe we should have. God knows how many criminals have been walking around free while I've been away from the business. Besides, there must be a long line of rich widows waiting for me to defend them."

Annie put her hand on top of his, not fooled for an instant by the bravado. Her voice softened. "You gave it a real good try, Billy, but it would have been a miracle if we'd succeeded where the police and the FBI had failed."

He tried a little smile. "I know." There was a pause and he said, brightening, "Promise me one thing: If I ever mention that airplane again, throw a law book at me, will you?"

"I'll get one out of hock specially."

Verecker raised his glass. "I love my wife but oh you kidnappers." Annie giggled. He said, "Wait, I want to make a toast. Hello, young hijackers, whoever you are. Tonight you may rest easy. Bulldog Verecker, sworn nemesis of crime and corruption, has just quit the case."

They ate their chili and drove back to San Francisco.

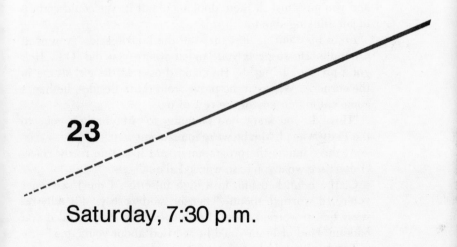

23

Saturday, 7:30 p.m.

Clarke jumped out of his chair and paced furiously up and down for the second time in two minutes. The others watched him, waiting for the outburst they knew was coming. He fumbled a cigarette out of the pack, jabbed it in his mouth, then snatched it out again and pointed it like an accusing finger at the skycap sitting on the end of the sofa. "I tell you he's going to screw things up just as sure as God made little green apples. If we don't do something about it we may as well kiss those rocks goodbye."

The skycap examined the can of beer he held in his hands. The big baggage man said to everybody in general, "He may be right."

Clarke whirled around angrily. "*May* be right? He figures out—I don't know how—that I landed on that course. He comes looking for me, hands me some ridiculous story and steals a picture of Ingrid. Then he goes looking for her, too. So already he's got a nice fat tie-up; already he knows who two of us are, and you guys just sit there thinking about it. We could end up in jail thinking about it."

From his chair against the wall the bookie said, "Now wait a minute. He suspects you landed where you did. O.K. He's got a picture of Ingrid." He glanced over at the girl sitting in the corner. "What can he prove from that? Besides, he hasn't come calling on any of the rest of us."

"How do you know he's planning to? Maybe he's gone to the Feds instead. Maybe we're too late anyway."

At the window the programmer said in a thin reedy voice, "I don't see what you're so worried about."

Clarke mimicked him in a high falsetto. "I don't see what you're so worried about." Then he said nastily, "I'll tell you what I'm so worried about, Brighteyes—my share. And if you had any kind of brain you'd be worried about yours, too."

The bookie told him to take it easy.

"Take it easy? This guy doesn't know what I'm worried about, our fat friend over here's so concerned he's reading a comic book, and you think I should take it easy. Every minute we sit here doing nothing that shyster lawyer's going to be getting closer, and if he figures it out before Monday night what are you going to tell me then?"

The big baggage man said, "Like he says, maybe we should do somethin'." He looked at his partner for confirmation. The fat man turned a page, his eyes eating up the colored drawings. The comic was snatched out of his hands. "This is important," the big man told him.

Speaking to Clarke, the bookie nodded toward the skycap. "He spent the best part of a year thinking this up. Let's not blow it in a couple of hours. If we stick to the plan we'll do all right."

"Listen. According to the plan nobody was supposed to come after me and Ingrid, but somebody did."

The bookie bent toward the skycap. "What do you think?"

The beer can revolved slowly, tipped to his mouth, then came back to his knee. "Let's wait," he said softly.

Clarke yelled at him. "We'll wait ourselves right out of the money."

"It's only three days," the programmer said to the window.

"Three days, two days, what's the difference if the guy finds the plane tonight?"

The room went silent; the pilot seized his advantage. "Let's vote on it." He thrust his hand in the air. "All those in favor of protecting our money."

The big man's hand went up. His partner followed his example.

"Three," the bookie said. "It's a stand-off."

"Hold it. There are seven of us in this room." Clarke was pointing at the stewardess. "She gets a vote, too."

She looked up quickly, her face frightened, pale under the yellow hair, dark lines underscoring her eyes. "What . . . what are you planning to do?"

"Nobody's going to get hurt, baby. We'll just grab that cute little wife of his and hold her till Monday night. We'll tell Verecker to cool it if he wants her back, that's all."

She looked miserably uncertain. Clarke crossed to her in two strides and gripped her arms. "Look, kid, we'll never have another chance like this. If they find that plane we lose everything. This is our future we're talking about." His fingers made sharp white depressions in her flesh. He spoke from the back of his throat. "Make up your mind, baby. Yes or no?"

She bit into her lip. "Yes."

He swung around to face the others. "Four against three. We pick her up."

The bookie looked disgusted. "You could be throwing the whole thing out the window."

Clarke said, "We could be saving it." He went over and pried a can of beer out of a six-pack, ripped the seal off and gulped at it.

The programmer turned from the window and caught the

193

bookie's eye. "It's crazy," he said, though not so anybody could hear. The skycap, his eyes closed, appeared to be thinking about something that had happened a long time ago. A clock ticked somewhere. Traffic sounds, half a block away, came in through the windows and walls.

The bookie asked, "Who's going to do it?"

"Me and the big fella. And Ingrid."

"Lee . . . "

"Relax. All you have to do is make one little phone call. You can do that, can't you?"

The bookie said, "How are you going to work it?"

"She wanted to talk to Ingrid, so we'll make it easy for her. Ingrid will call her and tell her she wants to see her, only by herself. Ingrid will arrange to pick her up in her car outside the apartment. We'll grab her when she comes out."

"How do you keep Verecker out of it?"

"They live at the same address but they've got separate phone numbers. I checked. That'll make it a lot easier. If she tells Verecker anyway, and he tries to get in on the act—" he glanced over at the baggage man—"we'll take him out of it, that's all."

The programmer asked a nervous question. "When do you plan to do it?"

"Tonight."

Saturday, 10 p.m.

Verecker let them in the front door and stooped to pick up two letters lying under the mail slot. He handed one to Annie. "Looks like Mrs. Grabowski's scrawl. This is for you, too." He eyed the postmark. "You got an admirer in San Jose?"

Annie took it. "From my sister, probably." They went into her apartment and she walked into the bedroom, tearing open an envelope. She came back into the room a minute later reading a letter. "My aunt's ill again, poor thing."

"Oh, I'm sorry to hear it. Bad?"

194

"No, but she gets miserable when she has these bouts. I'd better go down there for a few days, Billy. I may as well go tonight."

"Sure. I'll get out of your way."

"No, have a drink if you like. I'll just throw a few things together in a bag." She went back into the bedroom.

"What did Mrs. Grabowski want?"

Annie put her head round the door. "She's gone away for the weekend. She asked me to let Lulu in and give her her dinner tomorrow. Would you mind doing it?"

"I'll fix it." He moved to the door. "Stay down there as long as you think you should and don't worry about the office."

"Thanks, Billy."

"See you."

"Bye." She went back into the bedroom and finished packing a bag.

As Annie snapped the lock on her suitcase a white Toronado pulled up silently outside the house. The headlights winked out. Up the hill and around the corner the stewardess was standing in a phone booth. She reached for the phone and brought a coin up to the slot, dropped it in. A bell dinged and the dial tone buzzed in her ear. Carefully, exactly, she dialed seven digits. The phone rang twice, then a woman's voice said, "Hello?" The girl drew a breath in to speak, stopped and, as if it were starting to burn her fingers, dropped the phone on its cradle. She stood for a second with her eyes closed, then left the booth and walked slowly to the corner of the street where the car was parked. The yellow glow of a street light washed over her.

"O.K.," Clarke said. He got out, went around to the back of the car, opened the trunk and pretended to fiddle with something. The big man moved in the opposite direction.

Inside the house, Annie remembered something. She went out of the front door and onto the steps. "Lulu," she called softly. She made a kissing noise. "Come on, girl."

There was the sound of a car trunk closing. A figure moved

195

out of the night. A man's voice said, "Hello, Mrs. Verecker. Remember me?"

Annie couldn't quite see his face. He walked into the light coming from the front windows. Her eyes widened in surprise. Whatever it was she began to say was stifled by a hand clamping hard over her mouth from behind.

Clarke leaped for the car, jerked the door open and shoved the front seat forward. The big man wrestled Annie across the sidewalk and backed into the rear seat, dragging her in after him. Clarke dived behind the wheel and shot the car away from the curb, roared up the hill and stopped five feet away from the stewardess, who'd watched the scene rooted to the spot.

"Get in." She stood like a statue. *"Get in."* It came like a slap in the face. She ran to the car and the door slammed behind her. The Toronado bucked and screeched away, wheeled around the corner and was gone. It left behind a hot, harsh rubber smell that hung in the air for a moment, then drifted away on a late-evening breeze coming up from the bay.

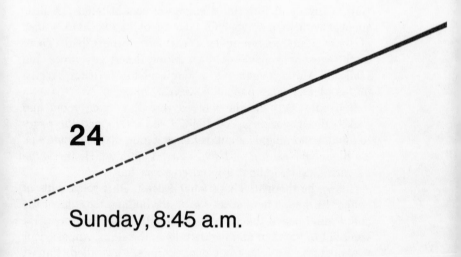

24

Sunday, 8:45 a.m.

Verecker woke up feeling as though he'd never been asleep. Sunday stretched endlessly in front of him. He'd go into the office and do a little work if he had any. Now that he was out of the airplane-finding business and Annie was out of town, what was he going to do with himself? She'd been gone only twelve hours and already he missed her.

He reached mechanically for a cigarette until he remembered he'd given them up. That was depressing enough but to start again would be even more so. He got out of bed and brushed his teeth instead, substituting one taste for another. Nicotine-flavored toothpaste—no risk and all the stimulant—he could make a fortune. Why not? Get some manufacturer interested, get an advertising campaign going, Smoke Pepsodent, something catchy like that. Or bring out a new brand of toothpaste, Koolgate maybe. O.K., so much for big ideas; that still left him with Sunday to be lived. Invite himself over to the Hackneys' for breakfast—Ramos Fizzes and Eggs Benedict on the patio? Call Warren and Judy for a couple of sets of tennis? A little snooker with John maybe? Or take a look at *TV Guide*—some of those Sunday-morning kids' cartoons weren't bad. There might even be a movie on, an exciting desert adventure, Jon Hall and Maria, maybe. Or a jungle picture—Johnny Weissmuller and Cheetah punching German spies.

Buoyed with hope, he walked into the living room and picked the magazine up off the TV set. He flipped the pages to Sunday morning. His smile of expectation died. *"They Came To Blow Up New Jersey, 1969,"* he read out loud. He threw the magazine aside. "About a hundred years too late."

Coffee, he thought. That's what I need; can't think without coffee. In the kitchen he set the water boiling, took down the coffee and opened the refrigerator for the milk. Fresh out. He went out of the door and padded down the stairs. Annie's door was open. So was the front door. "Annie?" he called. Funny, must have left in an awful hurry; didn't even turn the lights out. He switched them off and closed her door and went out onto the stairs for the milk. Milk . . . something pinged off the fringes of his memory; he had a vague sense of something left undone. What? He remembered: Mrs. Grabowski's poodle. God, he'd forgotten to call her last night.

"Lulu, there's a girl. Come and get it, Lulu." She should have been waiting there on the steps, scratching the door to pieces, panting like a crazy thing the way she always did when Mrs. Grabowski let her in.

"Loooo-loooo." He looked up and down the street. Nothing. He picked up the paper and the milk and walked back up to his apartment. Must have found a boy friend, he thought. He dropped bread into the toaster and scanned the headlines while he waited for the coffee to perk, then read the opening remarks of a columnist. He shook his head in wonder and muttered, "His father brought him down for a day on the cable cars and he's never got over it."

The toast popped up. He buttered it, ate it, drank his coffee and still felt hungry. He looked inside the refrigerator: two packs of frozen corn on the cob, three TV dinners, a six-pack of beer and a can of chocolate syrup. Eggs. Milk. Nothing appealed. He figured he'd grab a doughnut somewhere. He went into the bathroom, stripped and stepped into the shower.

The phone rang.

"Hello?" He brought the bath mat with him and stood on it, irritable and dripping.

The voice on the wire asked him a question. "Lost anything lately?"

"Hello?" Verecker said again.

"We've got her, Verecker."

"Got her?"

"Where you'll never find her unless you play ball."

It dawned on Verecker what the man was talking about. "You crud! If this isn't the lowest—what is this, some kind of new racket?"

The voice mocked him. "Something like that."

"How much do you want? Let's have it."

"It's not a question of money, you know that."

"Quit stalling. I'll give you twenty-five bucks."

"Twenty-five . . . " The voice snagged on something.

"Not a penny more," Verecker said firmly. "She's not worth anything, you know. She wouldn't win any prizes or anything —simple sentimental value and not much of that. As far as I'm concerned she's just another dog."

"Stop clowning, Verecker. We've got her and you won't see her again unless you do what we tell you."

"You heard me, I've made my offer. Twenty-five dollars and no questions asked, or I'll go to the cops."

There was a long silence. An amazed voice said, "You're not clowning. You really mean it."

"Damn right I mean it."

The line went dead.

"Hello? Hello?" Verecker slammed the phone down. "Punks!"

199

He crossed to the bureau and took out his wallet. He counted off some bills. "Seven dollars," he said. "I wonder if they'll take a check."

Clarke burst into the room, his face twisted with anger. "The bastard's not going to play ball. He offered me twenty-five bucks. Can you tie that? Twenty-five lousy bucks." He socked a fist into his hand. "He laughed at me, just plain laughed at me. I told you he was on to us. He's going after the whole lot—he's going to try to ace us out of everything, make his own deal with the airline."

The bookie's hand had stopped halfway to his cigar. "He must have figured it out. But how?" He addressed the question to the skycap. "The thing was foolproof."

The skycap said, "Maybe he just got lucky," almost as if he were unconcerned.

"We gotta do somethin'," the big man told them. "We gotta stop him."

"There's only one way," Clarke said. It sounded very final.

The programmer turned scared eyes on the room. "Kill him? You don't mean kill him?"

Clarke screamed at him. "He's going to take our dough away. Unless we stop him for good."

"Nobody's takin' my dough away," the big man muttered.

The fat man said, "Me neither."

"But killing . . . " The programmer looked across at the bookie.

Clarke was still yelling. "It's O.K. with you this guy helps himself to the lot, huh? What the hell, you're still facing the rest of your life in stir, you know that, don't you?" He looked balefully around the room. "We all are. The only thing that's going to stop the Feds from shaking us out of bed one of these days is enough money to get so far away they'll never find us."

"Still . . . murder . . . "

"Listen, dummy, it's the same rap. What's the difference between life for murder and life for kidnapping? We get caught now we won't see daylight again anyway. So what have we got to lose besides twenty-five million bucks?" Clarke threw himself into a chair and massaged his fist. His glance fell on the stewardess in the corner. Fear was stamped all over her face, her eyes quick, wild-looking. She was twisting a ring on her finger around and around and around. "Hey, baby," he called. "How about checking on our guest, huh?"

She got up and went toward the door. Clarke got up with her and caught her wrist as she passed. He leaned forward and kissed her cheek and whispered harshly in her ear, "Buck up." She left the room, Clarke's eyes tracer bullets in her back.

The room grew quiet again. A cloud of cigar smoke rose toward the ceiling, fanned out on a draft and crept toward the top of a window. The bookie considered the pilot's argument. He said, "It might not be so easy, you thought of that? He might just be expecting us."

Clarke answered him. "I'll tell you who else might be expecting us. The FBI tomorrow night, if we don't get to Verecker first."

The programmer said, "But they don't know where we're picking up the stuff, and they won't know."

"Sure, but what if Verecker makes a deal with Calair? The Feds will fake the delivery and when we make our move they'll hit us with everything they've got."

The big man stood up. "That makes sense. It makes sense, right?" He nudged his partner, who agreed with him.

The bookie chewed his cigar and shot a glance at the skycap. The guy seemed out of it, huddled deep in a chair, his chin on his chest. He looked like a seated statue of depression. The bookie thought about him. He'd come up with a plan that was dazzling in its concept—simple, fast, beautiful. But it had taken him the best part of a year. That's the way the guy was, slow and methodical. Now he was being asked to make a snap decision, and he didn't have that kind of mind. The bookie realized he'd have to do the thinking for him.

201

The stewardess came back into the room.

"She O.K.?" Clarke asked.

The girl nodded and sat down in the corner again, miserable. She dropped her eyes and the pilot swore under his breath.

The bookie ashed his cigar very carefully on the side of a saucer, twisting it in his fingers as if he were taking paint off a brush. "It'll have to be done right," he said. "What do you have in mind?"

Clarke told him. The bookie and the two baggage men seemed impressed. The programmer was doubtful; he claimed they should think of another way out completely.

Clarke appealed to the bookie. "Jesus H. Christ, do we have to listen to this sob sister all day?"

"If we do this we all do it," the man told him coldly. "He's taking just as much risk as you are."

"He's getting paid for it, isn't he? Overpaid if you ask me. Two million bucks just for fiddling with a lousy computer. I supply a plane and risk my neck in a night landing for the same dough. You call that fair?"

"You agreed to the price," the bookie said. "If you're not happy with your end, too bad."

"O.K. for you, you're making five times what we're making, you and the skycap."

"He gets five million and you know it. And if that sounds a lot, remember, without him there wouldn't have been any job and you wouldn't have stood to make a nickel." His eyes drilled into the pilot's. "And I make the most because I'm bankrolling this thing. Without me you couldn't have even started. Even then I'm only taking forty percent and you know what a professional financier takes—I mean legit business? You know how much? Eighty percent, that's how much. So, believe me, you're doing all right."

The big man cut in. "Hey, you two. If we don't decide quick, nobody'll get a cut of nothin'."

The bookie spoke to the programmer. "As I see it we have to safeguard ourselves. I'm not crazy about killing a guy, but

I'm not crazy about being picked up and having nothing to show for it, either. If you want to back out now, I'll give you ten grand cash for your share."

"Ten grand? For two million dollars?"

"That's my offer. Take it and you can put on your hat and leave now—out of it. Otherwise you're in. You won't have to do anything personally—the pilot and the big fella will take care of it."

The programmer looked bewildered. "But ten grand . . . "

"In, out," Clarke said impatiently.

The reply was a long time coming. "In."

Clarke snorted. "What a surprise!"

The big man moved to the door. "Let's get started," he said.

"Sit down. Nobody's going anywhere yet; we'll have to wait till it gets dark."

"But that's gonna give him all day."

The pilot said, "So let it. I'm not getting under a guy's car in broad daylight."

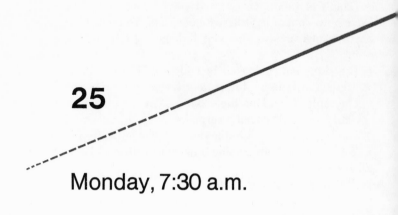

25

Monday, 7:30 a.m.

"I draw your attention to exhibit A," Verecker intoned, pointing to a small, thick wooden box. There was a tiny glass tube swaddled inside it which he picked up with infinite care. "Is this the vial of nitroglycerine you took from the defendant on the night of the sixteenth? Examine it carefully, please."

The dark man in the witness chair peered at it. The courtroom was hushed, the jury leaning forward in their seats. "It is," the man confirmed.

"You're absolutely sure?"

"Absolutely."

"Then if it is," Verecker cried, "we should all be blown to Kingdom Come," and, as the courtroom shrieked with one voice, he raised his hand and dashed the vial to the floor.

Instead of an earth-shaking explosion there was a tiny tinkle of glass. Verecker crouched down quickly, put a finger to the colorless liquid that had run from the vial and touched his finger to his tongue. "Water," he cried.

The courtroom gasped.

"Your honor"—he straightened up and advanced to the bench—"I submit this case be dismissed due to false evidence."

The judge banged his gavel down and said in an astonished voice, "Case dismissed."

Pandemonium broke out. A great cheer went up from the public gallery and newsmen and photographers bounded down the aisle, surrounding Verecker in a question-shouting throng.

A beautiful blond woman dressed entirely in black rose from behind the defendant's table and pushed to the edge of the crowd.

Verecker said deeply, "Let her through, boys." The newsmen parted, grinning.

The woman threw herself into his arms. "Oh, Bill, you were wonderful." She kissed him flush on the mouth while flash-bulbs popped.

Gently, Verecker disentangled her arms. "Easy, baby," he said, smiling down at her, "we'll get around to that later."

A portly, distinguished-looking gentleman wearing a cut-away with dollar signs on his vest struggled through the crowd.

"Oh, Daddy, isn't he wonderful?" the woman shrilled.

"My boy," he said, wringing Verecker's hand, "you've done a great thing here today. A great thing. The firm of Windbreaker, Jeans and Sneakers can always use a smart young lawyer. Would a hundred thousand. a year and expenses be acceptable?"

"A hundred thousand?"

"All right, you drive a hard bargain, but make it two hundred thousand and a beach house at Malibu."

Verecker was about to reply when an irritating jangling noise caught his attention. It got louder and louder until it seemed to fill the entire courtroom. The alarm clock beside his bed was letting go the tinny scream it had kept bottled up inside it all night.

He reached out a groping hand, found the stop button and patted the clock into silence. He opened his eyes and groaned. His mouth tasted as though he'd eaten a box of pencils. What had he been doing to . . . ? The memory of the night before came flooding back. A Sonja Henie movie on the Late Show, followed by Deanna Durbin on the Late Late Show. His stomach felt a little queasy, too, although he knew it couldn't have been his dinner: a can of Campbell's frozen New England clam chowder and a Sara Lee chocolate cake—all good, nourishing stuff. It must have been the bottle of bourbon. Another thought struck him: Mrs. Grabowski's poodle. She worshipped that dog. How was he going to tell her it had been kidnapped?

He rolled out of bed and scuffed across to the window. "Lulooooo . . . " To his great surprise a furious yapping came from outside the front door and a small black poodle danced out into the street and disappeared again. "How about that?" Verecker said, delighted. He went down and let the dog in, brought her upstairs and fed her. "Just goes to show," he said, watching the poodle gulp the food. "If I'd backed down they would've got a hundred bucks out of me, maybe more."

The thought cheered him immensely, and he went into the shower singing. He was still humming when he came back into the room with a towel around his waist. I've got it, he said to himself. I'll go around to the driving range and straighten out that fade. Annie will never know. He made a few practice swings, then went into the bedroom and dressed.

On his way out the door, he patted Lulu, sleeping on a chair. "Brave little doggie," he said. He grabbed up his golf clubs and went down the stairs.

The moment he got to his car he knew there was something different about it, something strange. He got the curious idea it was somebody else's. He slid in behind the wheel and the feeling of strangeness increased. Something was wrong—he seemed to be too low in his seat or something. He shrugged the feeling off and brought the key up to the ignition. He pushed in the ignition key, stopped and sniffed something—a smell he couldn't quite identify.

He dismissed it and turned the key.

The engine started first time and he revved it to warm it up.

The car was pointed down the hill, a long, steep, fast-plunging hill. He checked his rear-view mirror, swung the wheels away from the curb. The steering felt abnormally sluggish. At the same time he nudged the gear selector into Drive and the car moved away from the curb and started down.

His foot hit the brake pedal.

It was like treading on marshmallows.

He tried to pump it but the pedal thumped lifelessly against the floorboards. The hand brake came out like a dead stick in his hand.

Even with the fine sharp edge of panic that was shooting through him like electric needles he realized something crazy: the car should have been hurtling down the hill. But it wasn't. It was moving instead like a bumpy escalator. He jerked the selector into low, rammed the steering wheel over, jamming the front wheel against the curb, and brought the car to a clunking stop against a telephone pole. He cut the engine and sat there breathing hard, the sweat still coming. Then he got out and examined the car.

All four tires were flat down to the rims; they'd been slashed with a knife.

"*Ryder. You son of a bitch!*" Verecker bawled. "Insane, the guy's insane. Stark raving mad. He cuts the brakes, he slashes the tires—this time he's gone too far."

He stormed angrily up the hill and confronted Ryder's Buick, looking for a suitable protrusion to tear off. He got a better idea and ran back up to his apartment. He dived into the kitchen, threw open the cupboards and started pulling out everything he could find: salt, pepper, sugar, Worcestershire sauce, cornflakes, instant coffee, strawberry preserves, a can of tuna fish and an old package of cake mix. He tipped the lot into a blender, added two eggs, a cup of milk and some

207

flour, set it at its highest speed and turned it on. Three minutes later he raced down the stairs with the concoction, strode over to the Buick, lifted the hood, unscrewed the oil cap and tipped the mixture into the engine.

"There," he said triumphantly. "Let's see if that brings you trouble-free motoring."

Back upstairs he called the garage and asked them to send around the tow truck.

"Are you sure you need the tow truck?" the mechanic asked him. "Maybe it's just flooded."

"It has four flat tires, no brakes and I rammed a telephone pole."

"You need the tow truck."

"I could use two," Verecker said.

On his way to the cable car he stopped outside Ryder's apartment and called up to an open window, "Ryder, may your bones turn to yoghurt."

The bastard had destroyed his day; now he had to go to the office.

For a change, there weren't any bills waiting for him when he got to the office, which he thought was just as well. With Annie out there was nobody to type any stalling letters anyway. He looked over at her empty desk, the cover on the typewriter. The office was like a morgue without her. He thought of calling her, then decided against it. Why disturb her if her aunt was really sick? And the poor woman must be sick; she was still down there and this was Monday.

Monday! The airline would have the second note.

He grabbed up the phone and called Rinlaub, said good morning and asked him if they'd had any fascinating mail lately. Rinlaub told him yes, but he certainly couldn't discuss it over the phone. Verecker said he'd be right over and hung up before the other could protest.

He walked over to the Calair building where Rinlaub had

208

his office, three floors above the main reservations desk. A secretary showed him into a big carpeted room and Rinlaub came around from behind a mahogany desk and shook hands.

"Glad you could make it after all," he said.

Verecker said, "Today's the day, right?"

The other man confirmed it. "I heard you were up at Washoe."

"Yeah, a lot of good it did me, too."

"It didn't do anybody much good."

They sat down and looked at each other. "Well, you going to tell me or not?"

"Tell you what?" Rinlaub asked with a trace of a smile.

"Come on. I'm practically one of the gang by this time. Even the FBI knows me."

Rinlaub looked serious. "Billy, I know you've been doing a little snooping on your own time, and I think you were on to something. You started to tell me about it the day we had lunch. I assume it turned out to be nothing."

"A big fat nothing." Verecker introduced him to his golf-course theory and the pilot and stewardess and told him how it had all been a dead end. Rinlaub said he still should have reported it, even though it did sound a little fanciful. At any rate, it was too late to start checking on it now.

"Tell me about the note, Phil."

"If I do you're going to have to promise you won't try to interfere. Figuring out that lake idea was pretty smart, and nobody was upset you did, but we'll be dealing with the safety of maybe three hundred and sixty people tonight. You wouldn't try any heroics, would you?"

"Believe me, Phil, I'm out of it now. I was never really in it, come to think of it. I just ran around in circles."

"We all did that. O.K., then I have your word. It came this morning, the second note, mailed from Kings Beach at the northern end of the lake."

"I know it—about eighteen miles from Glenbrook."

209

"Right. We have to drop the diamonds from a small plane."

Verecker said, "Our friends seem to be aviation mad. Where do they want it?"

"We're not sure."

"They haven't told you?"

Instead of answering, Rinlaub pulled open a drawer and took out an Esso road map. He smoothed it out on his desk. "Take a look at this." His finger pointed to a thin red line that ran from San Bruno to Reno. "I drew this myself. It's the compass course they sent us. At eleven tonight a small plane with blue navigation lights is to take off from the airport and fly on that course— seventy miles per hour and keeping a thousand feet up. When the pilot sees a green flare he's to drop the loot immediately."

"Parachute?"

"Yep. The rocks are to be packed in egg boxes and placed in a Montgomery Ward tool box wired shut."

"You mean the big blue steel ones?"

"You got it."

"It'll hit the ground like a ton of bricks. Any other instructions?"

"The tool box has to carry a small white flare."

"Pretty cute," Verecker said. "The FBI will have to cover a lot of territory not knowing where the drop will be."

Rinlaub said, "It's slightly over a hundred and ninety air miles from the airport to Reno. They figure they'll be able to put a man about every half mile where the terrain permits."

Verecker leaned over the map. "But look at the area it covers. They could be waiting anywhere." His finger traced the red line. "From San Francisco airport over the bay to Oakland airport—how about that for a start? If I'm right about the golf course, and they have access to a small plane, wouldn't it make sense to have the box dropped on a runway, pick it up and use the plane as a getaway car?"

"And have to dodge all the Boeings landing and taking off? I don't think so. Besides, the line goes through Rio Vista here, forty miles to the east. There's a small-plane airport there; that

210

would make more sense. It runs close to Truckee airport, too, for that matter."

Verecker's finger moved to Oakland and followed the line east again. "Moraga, Walnut Creek, Pittsburgh, Rio Vista, across Ninety-nine—that could be something. A highway. Drop it near a waiting car, they could make a fast exit."

"But that would be the easiest place to hide an FBI agent, and they'd know it. It's a fine line we're treading. The FBI can't risk endangering those passengers, but at the same time they'd give their eye teeth to grab the kidnappers. So they'll try to follow them without being seen. Once the passengers are in the clear they'll move in. The gang obviously figures that—that's how come the elaborate delivery system."

"Phil, do you think they'll try to bug the diamonds, use a homing device, something like that?"

"I doubt they'll take the chance; the note warned specifically against it. This mob seems to have figured all the angles."

Verecker returned to the map. "Well, if Ninety-nine's out, Fifty's out for the same reason. Hey, it passes over a town called Rescue. I wonder if the gang has a sense of humor."

"Not with this kind of money involved."

"From then on it gets tough, doesn't it? Within thirty miles you're over the Sierras, right over the top of Granite Chief and Squaw Valley." He stopped for a moment, then dismissed the preposterous idea that had flashed into his mind. "It touches the tip of Forty, then over the border and across Nevada for ten miles to Reno. At least that's one place they won't drop it."

"The FBI won't discount any place; they'll try to cover as much as they can."

Verecker stabbed the red line. "You've got a hundred miles between Oakland and Clarksville before it starts to rise to the mountains. I'd say somewhere in that area is the best bet."

"Maybe," Rinlaub said, folding up the map. "Anyway, it's the Bureau's worry now. I'm just as much out of it as you are." He threw the map into a drawer and closed it with a snap. His eyes came up. "And you are out of it, aren't you, Billy?"

"Yep," Verecker said with resigned finality. "The hours are too long and the pay's too low."

They both moved toward the door. Verecker said, "You know, it's costing your airline a fortune, but at least you'll get to find out how they did it."

"It's a pretty expensive piece of information, isn't it? But you're right; it's the only consolation. There can't be more than one way to steal a 747 full of people—sometimes I don't believe there's that many—and when we find out what it is at least we'll be able to stop its happening again. I hope."

"You still don't think you can keep it quiet?"

"Not a chance. It's a miracle we've been able to hold the story as long as we have."

"Will you do me a favor and call me when you get the answer?"

"Sure. But it'll be a fast call. I'm going to be busy for the next couple of weeks."

"Phil"—Verecker held out his hand—"you're a prince."

"I seem to tell you everything, don't I?"

"I guess I have ways of making you talk. I'll see you."

Verecker went down in the elevator feeling depressed. The visit to Rinlaub had been a mistake. He felt as though he'd been eliminated from a giant quiz program and had been allowed to sit in the audience to watch somebody else go for the big prize. That damn jumbo jet. He wished he'd never heard of the thing. He wished he'd never heard of a lot of things.

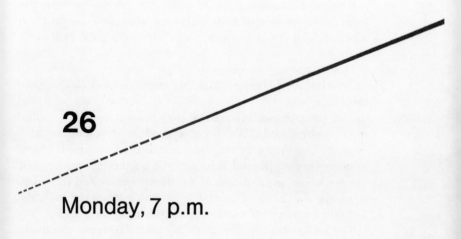

26

Monday, 7 p.m.

The bookie leafed through the pages, opening and closing the paper as if he were pumping a bellows under a stubborn fire. "Nothing in here either. And nothing on the radio. It looks like Verecker stayed in bed today." He tossed the paper to the pilot, who snatched it out of the air.

"You saying we didn't fix that car?"

"I'm saying whatever you did do it didn't work."

The big man made a fist, ran it up and down his trouser leg. "We shoulda done it personal and made sure. Fixin' his car was a lousy idea."

Clarke took a step toward him and the big man raised his eyebrows. "Don't tell me . . . "

Clarke turned away and swore violently.

The fat man asked what they were going to do now, and the bookie said they'd go ahead as planned. What else could

213

they do? The programmer wanted to know about the woman in the next room—what were they going to do with her?

Clarke produced a stick of gum and peeled the wrapper from it, tearing it in thin vertical strips. He rolled the gum into a ball and bit down on it. He said, "She got a good look at all of us."

"Yeah," the big man agreed.

"Maybe we'd better take her with us—as last-minute insurance."

The programmer opened his mouth and closed it again.

The bookie said, "We've got a good hour before we start moving. The only way we can operate is to assume this guy Verecker hasn't queered it for us. We go through with it just like we never heard of him. If we stick together and do things right, we should all of us end up a whole lot richer tonight." Nobody commented; the skycap might have been asleep.

The bookie looked over at the big man. "You sure you made out O.K. this morning?"

"Like I said, nobody saw me take it."

"And you?" he asked the pilot.

"Don't worry."

The stewardess rose and moved toward the door.

"Where you going, baby?"

"The drugstore."

"What for?"

"I need some things." She turned and went out the door.

"Why don't you stop riding her?" the bookie said. "She's doing a good job."

Clarke advised him to stay out of it.

"Mr. Verecker? This is Ingrid Arosund."

"Who?"

"Don't drive your car. They've done something to it."

On the other end of the line Verecker's brain spun like a dynamo—the girl, "they," the car—what was it supposed—? The realization numbed him.

"*They* did that to the car? They're after *me?*"

214

"They're not joking about your wife. They may kill her."

The shock hit him in the stomach like ice pellets fired from a shotgun. His legs felt boneless, jellified. He understood with a horrifying suddenness what yesterday's phone call had been all about.

"Annie? They've got Annie?" His voice sounded dry, desiccated.

The girl said quickly, "They're taking her with them on the pick-up. I'll try to get her away, but I'll need help."

"Where? Tell me where?"

"You've got to promise you won't bring the police. I'm not going to jail for the rest of my life."

"Ingrid. I just want Annie back."

"You'll come alone?"

"I swear."

She said, "You know about the instructions?"

"Yes."

"They're going to fire that flare from a boat in the bay."

"The bay? But the tool box—"

"We'll be about two miles off Oakland airport on that compass course. You'll have to get hold of a boat and try to get near without them seeing you. Blink your lights so I know it's you. I'll signal back. I can't promise anything. They're . . ." That was as far as she got before the door was wrenched back on its hinges.

Clarke was standing there.

He held his hand out for the phone. The girl drew it closer to her, protectively. His hand caught her arm and drew it toward him. He peeled her fingers from the phone and put it to his ear, his eyes locked onto hers, and spoke into the mouthpiece. "Hello?"

There was a click as somebody hung up at the other end.

He handed the phone back to the stewardess. "Looks like your party's hung up."

"It was my sister," the girl gabbled. "You know she's pregnant, Lee. I was just checking on her, that's all."

"Take it easy, baby. It was your sister." His voice was slow,

215

syrupy. "She's pregnant. You called to see how she was. Now hang up the phone."

She was clutching it to her like a child with a doll. She dropped it back on its hook, not quite straight. It slipped off and she fumbled it back on again.

He drew her out of the booth and said in the same weighted voice, "You've got to get a grip on yourself, kid. You're coming apart at the seams. After all, it was just a phone call to your sister, nothing to get upset about."

The girl's frightened eyes blinked, grew moist. She lowered her chin. "I'm sorry, Lee. It's just that this whole business has—"

He cut her off sharply, looked around the store. A clerk was stacking merchandise, a woman was examining a lipstick. Nobody was paying any attention to them. "Why don't you buy what you came in for and we'll go have a drink? How about it?"

She nodded, not looking at him, and turned toward the counter.

"And, Ingrid . . . " She stopped. He spoke to the back of her head, his eyes hard. "No more calls to your sister."

The moment a man's voice had come on Verecker had reacted instantly. He'd jabbed his finger down on the button and held it there, as if to let it go would release something noxious into the room. Then he gingerly lifted his finger and listened to the monotonous note of the dial tone.

The initial shock was replaced by a geyser of fear bursting through his body, flooding his brain. He'd been right about Clarke and the golf course—they'd tried to kill him to keep him quiet. It hadn't worked, so they'd taken Annie to ensure his silence. That's what that phone call had been all about. And to think he'd congratulated himself on being so smart, on backing down some small-time punk.

Forget it, he thought. He needed a boat. Cliff!

He grabbed his diary, flipped to the W's, dialed the number and told the answering voice he needed his boat and needed it fast—tonight!

216

He rushed into the bedroom and threw on all the warm clothes he could find. His mind churned with horrible possibilities: Who'd interrupted the girl—Clarke? Had he heard her? Good God, Annie's life depended on some vague plan Ingrid Arosund had which he hadn't the slightest idea of. And what was worse he couldn't be sure she was even going to get a chance to try it.

He thought of calling Rinlaub, the FBI and discarded the idea immediately. He had to go along with the girl; whatever her plan was it was the only one.

He bolted downstairs and across to the car. He'd picked it up only half an hour before. Thank heavens it had been ready.

He drove toward the Golden Gate, trying to shake off the thoughts that sank sharp teeth into him. On Lombard, a green light changed to amber. He hit the gas pedal and shot through it seconds after it had changed to red. This was crazy; he wasn't going to do Annie any good if he panicked. He slowed the car, forced himself to calm down, think.

The road curved into the bridge approach. He stopped for the toll gates, sped away over the bridge, a high avenue of swirling yellow light. A sudden gust whipped through the open window, ballooning the convertible's top. The wind died as the car plunged through the cut at the end of the bridge, up over and down the grade on the other side. He took the second Mill Valley turnoff, drove through the small village and started up a thin ribbon of road that curled up the slope of Tamalpais.

His friend met him on the drive, the boat keys in his hand. He said he didn't know what all this was about but he'd called the yacht club and told them to expect him.

Verecker snatched the keys and yelled that he'd explain everything later, then drove back down the winding road, passed the highway and took Tiburon Boulevard.

Fifteen minutes later he pulled up outside a high fence that shielded a two-story wooden building from the street. The top floor was lit up, music coming from the open windows. He hurried through a gate and along a walk that led around the side of the building and down to a series of flat jetties spread

217

out over the water like long square fingers held a few inches above the surface. They were jammed with boats moored hull to hull on either side—a huge floating parking lot.

A man came up, flashlight in hand. Verecker identified himself, told him Mr. Wilton had called about his borrowing his boat. The man led the way down a wooden finger and stopped in front of a sporty-looking cruiser. Verecker handed him some money, hopped up onto the bow of the boat, walked around and stepped down into the open deck. He ran his hands over the dashboard and flicked a switch. Lights came on. He ducked his head and went down into the cabin. There was a small galley—refrigerator, sink and stove—a dinette area, bench bunks up ahead. It'd been a couple of months since he'd been out on the boat, but he had a pretty good idea where everything was. He clicked on an overhead light and pulled open drawers till he found one jammed with rolled-up charts. He chose one that took in the entire bay. He grabbed up dividers, protractor, a ruler and a pencil and spread the chart flat on the table. He drew a line across the bay from the center of San Francisco airport to the southern tip of Oakland airport—he remembered the detail from Rinlaub's map. He rested the dividers on the mileage scale, set the points to two miles and measured it off along the line from Oakland airport into the bay. He marked the point with a cross, reached for the ruler and lined up the cross with a point in Belvedere Cove where he was sitting. He ran the pencil along the ruler's edge, slid the protractor over the line he'd made and read off the compass course he had to steer. It was only approximate but he figured it should get him within half a mile of that boat—close enough to spot a signal.

He brought his wrist up to his face: 9:48. He had about twelve miles of water to cross. Allowing for winds and tides, he figured thirty minutes. If he left now it would give him a little over half an hour to spot the boat before the plane took off.

He flicked off the light, went out on deck and started the

218

engines, revving them. He let go the forward and stern lines, switched on the navigation lights, shoved the gears into reverse and backed away from the jetty.

He took the boat out of the cove at a moderate speed, throttled up past Peninsula Point and sped toward the dark western tip of Angel Island half a mile ahead. The island came up at him, moved by him, a liner with its lights out.

The boat knifed through dark water.

Alcatraz came out of the night on his starboard bow, its ends awash in the swell that rolled five thousand miles to siphon through the Golden Gate. Above the bay's entrance the orange avenue of the bridge looked like lanterns strung across the sky. The city got closer, a glittering forest on his right.

A second noise joined the beat of the engines—a deeper, thicker sound—the roar of the traffic pounding over the Bay Bridge. It grew louder as the boat passed underneath. The traffic noise boomed down; the sky seemed to quiver. The engine-throb bounced back as if the boat were entering a steel cave.

Verecker reckoned he had about eight miles to go.

The cabin lights were out and they sat in the green glow coming from the uncovered starboard light. Annie sat next to the stewardess, the white gauze bandage they'd wrapped around her mouth looking like a surgical mask. Another bandage bound her wrists together in front of her.

The stewardess was silent, her eyes flickering from the window to the starless night that hung like thick black drapes at the open doorway.

Annie watched her. When she'd brought her her meals back at the apartment she'd tried to draw the girl into conversation, but she'd just shaken her head and left the room. Annie hadn't needed to ask why she'd been brought there; she'd guessed the answer a moment after she'd recognized the pilot and been bundled into the car. Later, lying locked in the tiny room, the initial, heart-stopping fright receding, she knew that if there

219

was a way out the stewardess was the key. The girl seemed almost as scared as she was, miserably unhappy, with no stomach for what she was doing. But the contact Annie had tried to establish over the next few days never came, and the dark fears she'd managed to keep from smothering her completely had crept toward her out of the corners of the room.

An hour ago, approaching the Bayshore Freeway, she'd got the stupid idea they were taking her back. For one stupendous, overwhelming moment a high tide of relief had gushed through her, only to dry up the next second like a river in a desert. Instead of turning north on the freeway toward San Francisco the car had turned south toward San Jose. It had left the highway five or six miles farther on and driven along a road that skirted what could have been a golf course. She'd got a wild idea about Clarke's plane being there, but the car had left the course behind and pulled up at a boat marina.

It had come to her the moment they'd hustled her on board a big power boat. Today was Monday—she was going with them on the pick-up. She figured they'd arranged for the diamonds to be transferred by boat, somewhere out in the pitch-black bay where they couldn't be followed. She'd obviously been brought along to make sure there were no tricks.

Then she'd thought of something else, something she was still thinking about: How about after they'd picked up the ransom —wouldn't her usefulness be over? They wouldn't just let her go.

Her eyes were drawn to the dark waters of the bay. She knew about the bay; except for the dredged channels it was only about twenty feet deep, filled in over a million years by the mud the rivers washed down—thick, oozing mud as black and heavy as molasses. And there were tides, fast vicious rips that could suck you under, then sweep your body out to sea, the way it had happened to most of the prisoners who'd tried to make it from Alcatraz.

A cold wind whipped into the cabin. She shivered, porcelain in her bones. In spite of the gnawing fear inside her she was conscious of the girl. She seemed like a hostage herself. Her hands twisted a ring around and around her finger and she kept swallowing dryly, her eyes flicking between the two windows. She checked her watch for the third time, holding it up to the green glow.

Annie looked, too. It was 10:50.

Out on deck a voice shouted, "Something over there." Annie heard another voice—it could have been Clarke's—say, "Take it easy. We're not the only boat on the bay."

She felt the girl beside her stiffen, watched her as she glued her face to the window following the lights of the other boat about a hundred yards east of them. The girl watched it swing by as if it were an old, unexploded mine that might bump against them. Its lights wavered and Annie lost them, then saw them reappear a moment later as if the boat had passed behind a buoy.

The girl's hands dropped to her bag. She slipped something into her pocket, stood up, grasped Annie's elbow and motioned toward the stairs. "Come on."

Annie was too frightened to resist. She did as the girl told her, moving on leaden legs. Together they went out into the night wind that swirled over the open deck. The men were clustered on both sides of the cabin, their eyes sweeping the sky ahead.

Clarke yelled from the wheel, "What do you want? Get back in there."

"She's going to be sick."

"Use the john."

"It's broken," the girl lied.

"I'll give you two minutes. Hurry."

The stewardess pushed Annie to the stern seats, reached into her pocket and came out with a pair of nail scissors. She snipped the bandage from her mouth and moved to cut the one at her wrists.

"Leave it," Clarke shouted.

The girl spoke in a whisper. "Lean over the side."

221

Annie knelt on the cushions and bent her head over the transom. An icy salt spray showered up in her face, stinging her eyes, and she coughed exhaust fumes out of her throat.

The stewardess bent over with her, her arm around her shoulder. Annie sensed rather than saw her other hand digging into her pocket, fumbling for something. She brought it quickly below the gunwale.

"*Ingrid!*" It was like a whip cracking behind them. Clarke grabbed the girl's arm just as whatever she'd thrown over the side, something bright and metallic, vanished in the wake.

He jerked her to her feet. "Grab the wheel," he called over his shoulder. "Hold her steady." His eyes hadn't left her face. "What was it?" He made one fast word of it.

"What was—"

His hand flashed up, smacked her hard. He gripped her arms, shoved his face at her, bawled at her. "What did you throw over the side? Answer me."

She sobbed, tried to shake her head. "Nothing, Lee. Nothing."

"You lying whore." He shook her like a rag doll. "You lying little—" He threw an arm around her neck, jerked her toward him and drove his fist viciously into her stomach.

She fell back on the cushions, her mouth open like a fish, trying to suck air in great airless gasps.

Annie got her bandaged wrists over the girl's shoulders and cradled her head in her lap, trying to ignore the man standing over them screaming obscenities. Clarke switched his tirade to her and she hid her face and gritted her teeth for the fist she knew was coming.

It never landed.

Five voices cried as one, "There it is."

Across the bay, directly in front of them, a bright blue star was rising in the sky.

The pilot dived for the wheel, shouting orders. "Get ready with the gun. Grab the hardware." The men scuttled about. "Get those boat hooks out. Get 'em out."

The light filtering down from the masthead illuminated the deck in a tiny twenty-watt glow. The bookie nervously fingered a Very gun. The two baggage men grasped boat hooks. The programmer held garden shears in his hands.

Everybody watched the blue light getting closer.

Clarke nudged a lever and the boat slowed, settled back on its wake. He watched the pennant flapping in the crosstrees, trying to judge the wind. The blue light in the sky began to widen, became two lights, then three. His eyes were stitched to it. "Not yet, not yet . . . "

The lights grew larger; they heard the drone of the engine. "*Now!*"

The pistol in the bookie's hand exploded. There was an instant of absolute stillness, then, from far above, a soft popping noise echoed back to them and a shimmering, violent light burst into flame. It drifted down the night, a green Martian sun dripped from a spoon, and disappeared into the black waters of the bay.

Clarke had allowed the plane's pilot five seconds to get over his surprise; he should have allowed him more. The plane was closer than he wanted it when something white spluttered under the wing and lit from below a ballooning parachute that filled with air and seemed to be growing in the night like a huge phosphorescent mushroom.

"You're going to go by it," somebody yelled.

Clarke wrenched at the wheel and heeled the boat over in a great sweeping turn. It circled back on itself and plowed through its own wash.

The chute was huge in the sky, its airy, floating appearance gone; it hurtled down like a brick thrown from a bridge. Clarke throttled back, threw the gears into reverse. The boat shook itself, shuddered, tried to stand on its bow. With superb judgment he'd maneuvered the boat so close it seemed the white plummeting light would crash right through the deck.

There was a loud, hissing splash ten feet away, the parachute settling over the water like a dark waterlily.

223

Everybody yelled at once. The two baggage men slapped at the water with the boat hooks, grappling for the chute. The skycap was leaning over the gunwale, almost out of the boat, his hands reaching. The boat hooks came up under the silk, the air bubbling out from underneath.

"Keep 'em down," the pilot screamed.

The skycap's fingers touched cords, grabbed a handful, held on. The programmer joined him. The big man dropped his pole, snatched at the strings, hauled them in hand over hand.

The metal case came out of the water like sunken treasure. Water poured off it, poured out of it as it was lifted over the side and dropped onto the deck. Garden shears chomped on the cords, ate through them in three enormous steel bites. They slid over the side, dragged by the waterlogged chute, the severed tentacles of a giant squid.

The boat rose up on its stern and surged up the bay.

Wire cutters snapped in the big man's hands and sliced through the wire that bound the handles of the tool box. The bookie hinged the lids back, thrust his hands in and brought out soggy egg crates. He switched them to a cloth suitcase. The big man hurled the steel box over the side along with all the other tools. Clarke cut the lights and the boat roared through the night.

Lying in the back of the boat, Annie had watched the whole operation with the stewardess's head in her lap. The girl made a move to get to her feet. "No, stay there," Annie said.

The stewardess put her lips to Annie's ear. She whispered in a weak, gaspy voice, "Over the side. There's a rope there. There's a gun on the end of it." Pain misted her eyes. Annie stared at her. "Get it," Ingrid urged.

Annie slipped her arms from around the girl and crawled up onto the cushions. She knelt, bent her body over the stern rail, braced her thighs against it and felt for a rope.

Behind her the stewardess pulled herself painfully to her feet, reached for Annie's ankles, heaved them up off the seat and tipped Annie into the bay.

224

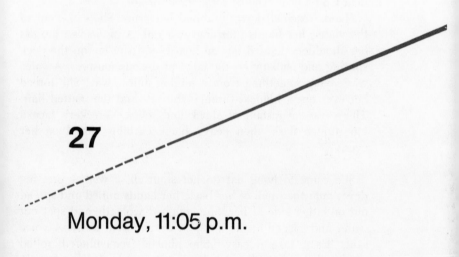

27

Monday, 11:05 p.m.

The bay came up like a hard, icy fist and belted the breath out of her. She skidded over the surface like a flat stone, a surging dizziness shocking through her, then knifed into a hole in the water, shooting under. She fought, kicked her way to the surface, black water in her mouth, her hands still tied in front of her, jerking at the water as if it were a raft she could haul herself out onto. The bay streamed into her eyes, cold darkness; she felt the mud reaching for her. Her clothes dragged on her, pointed the way down. She bit frantically at the bandages shrinking around her wrists, kicked at the slimy wet fingers that reached up for her from the bottom. The water got thinner, a cardboard floor that had soaked through, unable to support her. She stretched her neck, sucked at the night, her body getting heavy. She thrashed her arms, smashing at the water, trying to beat it off. There was a roaring in her ears; her hands struck something solid—a boat, dear God a boat. They'd come back for her.

Hands reached down, grabbed her arms. She came out of the water, her hands grasping at a rail. Arms locked around her shoulders, hauled her on board, and she lay on the deck spitting and choking on the edge of unconsciousness. A voice was saying something from a million miles away. She forced her eyes open, blinked through the salt and the matted hair. There was an instant of shock and relief, Verecker's face a too sudden flash, then heavy black curtains closed on her eyes.

She came to lying flat on her stomach, a weight pressing down onto the small of her back, her hands untied and spread out on either side of her. She coughed violently and spat out water and gasped at the air. The weight went away. A voice said, "Easy, take it easy." She blinked, remembered, rolled over on her side, still not believing it, and buried her face in Verecker's chest. "Billy, Billy, Billy," she sobbed.

His arms wrapped around her. "You're O.K. now. You're O.K."

She let the horror of the last five minutes flow out of her in a series of moaning cries. "I thought I was dead. I thought I was dying."

He let her get it out of her system. Then she quietened, ran a hand through her hair and said in a voice still wet around the edges, "This is some way to run a railroad. What on earth are you doing here?"

Verecker told her about the stewardess and the phone call. "She said she'd signal, but I didn't see anything, so I just stayed on the course and hung around. When the chute came down I was waiting for something but I didn't know what. I had no idea she'd try something as crazy as this. I almost went by you."

"Clarke caught her throwing something overboard," Annie told him. "It must have been a flashlight. I didn't know what

226

was going on. Then she told me there was a gun over the side and pushed me in. I thought she'd tried to kill me." She said quickly, "Billy, she's in trouble. Clarke suspected she was up to something; he beat her up. She'll say I fell overboard, but he'll know. We've got to try and help her."

"I should get you home."

"No, Billy. He's a psycho; he'll kill her."

"You sure you're all right?"

"Fine. Just a little frozen."

"Do you know where they were going?"

"I heard them say something about Mexico. The boat was headed north."

"North? Then they're making for Novato and Clarke's plane."

He jumped for the wheel. "Get out of those wet things," he called. "See what you can find in the cabin." He took the boat roaring up the bay, his thoughts whirling with the propellers. He was pretty sure Clarke had crossed up the FBI—nobody would have expected anyone to drop a ten-pound steel box into the bay. The delivery plane would have radioed back immediately, but he doubted it would have done the FBI much good. With its lights out a boat could go a thousand places around the bay undetected. Clarke was smart. He wasn't just one jump ahead; he was leaps and bounds.

They caught the watchman just as he was locking the yacht-club gate. If he wondered where Verecker had picked up a companion, a disheveled young woman wrapped in a blanket, he kept his thoughts to himself.

They ran to the car, the road hurting Annie's bare feet, her shoes at the bottom of the bay. Verecker pulled an airline bag out of the trunk and slung it into the back seat. He told Annie to hop into the back and see if she could find anything in the bag she could fit into.

He swung the car onto Tiburon Boulevard and headed toward the highway. Over his shoulder he said, "How many on board that cruiser besides Clarke and the girl?"

"Five men."

"Is that everybody?"

"It's everybody I saw. They took me to a rundown apartment house in San Bruno or Millbrae and locked me up in a dingy little room. Ingrid looked after me."

"Seven altogether," Verecker said to the windshield. "Even if I'm right and they are headed for Novato I don't know what we can do. We could call the FBI, but they wouldn't dare move in, not till the passengers are safe. If Ingrid Arosund is in trouble all we can do is pick up the pieces."

"But she saved me, Billy. We owe her."

"She tried to save me, too." He told her about the attempt on his life and the slashed tires. "If it hadn't been for that idiot Ryder they would have still been hosing me out of this car."

"My God," Annie breathed.

"She called me next day and warned me about it, so we owe her more than you thought. But you can't balance off one person against hundreds, no matter what they've done for you." Annie climbed into the front seat. She was wearing a gray track suit and white socks and sneakers five sizes too big for her.

Verecker said, "Come to think of it I guess I risked screwing things up coming after you. But then that was a purely emotional reaction. All we can do is hope she can talk her way out of it."

They'd left the boat at the yacht harbor at Sausalito, hot-wired a car on a side street off Bridgeway and started north up 101.

Clarke held the car at a steady sixty. There was no need to hurry now; nobody knew where they were or where they were going. They'd got clean away with one of the biggest hauls of all time. After the incredible tension of the last few hours relief fanned the men like a cool breeze.

228

For the second time the big man said, "Twenty-five million bucks." He held a dirty gray stone in his hand, marveling at it. "They certainly don't look like much."

The bookie took it from him and returned it to the case at his feet. "When they clean it and cut it and polish it it'll look like the moon, don't worry. So will all the rest."

"Twenty-five million bucks."

The bookie chuckled. "Biggest payoff I ever had." He slapped his hand down on the skycap's leg. "Fantastic," he said.

The skycap nodded toward the pilot. "The pick-up was his idea."

"And it worked like a charm," said the bookie. "You're both smart cookies."

The big man settled himself in the seat. "First thing I'm gonna do is get me one of them big Cadillac cars. An' a house with a pool with broads runnin' around. South America maybe."

The fat man piped up. "Me, I'm getting the first plane to Mauritius, right after we get the dough. There's a flight from England. I checked."

The big man nudged the programmer. "How 'bout you?"

"What? Oh, like you said—a car, a house, you know." He lapsed back into melancholy silence.

"C'mon, will ya? Forget the dame. She slipped over the side, didn't she? Nobody shoved her or nothin'."

The bookie said, more for himself than the programmer, "Sure, that's right. We jerked forward, she hit the rail and over she went. We couldn't have gone back for her; we'd never have found her in the dark anyway. Just one of those things, that's all."

Clarke, who'd remained silent since they'd been driving, glanced at the girl beside him. She was bent forward a little, her arm across her stomach. "That's right, isn't it, baby?" he said. "Just one of those things. You were standing with her back there, so you know best what happened."

229

She wet her lips. "She stood up—I don't know why—to get a better look at the diamonds, I guess. Then she was gone, just like that."

"And there was nothing you could do to save her."

She looked at him coldly. "I was lying on the deck if you remember."

"Sorry about that, kid. I guess I was a little excited, but I could have sworn you had a flashlight in your hand."

In front of them a sports car winked its right rear light and took the turnoff to Sonoma and the Valley of the Moon. A delivery van barreled past them in the outside lane. Inside the car there was an electric silence. Clarke broke it. "Must have been seeing things. Funny, though, I got the crazy idea you were trying to signal somebody."

"She said she was going to be sick. I was helping her. There wasn't any flashlight. What do you mean?"

The pilot spoke to the rear-view mirror. "I didn't tell you guys, but just before we left tonight I caught her calling somebody from the drugstore."

The big man said, "Huh?"

"She said she was calling her sister."

"It was my sister. You know she's pregnant. I don't understand all this."

"What are you getting at?" the bookie asked.

Clarke broke the words up into little sections. "I mean I think there was a boat trailing us tonight. Oh, not the Feds, otherwise we'd have an escort right now. I think it was the guy you called, Ingrid. And I think you called Verecker."

"It's not true. I called my sister."

"And was it your sister in that other boat—the one that blinked its lights? I didn't think anything of it at first. I still didn't tie it when you said the girl was sick, but that was before I saw you ditch the flashlight. It was just a cute excuse to get out on deck, wasn't it, sweetie?" He took a hand off the wheel and brought it lazily around behind her. He closed his fingers on a handful of her hair and gently pulled down so that

230

her head came back and rested on the top of the seat. "Wasn't it, sweetie?" he said through his teeth. His eyes were still on the road; his hand tugged harder.

For a second she fought the tears back, tried to deny it, then all the tension and fear and pain of the last five hours seemed to erupt within her and her hands flew to her face and her body shook with great racking sobs.

The big man, more in surprise than anger, said, "Double-crossin' little bitch."

Everybody stared at her hard, even the programmer, his mouth set in a thin, tight line of disapproval.

The bookie thought about it. A minute ago he'd called the woman's death an unfortunate tragedy. But he hadn't been kidding anyone, least of all himself. Her accident had seemed like a lucky, guilt-free way of solving a tough problem. He knew they couldn't have let her off that boat alive, not after she'd got a close-up of them. It was true the FBI would identify them sooner or later; the passengers had got a good look at three of them after all—the stewardess, the two baggage men, possibly the skycap—but it would have taken time—time they needed to lose themselves. But they weren't going to have it. Now, instead of just smuggling a suitcase off at Cuxhaven, they were going to have to smuggle themselves off as well. It wasn't going to be easy.

The girl's face was still buried in her hands. Clarke snickered. "I can sure pick 'em."

A mile farther on he swung the car off the highway and onto a little feeder road that ran through an open gate and up to long, high, windowless structures, a paved runway stretching in front of them, a double row of lights stitching its sides. Clarke parked the car beside a coffee shop and led the way across the strip toward a plane standing dark in front of a hangar. In one hand he carried the suitcase he'd taken from the bookie; the other held firmly onto the girl's elbow.

"I'm really disappointed in you, baby. You really could have screwed us, you know that?"

231

In a quivering voice, tears still on her face, she said, "You don't understand. Verecker only wanted his wife back. He wasn't going to bring the police. I made him give me his promise he'd come alone."

"His promise? And you believed him? You could have been selling us out, baby."

"I wouldn't do anything to hurt you, Lee. You know that."

"You told him about his car being booby-trapped, didn't you?"

"It didn't make any sense killing him."

"What's the matter with you? You were there, you heard. We figured he was going to make a deal with the airline. O.K., so we were wrong. We didn't know that; we had to cover ourselves. You and your Florence Nightingale act could have landed us all with a one-way ticket to Quentin."

He pushed her in front of him to the plane, unlocked the cabin door, climbed in and tried the engine. Twice it spluttered briefly; the third time it fired and held. He revved it, throttled back, jumped down onto the strip and motioned the men inside. The big man was last. As he put a foot on the step he spotted something.

"Hey."

His arm pointed to a convertible that was rolling to a stop next to the car they'd stolen. Two figures scrambled out, looked over at them for a second, then bolted into the coffee shop.

Clarke whipped his eyes back to the girl; her head was shaking in a frantic denial.

He said one word sharply, coldly triumphant: "Verecker."

"C'mon," the big man cried and clambered up into the cabin.

Very precisely, Clarke lowered the suitcase to the ground and stepped back a pace so that a good six feet separated him from the stewardess.

She yelled over the roar of the engine, "I didn't tell him, Lee, I didn't tell him we were coming here. I swear it. He must have guessed. I didn't—" She broke off, her eyes on his hand.

It had come out of his jacket holding a gun.

She backed away, hypnotized by the small, round, unblinking eye staring at her body.

His laugh surprised her. "You really went for the long bomb, didn't you? You're cuter than I thought—way cuter. That must have been some phone call you two had. Verecker gets his wife back and you and him split twenty-five million dollars. Only something went wrong. What happened, he miss us at the dock or something? I'd say he's a little late."

Above him the bookie yelled, "Come on, the place's gonna be crawling with cops."

"No, no cops," the pilot said evenly. He spoke to the air in front of him, his words caught up and sucked away by the engine noise. "He's not going to share those rocks with anybody except Ingrid here, right, Ingrid?"

She gave a small cry like a wounded animal in a trap, turned and ran clumsily toward the buildings.

The gun came up and his finger squeezed the trigger. He cursed, fumbled at it, flipped the safety off and tried again. The hammer clicked on two empty chambers. The third and fourth went off with high, sharp cracks, one, two, and the girl stumbled as if she'd been shoved from behind. Her knees buckled and her body thwacked hard on the cement.

She lay quite still, a tangle of arms and legs. She looked as though she'd fallen from a roof.

The big man charged out of the plane, the bookie behind him. They jumped to the strip and pulled up short as the gun swung around on them.

The bookie cried urgently, "We've got to go. Now. Put the bag in and let's go."

Clarke looked at them crazily, held the gun on them. His lips came back on his teeth. "Verecker's coming out here in a minute," he was yelling at the top of his voice. "He wants that suitcase. He's going to get his chance."

233

The two men shouted back at him, pleaded with him. The minutes ticked by.

"If he's coming after the suitcase, why hasn't he come?" The bookie pointed furiously. "He's still in there, isn't he? He's calling the cops, you damn fool."

Clarke seemed to shake himself, straightened a little as if he'd just emerged from a tunnel. He wiped a hand over his face and examined it, then glanced behind him. Verecker's car looked empty; the lights burned in the coffee shop.

He tucked the gun into his belt and reached for the suitcase. The big man beat him to it; he snatched it up, threw it into the cabin and jumped in after it. The bookie scrambled up next and Clarke followed, slamming the door closed. He taxied the plane down the runway and turned at the other end.

A moment later the plane began its run into the wind.

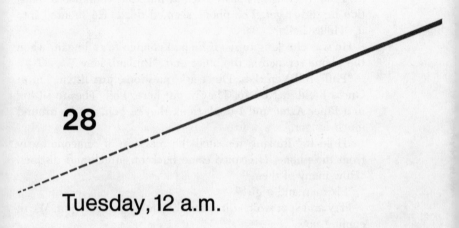

28

Tuesday, 12 a.m.

They had spotted the gang by the plane even before they were out of the car. They ran for the coffee shop.

Verecker stuffed himself into a phone booth, grabbing for his wallet and the card Rinlaub had given him. As his fingers flew over the dial he wondered if they had an all-night answering service.

The phone was picked up after the first ring. Verecker gabbled into it. "This is William Verecker. I've got to talk to Rinlaub, quick."

The crisp voice on the other end gave him a number to call. He hung up, dug for more coins and dialed again.

"Calair. May I help you?"

"Listen, this is an emergency. My name's Verecker, have you got that? Verecker. I've got to talk to Phil Rinlaub. Now."

"Rinlaub," the voice repeated. "One second." The voice went

away and was replaced by a series of clicks. Verecker drummed his fingers on the phone directory, peered through the glass at Annie peering anxiously back at him. She mouthed a question he didn't get. The phone seemed dead. He shouted into it, "Hello, hello?"

He was checking to see if he had change to call again when the phone scraped at the other end. "Rinlaub here."

"Phil? Bill Verecker. Don't ask questions, just listen. I'm at Gnoss Field at Novato. They're out here, Phil. They're sitting in a Piper Aztec and I don't think they're going to be around much longer."

"Hold it." Rinlaub repeated the message to someone away from the phone. His voice came back on, quick and distinct. "How many of them?"

"Six men and a girl."

"Try and spot which direction they take. You stay put. We're coming now."

"Phil, I've got a hunch they'll be heading for Mexico."

"Maybe. Hang in there anywhere. And, Billy, we found the passengers."

"The pass—? Where?"

"They never left the airport. Well, some did, some didn't. Tell you later."

The phone clicked in his ear. Verecker stared at it like a dead thing in his hand. "Never *left* it?"

The door of the phone booth folded back. Annie had seen the astonished look on his face and the way he'd taken the phone from his ear. "What is it? What's the matter?"

It broke the spell. He grabbed her hand and pulled her after him across the floor and out of the door.

The plane was taxiing away from them, almost at the end of the runway.

They saw something else on the runway—something lying crumpled in front of the hangar where the plane had been. A naked bulb under a metal shade shone down on yellow hair spread out like a sunburst.

Annie closed her eyes, her stomach turning over.

"The bastards," Verecker spat.

They jumped for the car, took off in a tire-burning shriek across the strip and pulled up a few feet from the girl.

She was moaning softly, her mouth against the concrete, her left wrist smashed and bloody. A moist stain the size of a saucer had seeped through her jacket over her left shoulder blade.

Verecker left Annie bending over her. "Get an ambulance," he called and dived back into the car, shoved his foot to the floor, cut across the runway and headed straight for the plane that was gathering speed, coming down the strip toward him.

Explaining his actions later, he said that doing a thing like that had been strictly a reflex action. He knew the passengers were safe, the stewardess out of it, and a plane containing a gang of kidnappers with a fortune in uncut diamonds was about to disappear into the clouds. Besides, he'd figured the risk was mostly on the pilot's side. A car could be maneuvered ten times easier than a small plane, especially one carrying just about its maximum load. The pilot had to know that with a full tank he was sitting on dynamite—a head-on would have been disastrous for both of them, but, psychologically, much more so for the man in the plane. As Verecker saw it, they were going to play a pretty one-sided version of Chicken.

But if he'd known Clarke a little better, he'd never have attempted it.

The plane was still picking up speed, coming down like an express. Verecker switched his hi-beam on, trying to dazzle the pilot, expecting to see the plane swerve, slow, do something.

It came on.

The wind rushed underneath it and the wings rose an inch, seemed to stretch themselves. The tail started to lift off the ground.

In a cold sweat Verecker knew that if anybody was going to swerve aside it was going to have to be him. Then a second later he saw that there might not be any need. There was an inch of air under the wheels; the plane was taking off.

For an insane moment he thought of ramming it, but even

as it occurred to him he realized that that was hopeless—the gap between the plane and the car wasn't closing fast enough, even though they were roaring toward each other.

The plane was going to pass a few feet over his head.

Right in the middle of a fit of frustrated anger, he got an idea.

He moved faster than he'd ever moved in his life, flipped off the hood catches at the top of the windshield and jabbed at the hood button.

A motor whirled; the hood rose and started up.

Wind rushed over the windshield like a fury, bellowed the hood, slowed the car as if it had been lassoed. The hood lifted higher; the cloth split and blew out like a sail in a storm, leaving the metal frame rising slowly above the seats.

The plane was only feet away, its wheels starting to fold into the fuselage.

As the car flashed underneath the top of the frame caught the plane's left tire just enough to bring the left wing swooping down toward the ground.

The pilot had only a few feet of air to correct in.

It wasn't enough.

The right wing dipped too far and smacked the runway. The plane seemed to pivot on the wing like a boomerang thrown through the air, slewed crazily around and crunched into the strip in a tremendous, tearing, popping scream of ruptured struts and ripped fabric. It sheared off both propellers, flipped over, ground sickeningly into the concrete for another twenty feet and came to rest on its back, crushed like a swatted insect.

Verecker fought the car out of a skid, braked, and brought it around on two wheels.

Up the runway red lights flashed and he caught the wailing note of sirens.

Three police cruisers skidded to a stop at the wreck while he was still fifty yards away. He saw the policemen, lit up by their own headlights, charging out of the cars at the run, grabbing bodies, dragging them from the wreck. One side of the plane had opened back on itself like a sardine can—the only reason they got them out in time.

Verecker was running for the plane as a patrolman hauled the last man out, hitched him onto his shoulder and ran at a staggering trot toward the cruiser. "That's all," he yelled. "Get back."

Verecker ignored him and ran to the wreck. His foot stumbled against something and he went down, belly flopping into a spreading pool of gasoline. He got up, winded, his clothes soaked like the wick of a lamp. He reached the gaping wound in the side of the plane. The cabin was a jumble of broken seats hanging like bats from the floor that was now the ceiling.

At the front of the cabin, lying half in, half out of a busted window, was a cloth suitcase.

He grabbed for it, tried to drag it out.

It wouldn't come.

He tugged harder, wondering how he could be so crazy. He was on borrowed time already. In the flick of an eyelid he could become a screaming sheet of flame.

But he didn't let go of the handle.

He tugged, jerked at it, finally stepped right into the wreck and pried it loose from the twisted pedals.

He struggled out with it, amazed he wasn't being incinerated. He made the door, made the strip, made his car. He rammed it into low and tore away.

Twenty feet behind him there was a loud, oxygen-sucking *harrumff* and a thousand suns came out.

He swiveled his head, shielding his eyes—a cresting tidal wave of fire was trying to burn down the sky.

There was an explosion, incredibly loud and incredibly long, then slowly the ink ran back into the night and the darkness closed around spluttering flames no bigger than a Christmas fireplace.

Over near the hangars, an ambulance was picking up the stewardess, Annie with her. It howled away and Verecker followed.

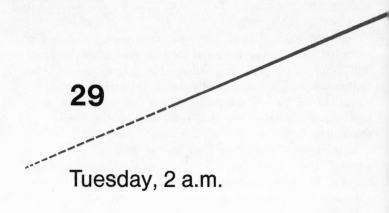

29

Tuesday, 2 a.m.

They sat together in the middle of a row of seats, alone in the room except for the nurse writing behind the reception desk. They sat like survivors of a shipwreck waiting for news of their fellow passengers. Verecker's clothes were soaked and torn and his face streaked with oil where he'd wiped a hand over his forehead. Annie's hair was still a damp, shapeless mop, and the gray track suit hung on her like a collapsed tent. She had her arms tucked under Verecker's and her head cradled against his shoulder. Her eyes were closed, furrowed at the edges as though she were having a bad dream. They'd been sitting like that for an hour, ever since Rinlaub and a group of FBI men had arrived, told them to stay put and had gone in to talk to the surgeons. Rinlaub wouldn't answer any questions; he'd said they both had a lot of explaining to do but they'd do it later.

A nurse brought them coffee, then a second cup half an hour after that.

Another twenty minutes went by before Rinlaub walked back into the room. "She's O.K.," he said. "The doctor's going to let us talk to her in a minute."

Annie, who'd sat up in her seat, slumped back down in it. "Thank heavens."

"And the others?" Verecker asked.

"Everybody's breathing, although between them they broke just about every bone in the human body. The guy who was flying the plane is the worst off—multiple skull fracture— but they say he'll pull through." He looked at the suitcase at their feet. "I see you picked up a souvenir."

Verecker didn't acknowledge the comment. Instead he said soberly, "Phil, for hours I've been sitting here going out of my mind wondering if I heard right on the phone. You found the passengers at the airport?"

"That's right."

"But where?"

"Locked in the boiler room underneath the terminal."

"Three hundred and sixty people in a boiler room?"

"There were only sixty people in there—just the First Class and the crew."

Verecker mouthed an unspoken "What?"

In an awed voice Annie said, "The Economy Class is still missing?"

"Yes, but not in the way you think."

Verecker said, "Phil, please . . . "

Rinlaub dropped into a chair next to them. "We were at the airport tonight getting everything ready. At about ten-fifteen there was a godawful explosion in one of the maintenance hangars. We came running and found a stripped Calair 747 with its head blown off. A bomb had exploded in one of the forward washrooms. Somebody had enough sense to take a look at the registration number and guess what?"

Verecker said, "You're joking."

241

Annie was having a hard time, too. "It was in the maintenance hangar all along?"

"In about two hundred different pieces," Rinlaub told her.
"The engines off, the tail off, the undercarriage—a complete
overhaul job. There was another 747 there in the same
condition."

"But how come nobody thought of looking there before?"

"Believe me, we're all kicking ourselves."

"Still," Annie said, trying to make it less painful for him, "if
you're looking for a plane you think's in the Sierras, who's going
to look in a hangar in San Francisco?"

"Thanks, Annie, but we should have. Anyway, seeing the
plane was there, it followed that the passengers were, too. We
found them fifteen minutes later."

Verecker couldn't understand it. "But you said only the First
Class and the crew."

"And twenty passengers from Economy. We searched every
inch of the airport—the supply hangars, the terminals, the
tower, even the nearby hotels. There wasn't a sign of the rest,
so we had to assume they were never kidnapped."

Aghast, Verecker said, "You're not suggesting that they were
in on it, are you? Two hundred and eighty people?"

Rinlaub scratched his nose. "Wild, isn't it?"

None of the words Annie started to say seemed to fit. "But . . .
so many people . . . And the plane . . . we know it took off.
How did it get back without anyone knowing?"

"That's what we hope the girl is going to tell us. Now you
answer me a question: How did you trail them here?"

Verecker started with the call from Clarke. "I thought Annie
was at her aunt's in San Jose, so when they called I assumed
they were trying to ransom our landlady's dog."

"Naturally," Rinlaub said.

"I offered them twenty-five dollars."

"That's all?" Annie asked.

Verecker patted her arm. "If I'd known it was you I would

242

have doubled the offer." He turned back to Rinlaub. "So apparently, in a fit of pique, they decided to kill me."

"How?"

"They cut the brakes on my car."

"What saved you?"

"My neighbor across the street. He slashed my tires."

"He spotted the gang working on your car?"

"Oh no, he just does things like that."

"Uh huh."

"Ingrid Arosund, the girl in there, called to warn me about it and tell me they'd got Annie. She had some plan to get her away, but didn't have time to tell me."

Annie chimed in. "She didn't have time to tell me, either, so it came as quite a surprise when I found myself swimming in the bay."

Verecker picked it up. "Annie said they were heading north, so I figured Novato, where I knew Clarke kept his plane."

Rinlaub got up from his chair and jammed his hands in his pockets. He said, mild admonishment in his voice, "You really should have told me about that golf course sooner, Bill. It's something we could have checked on. I'm not saying it would have solved the thing for us, but it was a lead and, as it turns out, a pretty good one."

Verecker made a little fatalistic movement with his hands. "I know, Phil, and I'm sorry. It's just that I wanted to go to you with all the ends tied up. Then, when they looked as if they'd never tie up, I got to thinking my whole theory was crazy and I'd be just wasting your time."

Rinlaub started to reply but stopped when a man, the same one Verecker and Annie had talked to at the lake, walked into the room. He nodded to them both, ran his eyes over them. They'd seen him arrive, but he'd rushed right by them then. Now he smiled and said, "Still helping us out, I see."

Rinlaub introduced him as Donald Rawlins, then took him aside and spoke to him privately for a few minutes. They came back and Verecker expected the man to give him hell, but all he said was that he'd like to speak to them both later, tomorrow maybe, if that would be convenient. Then he said they were going in to talk to the girl and invited them along.

Verecker indicated the suitcase and asked Rawlins if they shouldn't put it some place where it wouldn't get lost. Rawlins called a patrolman over to look after it and then steered them out of the room.

On their way down the antiseptic corridor, shoes squeaking on the white cushioned flooring, Annie asked about the stewardess. Rawlins told her that whoever shot her was either a lousy shot or his gun fired to the left. He'd busted her wrist and put a slug through her shoulder. She had a lot of pain but, compared to the others, she was fine.

A policeman got off a chair at their approach and opened a door for them and they went in.

Ingrid Arosund was sitting up in bed, the back of it winched up to support her. Her left side was swathed in a layer of bandages an inch thick and her arm rested in a sling. Underneath the strip of pink surgical tape across her nose her face was as colorless as the crisp white sheets that lapped her waist.

Annie went to her. "How are you feeling, Ingrid?"

She didn't answer.

Annie said awkwardly, "I want to thank you for what you did for me."

The girl replied as if Annie had apologized for something. "Forget it."

They seated themselves on chairs grouped around the bed. The door opened and two other men, dressed similarly to Rawlins, came in and stood at the back of the room.

Rawlins got right down to it. "Miss Arosund, the fact that you probably saved Mrs. Verecker's life and warned Mr. Verecker about his car is going to go a long way for you in court. If you'll cooperate with us and tell us what we want to know we might be able to do a little more for you."

Imperceptibly, the girl nodded her head.

Rawlins asked her, "You know about the plane crash?"

"Yes."

"There were six men in that plane. Are there any more involved in this?"

"No."

Rawlins leaned forward. "Besides the crew, you kidnapped only the First Class passengers and twenty from the Economy Class, is that correct?"

"Yes."

The entire room seemed to relax. Rawlins sat back and unbuttoned his jacket. "Miss Arosund, we'd like to know how those people got into the boiler room and how the plane got into the hangar. We found that, too, of course."

In a flat voice the stewardess asked him where he wanted her to start.

"Where did it start for you?"

"When Lee told me about it."

Rawlins looked over his shoulder at one of the agents at the back of the room. He held a notebook in his hand. "Lee Clarke," the man said, reading. "The plane was registered in his name. We found a gun on him."

Rawlins asked the girl, "Was he the one who shot you?"

"Yes. He thought I'd made a deal with Mr. Verecker to keep the diamonds."

"Clarke is your boy friend?"

She said dully, "We're engaged."

"I see. Go on."

"He answered an ad for a pilot who flew his own plane. The bookie ran it. I don't know his name."

"Describe him."

"Bald, about fifty."

"James Carlisle," the man with the notebook said.

"But you knew he was a bookie?"

"Yes. He put up the money."

"Then this was all his idea?"

"No. The skycap thought it up."

245

Everybody traded glances. Verecker couldn't stop himself from saying, "A skycap? You mean the whole thing?"

The agent flipped a page in his notebook. "Two of those men were carrying Calair ID cards and there's another man, a Negro. Would that be him?"

"Yes."

"George Spencer."

The girl continued. "The plan called for a stewardess. I wasn't crazy about the idea, but Lee insisted. I knew if I said no he'd leave me. I didn't want that to happen." She dropped her eyes, her voice trailing away.

"Go on," Rawlins prompted.

"The bookie recruited a computer expert and the skycap brought in the two baggage handlers."

Rawlins flicked his eyes to the back of the room. The agent looked up from his book. "Check," he said.

Rawlins came back to the girl. "Seven in all, then. But you also needed close on three hundred other people . . . "

"The bookie got them. He said they were small-time horse players who all owed him money. Not much, a hundred dollars maybe. He canceled their debts and gave them fifty dollars' credit on top of that."

"And in return they were to help out on the kidnap."

"They didn't know it was a kidnap. They probably thought we were after the baggage or something."

Rawlins frowned. "I don't understand. How could they not know?"

The girl didn't appear to have heard him. She was into the story now, telling it step by step as if she were going over it for her own benefit. "Three months ago he gave every one of those people money to buy a ticket to New York and told them the airline, the flight and the date. He got them to spread the buying out over a month. He chose the people carefully, real players he said they were. Every one of them went through with it."

"Exactly how many?"

"Two hundred and eighty-two. We left room for twenty genuine passengers in Economy so the airline would get some phone calls from people wondering where they were. We knew you'd check on them, so they had to be genuine."

Rinlaub said, "That's one of the things that puzzled me: eighteen phone calls out of an entire Economy section didn't seem enough."

"We wondered about it, too," Rawlins admitted.

The stewardess shifted painfully in her bed and looked around her. Annie got up and poured her some water. The girl winced reaching for it, took the glass and drank from it.

She continued in the same flat monotone. "The skycap and I had tickets, too. We were about the last to board. He didn't even sit down; he went up the stairs to the First Class lounge and when a stewardess went up after him he pulled a razor out of his flight bag and held it against her throat and got into the flight deck that way. Then he ordered the captain to call all the cabin crew up into the lounge."

Rawlins said, "So the plane was hijacked even before the doors were closed."

"It had to be. When the last stewardess had gone upstairs I took off my coat—I had my uniform underneath—walked into the First Class and made an announcement. I told them the plane was having engine trouble and we were going to transfer them to another flight."

"And they believed you?"

"Why not? It's true my uniform wasn't the same, but I could have been a ground hostess, something like that."

Rinlaub confirmed it. "Sure, people will always do anything a uniform tells them. They never ask why."

"Then what?"

"I went into Economy with the names of the twenty genuine passengers, read them out, said there'd been a mix-up and they'd have to change planes. I told them that to make up for the inconvenience we'd fly them First Class."

"And, of course, they went for it."

The girl nodded.

Rinlaub asked her where she'd got the names from, and she told him the computer man had got them. He'd worked with the airline at one time, so it wasn't any trouble for him.

"How did you get the passengers off the plane?"

"They way they got on—up the covered walkway. I took them to the end of the finger and down the emergency stairs."

"But how about the airline personnel? What did you tell them?"

"There was only the walkway operator to take care of. The rest of the personnel were at the other end of the finger at the departure gate."

Rinlaub agreed with her. "That's right. There'd be only one guy to get past."

"I waited at the door. One of the baggage men came up the stairs and into the walkway. I signaled when everybody was ready, and he got the operator out of the way for a few minutes. That's all I needed."

Rawlins said sharply to the men behind him, "I thought we checked everybody who had anything to do with that flight."

An embarrassed voice replied, "I'm sorry, sir, I didn't even know about that guy."

Rinlaub suggested that even if they had checked on him he couldn't have told them much—certainly nothing that would have pointed to what had actually happened. What was puzzling him was why the Calair staff down on the ramp didn't spot them coming down the stairs. The girl told him that the skycap had ordered the pilot, who had radio contact with the ramp crew, to ask them to check something on the other side of the plane. Rawlins accepted this and asked her what had happened after she'd got the passengers down the stairs.

"I told them we didn't have a bus available just then, so we'd take a short cut under the terminal to the other departure gate. There were a few grumbles but they went along. I led them down the stairs and into the passage and opened the door to the boiler room—the skycap had had a key made. I told them there was another stewardess waiting through the door at the end and to go on in. I closed the door after the last person and locked it."

Verecker couldn't keep quiet any longer. "But that's fantastic. How did you know nobody would go near the place for a week?"

"We took the chance. The skycap said the only reason anybody would do down there would be if the boiler went on the blink. And it was a pretty new boiler."

"But how did they survive down there for a week?"

Rinlaub answered the question. "There's a basin and a toilet in the back, so they had water and some kind of facilities. And there was a case of beans and a couple of dozen plastic spoons that the skycap must have left for them, right?"

"That's right."

"They slept on some broken seats that were stored there from the old terminal. They said they tried everything to get out— yelled themselves hoarse, tried for days to break down the doors—but nothing worked. As you might imagine those people were in pretty shoddy shape when we found them."

Impatiently, Rawlins said, "Let's get on. Miss Arosund, after you got the passengers off, what did you do?"

"I went home."

"And the skycap?"

"Everything went the way he'd figured. He made the captain tell the tower they were checking oil pressure in one of the engines. That gave me time to get the passengers off. Then he ordered the doors closed and forced the captain to go through the normal takeoff pattern. He gave him a compass course that would take the plane over Tahoe, then when they got near the lake he ordered the plane down, below radar level. Then he made him turn the plane around and fly back the way they'd come. He ordered the plane up to regular height again and gave the captain a new transponder code."

Annie appealed to Rinlaub. "A what?"

"A transponder. It's a radar device under the plane that

249

tells traffic control an aircraft's flight number and altitude."
Then he asked the girl, "What do you mean, a new one?"

She said, "We went out as Calair 422. We came back as
Calair 73."

"You came back as a different *flight?*"

Verecker and Rinlaub locked eyes. They both wore the same
expression—a dismayed realization that verged on pain.

Rawlins took a Kleenex out of his pocket for something to do.
He touched it to his nose and put it away again. "I want to get
this straight," he said. "You went off the radarscope flying east.
You came back on it as another flight flying west." He turned
to Rinlaub. "But as I understand it, when a plane flies across
the country a lot of different control centers look after it, each
one seeing it safely over its sector, then passing it on to the next
man. Am I wrong?"

"No, you're absolutely right."

"Then wouldn't the controller wonder at the new flight that
suddenly popped onto his screen? Nobody handed it on to
him. Why didn't he report it?"

Rinlaub said, "For one thing it's a fringe area up there—
strange things can happen, like radar images that look like
planes but aren't—and that works in reverse, too."

"Even with a transponder?"

"Not every aircraft has one. Also they were busy looking for
Calair 422 traveling east—not Calair 73 traveling west. Nobody
would ever have made the connection. I'm still having trouble
myself."

"It that the way you figured it?" Rawlins asked the girl.

"Something like that."

"How did you fix it when you reached the airport? They
weren't expecting any Calair 73."

"Yes they were." Rinlaub was way ahead of him. "The computer man, remember?"

The girl said, "He fixed it so the flight appeared on the day's
roster. He made it a charter flight from New York so it wouldn't
conflict with any regular scheduled flight."

There was a long second's pause while that sank in. Rawlins asked her what had happened then.

"Before the plane reached the terminal the skycap gave some instructions over the PA. He asked the first fifty people in Economy to move into the First Class section and collect the First Class baggage when the plane unloaded; they were to collect their own as well. He told them to take the First Class stuff straight from the airport to a parking lot in San Francisco."

"I see. So when the doors opened fifty people walked out of the First Class, two hundred and thirty-two from Economy. They claimed the bags, left the terminal and that was that—just another flight come in."

They started filling in details themselves.

Rinlaub said, "And the crew had to go along with it because one of the girls had a razor against her throat."

Verecker said, "And you needed the baggage men because all those bags were ticketed for New York and you had to have somebody who wouldn't point that out to anyone."

"They probably tore them off as they unloaded them from the containers," Rinlaub proposed. "That way, without the attached checks, nobody could have disputed anyone's claim on the baggage."

Rawlins said to him, "Only two baggage men for a 747?"

"It's not unheard of. It works out that way sometimes. But that's a detail they could have controlled easily enough." He said to the girl, "The computer man got the plane into the hangar, too, didn't he?"

She nodded.

Annie looked around. "I don't understand."

Rinlaub explained how the computer kept a record of maintenance for each aircraft. The programmer had juggled the tapes so that the 747 was due for an eighteen-month overhaul. It had probably gone into the hangar thirty minutes after it landed.

Rawlins wanted to know how the crew and skycap got off the plane. It turned out that the skycap had told the captain

251

what had happened to the First Class, and to prove it he had sent a stewardess down to verify it before takeoff. He also knew the captain would have to compensate for the lightened nose. When they landed he'd told the captain to go ahead and report in normally but to bring the crew straight down to the ramp afterward. He'd warned him that if he didn't play it straight, if any of them said anything or gave any sign, they'd be responsible for starting a massacre. They had no alternative but to go along with it. They'd turned in a fake log, met the skycap on the ramp and been locked in the boiler room with the passengers.

Rawlins looked around at the man at the back of the room. The man had his head down scribbling. He turned back to the stewardess, who was reaching for the glass of water, Annie helping her.

"Who stole the ticket duplicates and the flight manifests?"

The girl sipped with closed eyes, ran her tongue around moistened lips. "I did. I knew where the ticket stubs were filed in the Operations room and where to find all the copies of the manifest. It wasn't hard getting them. In a blue skirt and white blouse I was just another busy traffic agent."

"And, of course, the programmer wiped the names from the computer."

"Yes."

Rinlaub asked her about the watches and things. "When did you get them?"

"Lee had given the baggage men his gun. They were following on my heels. They let themselves into the boiler room, chose the nearest five passengers, got their names and took something from each of them. Then they drove over to the golf course where Lee was going to land and lit flares for him."

Verecker thumped his knee. "So I was right. But I thought he'd brought somebody in."

"No, he just picked up the watches and flew them to Carson City, drove to the lake, wrapped them and mailed them from

252

there. That way the package was mailed about two hours after the plane had gone off the radar, which we figured would make you think the plane was somewhere in the area."

"Which is also why you dumped the First Class baggage in that lake nearby," Rawlins suggested.

The stewardess seemed surprised. "You found it? The bookie didn't think you would, but he dumped it there just in case. Like I said, the people took it to a parking lot downtown. The bookie was there with a rented van. He piled the bags in and drove up to the Sierras that night and ditched them. He figured that if by chance you should find them it should be some place near the lake."

She delivered the last piece of information with her eyes blinking irregularly, a barely perceptible fuzziness creeping into her words.

Verecker didn't seem to notice; he plowed ahead and asked her where she'd been the day they'd come to see her. The girl said that Clarke had told her about them; she'd seen them from the kitchen window and hid out on the fire escape.

"Just two more questions, Miss Arosund, then we'll let you sleep," Rawlins said. "You feel up to it?"

Eyes closed, the girl said yes.

"One of the suitcases from the Economy Class made it to New York. We found a couple of house bricks inside. Any idea why?"

Her lids opened heavily. "I think a lot of the people the bookie got were pretty down at heel. They wouldn't have many spare clothes to put into a bag, so maybe some of them faked it."

"One last question: Where were they going in that plane tonight?"

"Mexico. Then a freighter to Europe. The plan was to have the stones cut in Antwerp, then sold on the London exchange."

Rawlins got up and the others followed him. "Thank you, Miss Arosund. We'll be talking to you again. And, as I said, we'll do everything we can for you."

253

She didn't reply. Her eyes were closed and she was breathing deeper, a small frown on her face.

As they trooped out of the room a starched nurse gave them a dirty look and went in after them. They walk in a thoughtful group down the corridor and into the reception area. The nurse who had been behind the desk was gone.

"A skycap." Verecker was still grappling with it. "I thought at least an MIT professor."

"It was a beautiful idea," Rawlins admitted, "and they might just have got away with it if it hadn't been for the bomb."

"How about that?" Annie asked. "Who'd want to blow up a plane in a hangar?"

"I think we'll find it was put on board before the plane went into maintenance. It was probably a home-made job—pretty unpredictable things. This one apparently decided to go off a week later than it was supposed to."

Verecker grunted. "The traditional quirk of fate. But instead of something small like the red traffic light or the changed lock it was an almighty explosion. At least it was in proportion to the size of the scheme."

Rawlins said to him, "By the way, I haven't thanked you yet. We would have got those men sooner or later but you certainly saved us a chore. Whatever made you go after the plane, anyway? You could have been killed pulling a stunt like that."

"Mr. Rawlins, I wish I could say I was acting as a public-spirited citizen, but it wouldn't be true. I saw twenty-five million bucks about to fly away, and I knew the insurance company would be grateful to whoever recovered it." He grinned. "See? I was motivated solely by greed."

Rawlins looked over at Rinlaub. "You didn't tell him?"

Rinlaub had something in his eye.

"Tell me what?" A sudden taste of ashes came into his mouth and a terrible, unthinkable suspicion crept into his skull and blossomed like a paper flower in water. In a shaky voice of doom he said, "I think I'm just about to have a severe attack of Verecker's Luck."

254

"I'm sorry, buddy," Rinlaub apologized. "I should have told you earlier."

Verecker saved him the trouble now. "You faked the rocks," he said miserably.

Rawlins explained. "We had a dummy set made up in the event something would break. We switched them at the last moment. We gave orders all along the line to move in when the drop was made, but we never figured the bay."

Verecker hadn't heard a word; he was still stunned. "I risked my neck for a case of marbles." Annie took his arm. He looked at her, sighed and said, "What the hell, money never bought anything except security anyway."

Rawlins was holding out his hand. "We'll be talking to you again, Mr. Verecker, Mrs. Verecker."

Rinlaub said, "I'll call you tomorrow, Bill. So long, Annie." They left them alone in the reception room.

A new nurse came out and moved in behind the desk. "Can I help you?"

Mournfully Verecker said, "Do you do brain transplants here?"

Annie propelled him out of the door to the car. The frame was twisted and bent where the plane's wheel had struck it, and it stood half folded up on itself three feet above the back seat. The hood had flapped itself into tatters, like a kite caught at the top of a telegraph pole.

Verecker said, "It looks like a dinosaur ate it."

"Will it be all right to drive back in?"

"It'll be a little cold for you. Is there anything else in my bag you can put on?"

"Just your jock strap."

"Well, it would keep your ears warm."

"Come on," Annie said, "we'll turn the heater on full blast."

They drove the half mile to the highway and headed south for the city, both thinking about the same thing, taking it apart and putting it back together to see how everything fitted.

"You know, Billy, it was a marvelous plan, but they did have

255

incredible luck. A lot of things could have gone wrong but nothing did until it was almost all over. For example, all those people buying tickets. Wouldn't an airline think it strange that almost three hundred people had bought tickets across the counter for the same flight—no travel agents?"

"Strange, maybe, but not unprecedented. A lot of people like to make their own arrangements. Besides, what were they going to suspect? One or two people on a flight might be potential hijackers, but an entire Economy Class?"

"How about those people, Billy? Will they be caught?"

"I don't see how. The bookie's the only one who knows who they are and I doubt he'll talk, being a bookie."

Annie had another thought. "Rawlins never got around to the fake watch. I guess some guy lost his wife's anniversary present and had one made up exactly like it so she wouldn't notice."

"I guess," Verecker said, not particularly interested. He was thinking about something else.

She said gently, "You were awfully close, Billy."

"Close but no cigar. And I'll tell you what really hurts—the fact that there was another 747 in that maintenance hangar. Remember when you said a 747 was a jumbo, an elephant, and where would you hide an elephant? There was an obvious answer I must have been crazy not to see: You hide one elephant behind another elephant."

"Sure. It's the obvious answers you never think of."

A mile farther on she asked him what was going to happen to the gang.

"Are you kidding? With time off for good behavior they'll be out of jail in two hundred years."

She sank lower in her seat, closer to the heater. She tilted her head and gazed at the stars, dim blue on dark black, clouds like shadows on a hot day moving through them. She said, "I'll tell you one thing. By hijacking that plane they saved a lot of lives."

"How do you mean?"

"The bomb. If that plane hadn't been stolen and was flying

256

a scheduled service, that bomb might have gone off in the air with hundreds of people on board instead of in a hangar with nobody on board."

"Hey, you know that's right? A smart young lawyer could build quite a defense around that. If the nuts started calling for the death penalty or torture or something, that's just the kind of thing you'd need. Yeah," Verecker said, warming to it, "however you slice it the gang saved a planeload of people. That's got to count for a lot. I just hope the bookie has some money left. I'm not working for free."

Annie started laughing.

"What's so funny? I'm going to need something to do, aren't I? Now that we're not going to the Riviera."

257

30

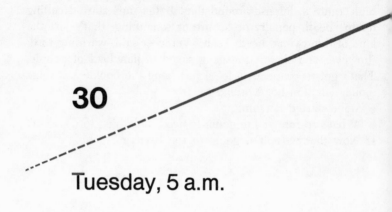

Tuesday, 5 a.m.

As they pulled up outside the house they were surprised to see Ryder standing at the curb. He had on pajamas and dressing gown and was holding a wheezing, overweight Dachshund on the end of a lead.

His eyes opened wide as he took in the wrecked top of the convertible. He asked Verecker, "You having trouble with somebody else on the block?"

Verecker got out and came toward him.

The man backed up, shortening his grip on the lead. "Take it easy, Verecker. One word from me to Fritz . . . "

Verecker grabbed his hand and shook it warmly. "Ryder, old man, thanks a million for the tire job."

"I told you I'd do it. I . . . Thanks?"

Verecker winked at him. "Boy, you can really slash 'em. Those babies were flat to the ground."

258

Ryder disengaged his hand and took another step backward. He didn't like this at all.

Verecker pointed his finger at the sidewalk, shaking his head in admiration. "I mean, they were down to the rims."

Ryder's face was a monument to non-comprehension. He reined in the dog, turned brokenly and walked back inside, a beaten man.

Annie said, "I don't think Mr. Ryder gets many kudos. I think you shocked him."

They went into the house and into Annie's apartment. Verecker made straight for the sofa and flopped down on it. Annie went into the bathroom and came back toweling her hair. She sat down next to him, rubbing at her hair and looking at him in a way he hadn't seen for ages. He tried to remember the last time she'd looked at him like that and what it had meant.

He said, "Do you realize that barely six days ago we were counting on catching the kidnappers to save the firm? Now we're counting on them paying us to defend them."

Annie moved a little closer. She seemed to be examining his face as if looking for something she'd lost. She said casually, "I guess I'll just have to make the supreme sacrifice and give up taking alimony from you."

"Oh great. They'll find out and put me in jail."

"Not if I get married. Then it stops."

"Oh, Annie, that's really sweet of you. But I couldn't let you marry a creep like Frank Golson just so I can stay in business."

She moved a shade closer. "I wasn't thinking of that creep. I was thinking of another creep."

"Which other creep?"

Annie rested a finger on his nose. "You."

"*Me?*"

"Think of it as an economy measure. As your wife you wouldn't have to pay me alimony or a salary. And I could give up this apartment and save the rent."

"You mean you'd move in with me? We'd be together at night?"

259

"A lot of married couples are."

"But, you said . . . What a switch! When did this all happen?"

"When I opened my eyes and saw you bending over me in the boat tonight."

"So that's it. A shipboard romance that won't last a week. I might have known."

She put her hands on his shoulders. "I figured you wouldn't have come after me, against a whole gang and everything, just because I'm good at filing, and that maybe it was because of some other reason."

"Is *that* what's been bothering you all this time? You didn't think I cared or something?"

"Well, what was I supposed to think, with you giving nude swimming lessons at parties?"

"But that was just high spirits. God, Annie, I've been crazy about you ever since I picked you up on that cable car. If I stop paying you alimony I'll be even crazier about you."

She came into his arms, all soft eyes and melting mouth. "No more swimming?"

"I promise. From now on I walk everywhere."

"In that case," she breathed, her eyes closing, her lips parted, "maybe you'd better sleep on the sofa tonight."

"The *sofa?*"

Her eyes shot open. "Billy, I'm not on the other side of the room."

"But, Annie, you've been telling me for ages you don't believe in post-marital sex."

"But we're getting married," she murmured, rubbing noses. "This will be premarital sex."

"Good thinking," he cried jubilantly.

"Billy, if you keep yelling and screaming like this I don't see how there'll be any kind of sex at all."

"Oh yes there will be. But I'm reeking of gasoline and I've got seaweed in my hair. Now that I'm finally going to sleep on your sofa I want everything to be just right." He ran for the door. "Give me three minutes," he said excitedly. "You get ready, too. Lie down or something."

He dashed up the stairs two at a time. He had it all planned: a quick shower and shave, a gallon of Florida water, the gray slacks, the Italian polo shirt, soft black slip-ons, then down the stairs again, suave, nonchalant, his eyebrows set the way Gable would have had them. It was going to be perfect.

He was so preoccupied that he didn't notice the men standing waiting in the shadows at the top of the landing—men with unfinished business.

The cry that welled up in his throat was choked off prematurely. Hands grabbed him, pinned him, jammed something tight and suffocating over his head and shoulders—a straitjacket, he thought wildly. He struggled frantically, struck out blindly. Rough hands pushed into his face, ran something moist over his cheeks—a chloroform pad searching for his nose? He heard the swish of an object swinging through the air and tried desperately to duck his head. It landed heavily over his eye, momentarily stunning, curiously soft and spongy. He knew what it was—a lead pipe wrapped in a wet towel.

He braced himself for the final blow.

Unbelievably, the clutching hands jumped from him as if he'd turned to fire. Bodies swept by him, footsteps clattered down the stairs, the front door banged and he was alone.

When Annie opened her door she leaped back, her hand flying to her mouth. A hideous phantom stood half hidden in the darkened hallway—long ghostly robes, staring eyes, macabre green face. And the hair. What was that in the *hair?*

In a blinding flash she knew.

It was definitely, unmistakably, without the shadow of a doubt, custard pie.

261